VANNALI

Book Seven of the Lissae Series

R. Lennard

Vannali

First published in 2024 by R. Lennard

Edited by Anna at CREATING ink.
www.CREATINGink.com

Published by Rebecca Lennard.
lissae.com

Check the trigger warnings by scanning the QR code below:

A catalogue record for this book is available from the National Library of Australia

To Ren,
You may have inherited more than you wanted,
but your heart is even bigger than Shari's.
Thank you for the many different ways you continue to change my world.

 PROLOGUE

Lissae

Zoeday

Seventh day of the final week of Nightcrest

4060

It all ends with a trip through a portal and a charging minotaur.

Shari Dawn, the Altoriae of Lissae, looked around her.

Samuel was staring aghast at the golden arrow which he'd just stabbed her mother with.

Jonathan, on the far side of the town square, stared at her with wide, horrified eyes.

Asterion was still charging towards them on soundless feet, mouth open in a silent bellow.

Grace's pale face was rapidly becoming flushed again.

Calem, her father, gathered Arilla in his arms.

And her mother lifted a trembling, blood-soaked hand upwards.

How had it all come to this?

Mere minutes before

Samuel's head snapped up.

"Shari!" Jonathan screamed at the retreating form of the Altoriae. Mainland soldiers sensed his distraction and swarmed the Guardian.

"Help her!" Jonathan yelled at Samuel.

Before he could take a step, blue skin filled his vision.

Temira met his gaze directly. "It's time."

"I need to..." Samuel gestured to the oncoming calamity.

The technomancer shoved the parcel in his direction. "Make it quick then."

Instinctively, Samuel grabbed the bundle, the Dark Innarn thrumming under the wrappings. Over Temira's shoulder, and past the swarm of mainlanders, Shari was standing back-to-back with Arilla and Calem, doing her best to guide her parents away from the growing portal.

"Asterion!" he yelled and jerked his head.

The minotaur took off running. Soldiers in the oily black mainland uniform took off after him.

Transforming the skin on his hand to scales, Samuel unwrapped the golden arrow. "I don't want to do this," he said.

Drawing herself up to her full height, Temira glared at him. "I won't let you help her until you do." She held her arms out to the side, completely unprotected.

"Fine," he snarled, and jabbed the arrow into her belly.

Gasping, Temira folded. "My... my thanks," she said, sinking to the ground.

As much as Samuel didn't want to ignore her sacrifice, he had an Altoriae to save.

Time seemed to slow as he ran to the portal. A doorway seemed to be forming behind it.

Several things clicked in his mind at the same time.

Mother Realm.

Blank.

Birth.

There wasn't breath left for swearing, but that didn't stop others from cringing away as he hurtled through the crowd like they were paper, careful to keep the arrow away from the unworthy masses.

Grace floated above them all, shooting bolt after bolt and downing those in his way.

Samuel rounded the portal and peered through the back, only to see nothing.

One way in. He came around the side and stabbed the arrow into Shari.

Only Cylanthar's chimes and a soft, startled noise told him it wasn't Shari he had imbued with the Technomancer's Innarn.

Pulling the arrow from Arilla's side, Samuel couldn't tell if the Realm had gone silent again or if he was about to die and this was just the precursor.

Asterion shook free of the mainlanders and opened his mouth in a soundless bellow as he rushed towards them.

Calem rounded on Samuel, sword raised, ready to strike him down.

Samuel bared his neck. He deserved the deathblow.

A soldier on the ground in front of Arilla groaned and sat up without looking.

Asterion stumbled over him.

Tripped.

Before Calem could swing his blade, he and Arilla were shoved through the shining light of the portal by the falling minotaur.

CHAPTER ONE

Portal

Arilla tried to place where she'd seen the grey walls of the endless hallway before. Doors of wildly different designs were branching off each side, and she would have loved to take them all in, if her flesh hadn't been on fire.

Dropping to her knees, she gasped. It felt like she was burning from the inside out.

"Arilla?" Calem's voice sounded close enough to touch, but so far away.

Forcing her eyes open, Arilla came nose to hood with a creature she'd only seen once before.

"Come on," he said. "Up you get." The robed being helped her to her feet, keeping her steady as she staggered by looping an arm under her shoulders.

"Calem," she said weakly.

"Here." Another arm wrapped around her waist, and the trio started walking.

It still felt like she was on fire, like her insides were too big for her skin. "Mitch?" she groaned. "Where are we going?"

The robed figure froze. "How did you…? Never mind. It's not important. But we have to hurry."

"Why?" Calem asked.

'*Thank you, love.*' Arilla's thought was loud enough to become a send.

Beside her, Calem stiffened. '*I heard you.*'

'*I would hope you hear me every time I talk,*' Arilla snipped. Pain was not her friend today, and if she didn't sit down soon, she might just explode.

"Two more doors should do it," Mitch was saying.

'*You aren't talking, love. You're sending.*'

Arilla gaped up at him, wanting to stop and stare at his face.

"You need to let go now, Calem."

Calem stared Mitch down. "Never."

"If you don't, you'll be drawn in too."

"Wherever Arilla goes, I will be at her side," Calem snarled.

Mitch sighed. "As you will it." He let go of her, and she sagged against Calem.

He removed his hood and looked every inch like the boy she'd thought lost. "Place your hands on the wall," Mitch said. "And state your name."

"Both of us?"

The grey-robed shoulders shrugged. "I've no idea. It's just meant to be one."

"We'll do it together," Calem said. He lifted her hand and interlaced their fingers.

Arilla groaned. "I… I need to sit." She blinked away tears of pain.

"Place your hand on the wall, and the pain will stop," Mitch said softly, scrubbing at his cheeks.

"Together," Calem repeated. Raising their joined hands, he pressed them against the wall.

"Ca…"

"...rilla."

Their names rang down the hallway, and a door sprouted beneath their hands; wooden, with steel bolts as bright as her polished swords, feathers carved into the door, and a rectangular knob reminiscent of Calem's favourite book.

A bronze plaque appeared at the side. Arilla wished she could read it, but between one breath and the next, the door disappeared, and she and Calem were freefalling.

Spinning in an endless sky, Calem reached out and grabbed her. She wrapped herself around him.

'*Think of the perfect world for Shari!*' Mitch's voice echoed in her head.

A perfect world.

One of joy, happiness, and fewer fights. One where there was no need to patrol, and they could live peacefully with all the neighbouring Realms. One where anyone was welcome, so long as they harmed none.

A chime sounded as the door far above faded from view.

Arilla kissed Calem, and let her eyes fall shut. She took one last breath in, and when she breathed out, they were everywhere.

Mitch rubbed at the tears tracking down his cheeks. '*You never told me I'd know them.*'

Pala laid a wizened hand on his arm. '*We can't always predict who will be the first one through the portal.*'

'*I never thought it would be them.*'

'*Finish the plaque, or their sacrifice will have been in vain.*'

Stepping up to the blank piece of bronze, Mitchel Hoffman, former apprentice to the Guardian of Lissae turned Ducibus protector, placed his hand on the metal. *Carilla* etched itself on the plaque in the neatest script he'd ever produced.

Pala nodded. '*It is done.*'

Mitch looked at the open door. Across the hall, he could feel the portal groaning. The familiar double doors of Lissae were temporarily relocating.

'*Might want to step back*,' Pala warned. The ancient Ducibus thudded his staff on the floor, and a swirling mess of Innarn appeared, linking the two doorways together. Beings started to stream past, then chunks of land.

On the other side of the portal, held back by an impenetrable Innarn barrier, a dark army shook their weapons and glared. One by one, the Ducibus from all over the halls came to stand guard.

Shifting to join their ranks, Mitchel smirked.

He might have failed Shari once, but he'd never do it again.

A dark being he didn't recognise, with tusks as long as his fingers protruding from his mouth and skin bluer than Lissae's sky, pounded on the barrier.

A crack appeared.

Not so impenetrable, Mitch had time to think before more and more dark beings started throwing whatever they could at the barrier.

Shifting his weight, Mitch steadied himself. The Ducibus had taught him how to wield Innarn in ways that were too dark for Jonathan to even imagine.

Their mantra... *his* mantra, now, played on loop through his head as the tip of a tentacle reached through a tiny hole and the barrier fell.

No life is worth more than the portals we guard.

His fellow Ducibus were ripping into the Dark Army like they were wet paper, beings dropping before their final breath could even leave their bodies.

Mitch, decidedly taller than his counterparts, stood in the back row, his Innarn lashing out and preventing anything from entering the stream of Innarn between Lissae and Carilla that wasn't meant to.

Blood from the fallen drifted by, pulled into the stream before he could stop it, and then there was no more time to think.

The blunt end of a staff smacked into his cheek, and Mitch howled even as he blasted the offending being away–the sickening thud as his attacker hit the opposite wall and slid down, lifeless, almost lost in the fray.

Lissae herself had no Innarn to spare, but the Ducibus did. They'd been laying traps in preparation for this attack for months.

'*Three*,' Mitch sent, reaching out to find the edges of the trap.

'*Two*.'

He could feel the Ducibus gathering their Innarn, could see grips tightening on weapons, could hear the cries of the wounded mingling with the rumble of the warning under their feet.

'*One*.'

The portal seemed to shift sideways as Mitch flooded the traps with as much Innarn as he dared. Plasma–a tribute to Shari, but lighter than anything she could conjure–arched from the floor. Lines of silver bounced and flowed between bodies, dropping each member of the Dark Army until all that was left was a sparking, oozing mass.

The Ducibus, safe behind their shields, grinned at him from beneath their hoods.

He glanced down at his hands. Was this mix of awe and disgust how Shari felt after each battle? Awe at the sheer amount of power flowing through his atoms, and disgust at how easy it was to wield said power in such a deadly manner.

Pala limped over to him. '*Well done*,' the older Ducibus said. '*Shari would be proud*.'

Mitch smiled grimly.

If only he would get a chance to talk to her again.

'*I believe that a single-handed defeat of the Dark Army deserves some sort of reward*,' Pala mused.

'But I *didn't*–' Mitch started.

A nearby Ducibus stomped on his foot and glared at him.

'*What do you suggest?*' Mitch asked instead.

Pala grinned.

Lissae

Samuel expected the sound to come back in a rush. He didn't expect Shari to grab his shirt and punch him in the face.

The silence dragged on even as Asterion staggered to his feet. In the process, the minotaur accidentally shoved the two with his horns.

Apprentice and Altoriae fell backwards through the portal.

A great sucking sound, and Shari and Samuel were elsewhere.

It didn't stop Shari from her attack. *'You killed my mother!'*

'No! I gave *her Temira's Innarn!'* Samuel blocked and defended.

Shari gave him an incredulous look. *'That's why you stabbed her?'*

'Temira gave me the arrow. Asked if I would finish the job, I started on Ulnan.' He blinked away the threatening moisture. *'I didn't want to. It was her or you. I thought you were standing where your mother was. Shari, I'm so sorry.'*

The Altoriae was staring into his eyes like she could see the reflection of his soul. Samuel held his breath, praying to Cylanthar that she would trust him.

'I believe you,' Shari sent.

Something large and horned slammed into them, sending them spinning. Asterion gave a garbled yell as he disappeared into the darkness.

More and more things were streaming past, bumping against them and sending the pair spinning. Samuel changed forms. Careful of his claws, he pulled Shari closer to him and enfolded the Altoriae in his wings. He'd have bruises on his bruises at the end of it but would be able to sleep easier knowing he'd kept her safe.

'Samuel!' The Guardian's send was louder than he'd ever heard before.

Blindly reaching out, Sanithane snagged Jonathan and pulled him inside his wings as well. Never in all his years would he have expected to have Lissae's two fiercest protectors so close to his vulnerable underbelly. Four sets of needle-sharp claws dug into his scales, and Sanithane angled his head to see Kemanyr holding onto his hide, gibbering in fear. Looking over the hatchlings shoulder, Sanithane's three eyes went wide.

The top of Ronah's castle was poking through the enlarging portal.

Giving birth, he thought.

As the castle broke free and started spinning towards him, he groaned. *This is going to hurt.*

The Realm went black.

CHAPTER TWO

Carilla

Birth Year

Adonday

First day of the first week of Waeghost

A voice was calling her name.

'Altoriae.'

Groaning, Shari rolled to the side and almost landed in the water.

Where did that come from? Groggily, Shari pushed herself up, trying to take stock of things.

She was lying in a heap of limbs. Judging from the golden skin and the brown hair, Jonathan and Samuel were part of the tangle as well.

"What happened?"

Brayden, hanging onto the edge of the land—the rest of his body in the water—tapped on her thigh.

Shari's blade was at his throat before she even thought about moving.

The Wisara's eyes went wide. "The silence, Altoriae. We've passed through it."

Lowering the tip of her weapon, Shari cautiously extracted herself from the others and stood.

They were on a small parcel of land in the middle of a heaving ocean. "What's going on?"

"The silence. We were what was hiding it in," Brayden said.

"That doesn't make any sense," Shari said crossly.

"The stories were wrong," Brayden ducked out of the way of a hunk of flying debris that looked suspiciously like a cooking pot. "The silence wasn't to be feared. It's the start of something new. The pause before a sentence, the wind before a..."

"Get to the point," Shari said, nudging Jonathan with the toe of her boot.

"The birth of a new Realm," Brayden finished.

"Wait. What?" Shari looked around again. Others were starting to wake and stand on the tiny dots of land scattered through the sea. As she watched, two collided, becoming bigger than their original masses had suggested. "I think you'd better get up here," she said. Reaching down, she helped pull Brayden to his feet.

Jonathan rose, unsteadily, one hand to his head. '*Anything broken?*' he asked.

Doing a mental check, Shari sent back, '*All in one piece. You?*'

'*My head is aching like a castle landed on it.*' Jonathan looked over Shari's shoulder. '*Oh. It did.*'

Glancing behind her, Shari's eyes widened. The sprawling chunk of land Ronah's castle inhabited was heading straight for them.

"Help me get Samuel up," she said. The last thing she needed was for him to have some vital body part smashed between two bits of rock.

Brayden reached down and hauled Samuel to his feet like the other man weighed nothing. The three of them braced for impact and managed to stay standing as the two bits of land smashed together.

"Huh?" Samuel opened bleary eyes and groaned. "What happened?"

"Lissae gave birth," Shari said shortly. She sent her Innarn out, intending to search for survivors, and gasped at the rush of power that left her.

"What was that?" Samuel was awake now and staring at her.

"Innarn rush." Shari took a breath, and years of reining her Innarn in was the only thing that stopped her from staggering backwards and off the tiny scrap of land behind her.

Another bit of land joined on beside Jonathan, sending them sprawling and voices crying out.

"If you can harness that much, better do something with it," Jonathan said.

Weeks of unpredictable Innarn made Shari doubtful, but she stilled. It was worth trying. Closing her eyes, she drew in a breath and let her Innarn out, seeking survivors and hunting the seas for other bits of Ronah, of the other Shifting Islands.

Searching for her parents.

Asterion burst from the castle, looking around frantically.

Shari ignored him.

Heartbeats.

The four around her. Three more off to the side. Another dozen in the castle. The slower, surer beats of Ginorti's Kumaru. The ancient thump of Akoren's head elder from under the water.

More and more surrounded her as Shari fought to pull them closer. The land swelled around her as it found the right spot to slot back into.

The Shifting Islands and their beings were whole and accounted for. Apart from three.

At last, she dropped her arms and opened her eyes.

Screams rent the air.

Shari slapped her hands over her ears, which did nothing to abate the sound. "What's going on?" she yelled over the noise.

Tania appeared in front of her. "Ronah! She's getting bigger!"

"Bigger?" Shari called back.

A fissure split the ground between them, smoothed over almost immediately as if by an invisible hand. Anywhere a being wasn't standing, the process was repeated.

Ronah's Linked had tears streaming down her face.

"How do we stop it?" Shari screamed.

"I don't think we can!" Tania called back.

"Jump!" Samuel ordered.

Shari's feet left the ground before she processed what he said. In the space of time she was suspended in the air, the island grew again. "Genius!" *'Everyone jump!'* Shari sent, hoping that they would hear her over the screams of the islands.

Wrapping her Innarn around the Blanks and the injured, Shari counted down from three and the population of the Shifting Islands took to the air as one.

A final scream, louder than the rest, pierced the air as chasms formed and closed. The ground beneath them swelled and shifted. Shari felt people gripping on to those closest to them, holding on tight. Jonathan and Samuel did the same to her. In the back of her mind, she was aware of the Innarn bridges tearing apart, the new growth too much for them to withstand. Rakemyst's floating islands toppled under their excess weight, falling into the ocean and sending massive waves upon the shore.

When their feet touched the earth again, the island groaned, long and low, then fell silent.

The castle, which had only been a few steps away, was at least a five-minute walk now.

Gaping, Shari spun in a circle. Mainlander troops, looking discombobulated, were huddled in a bunch where she expected the town square to be. Instead, the square was a blur of colour at the end of a very long street. Others were trying to come to their senses, the Returned seeming to be unflappable as they raised their weapons and surrounded the bulk of the mainlanders.

Tania dropped to her knees, making soft soothing sounds as she pet the ground. "Ronah?" she whispered over and over. Looking up at Shari, Tania blinked away tears. "She's not answering."

"Maybe she needs a rest?" Shari offered. Pushing her Innarn out again, she felt the deep weariness seeping into Ronah's bedrock. The other islands felt the same.

Dashing her tears away, Tania sniffed as Collis shifted in beside her. "I hope that's all it is," she said.

Gathered in the arms of her soul-match, Tania and Collis slowly made their way towards where the mainlander's troops were spewing curses at the others. With a sharp movement of her arm, Tania crafted walls of impenetrable ziom around the remaining army.

The sound cut off, and Shari glanced at Brayden.

"We're safe," he said.

She shook her head grimly. "Not all of us."

Shari pounded on the door in the middle of the field. She'd looked all over the island, but her parents were nowhere to be found.

"Open up," she demanded.

The door pushed open, sending Shari stumbling backwards. A grey robed figure loomed over her for a moment, before one hand grasped the doorway and the other extended to haul her to her feet.

'What is it you seek?' The voice in her mind was gentle, familiar even.

"My parents. They were the first through the portal and I can't find them anywhere," Shari said. She dug her nails into the back of her thigh. Part of her already knew what the Ducibus was going to say, but she needed to hear it. Or else it wouldn't be real.

'Two beings, their souls entwined, their spirits enmeshed. They created the base for the Shifting Islands.'

Something about the send was tickling the edge of her mind. "I know you," she blurted.

A light shone to one side of her. Glancing over, she spotted Wisp trotting through the field towards them, the glow from his chest warm against the darkening sky.

Wisp huffed a breath against her fingertips and turned to regard the Ducibus. Instead of the growl Shari was expecting, the Shadow Bringer leapt up and licked zir's face, knocking the hood back.

Shari's jaw dropped. "Mitch?" she whispered.

He gave her a wry grin that sent her to her knees. "Well met, Shari." To Wisp, he said, "You are a menace. I told you to watch over her."

"He's from you?" Shari sniffed, burying her hands in the thick white fur. Wisp leaned against her legs heavily.

"He'll watch over you when I can't," Mitch said, rubbing the Shadow Bringer's scruff.

Gaze running over his familiar face, Shari noted the bruise high on his cheek and the split lip. She wanted to ask but found she couldn't. He noticed her gaze anyway. "Dark Army. Decided to try and join the new Realm. We made sure they didn't."

She gave him a wobbly grin. "I bet you put them in their place. But what do you mean when you can't?" Shari rubbed her arm across her face, dashing away the falling tears. "Now you're guarding the doorway, I can see you all the time."

Mitch's lips quivered, and Shari had a sinking feeling.

"New Realms need time to settle."

"What?"

"Shari!" Jonathan was yelling her name and getting closer.

Looking in the direction his Guardian was coming from, Mitch sighed. "I have to go."

Shari grabbed his hand. "No," she whispered.

He smiled sadly. "I'm right here, Shari. I swear I'll do a better job of protecting you this time." Gently, he eased his hand out of her grip.

"Wait! How much time?" she asked.

"As long as it takes."

"It is you." Jonathan looked at his former apprentice, awed.

Tears sheened over the new Ducibus' eyes. "Well met, Guardian."

"Mitchel." Jonathan started forward, arm outstretched.

A deep chime sounded. Shari felt her bones rattle.

"We'll see each other again," Mitch promised. "Stay safe. I bid thee well." A tear dripped off his lashes and down his cheek as he closed the door with a *click*.

"Mitchel," Jonathan said again, laying his hand on the closed door and bowing his head. Standing on unsteady legs, Shari wrapped her arms around his middle and wept.

CHAPTER THREE

Inthday

Second day of the first week of Waeghost

Tania walked through the elongated streets of Ronah. The healers had been working through the night. The fields on either side of the town square were filled with sheet-covered bodies that glowed pinky-orange with the rays of the rising sun.

She was refusing to think about how they could have a sun in a brand-new Realm. What about the stars? The moons? Were there different planets around them? Would their seasons change? Pushing the thoughts to the side, Tania continued her walk alongside the never-ending bodies of the dead.

Collis and the rest of the Returned had been busy as well. The mountains along Ronah's beach had gone.

'*How fares your islands?*' Tania sent to the other Linked. Rakemyst, Ronah, and Akoren had suffered the majority of the attack, and she half-expected not to get an answer from them.

Zana was the first to reply, her send sounding like it was the middle of the day and not dawn's first blush. '*Rakemyst has suffered, mostly from our small islands falling from the sky. The elders and I have been working to replace them.'*

'Let me know if you need help,' Cyrus sent. *'Talhan is acting like a child hyped up on sugar, for all he won't talk to me at the moment. Crystal is literally spitting out of the ground. If anyone finds Temira, let me know. Maybe she can talk some sense into him!'*

Tania froze. A blue hand was sticking out from under a sheet. "No," she breathed. Slowly, she leaned down and pulled the cover back to reveal the bald head and closed eyes of the technomancer. *'I found her.'* Dropping to her knees, Tania shoved her fist against her mouth to keep from wailing.

Two beings appeared. Collis knelt behind her, wrapping Tania in a hug, while Cyrus sank to the ground on the other side of Temira.

Talhan's Linked took the cold hand of the technomancer in his own, murmuring nonsense words at her as he sobbed.

"I thought she'd live forever," Tania said.

The other Linked shifted in, holding vigil while Tania and Cyrus cried their grief out.

As Tania stood, she noticed the middle Q'Aralide hatchling sitting on the path, head drooping as if she too was mourning.

"Well met," Tania rasped.

'Well met, friend of Temira. I am Tormorylth. I am here to honour her in the way of her people.' The Q'Aralide licked at her falling tears before the acid reached the end of her maw. *'I did not wish to do this so soon.'* The send was barely more than a whisper.

"In the way of her people..." Tania furrowed her brow as she wiped the remains of her own tears away with the cloth Collis had handed her. "You're going to eat her?"

Tormorylth nodded. *'To show her the respect she deserves, yes.'*

Tania looked around. "Is there anyone else who would want to say goodbye?" she asked Cyrus.

He barked a laugh. "No one she would care about."

She'd half been hoping that he'd say yes, so she could deny the macabre request.

Tilting her head, Tormorylth gazed solemnly at Tania. *'You are her kin. If you do not wish me to, then I won't.'*

Looking at Collis for help, Tania found she didn't know what to do. In her grief, was she meant to deny what she knew Temira wanted? "I don't think I can bear to watch," she admitted.

'Could you shift her away?' Tormorylth asked.

"Yes." Tania scrubbed a hand over her face. "Yes, I can do that."

"She loved visiting Farm Land," Cyrus said. "It was her favourite spot, outside the Techno Centre."

"Would you do the honours?" Tania asked.

"I'll shift you both?" he said to Tormorylth.

'Thank you. My kin can watch and confirm, if you wish?' Tormorylth, despite her youth, seemed to know that some traditions were distasteful to others. Tania wondered if it had anything to do with the way Q'Aralides were raised, or if Shari was a good influence on the hatchling.

"I think she would have appreciated that." Tania sniffed, determined that her tears were done for today.

Cyrus shifted the Q'Araldie and the technomancer away, and Tania found that sometimes, determination wasn't everything.

Tania looked at the smooth, black ziom walls holding the mainlanders prisoner. "We can't just keep them in there."

Arms crossed, Shari tipped her head and glanced at Tania from the corner of her eye. "You were the one who made the wall."

"In anger." Tania flushed.

"And now you've had time to calm down?" Zana asked. The other Linked were standing in a line, all looking as tired and drawn as she felt.

Tania huffed at the Ilutri. She'd spent a restless night tossing and turning, so used to Ronah's running commentary that it had been hard to get to sleep. In the morning, guilt had woken her, plaguing her thoughts and making her gut churn.

"They barely have enough room to move in there," Tania said, hating how small her voice sounded.

"And we've barely had time to breathe," Shari countered.

"I'm sure if we just explain, they'll be fine," Tania said. She flicked her hand, intending to open a door, and instead an entire wall disappeared.

The mainlanders yelled and charged at the duo, weapons at the ready.

"I was wrong!" Tania shrieked as Shari glared at her.

Zana moved her wings and the wall reappeared, farther out, but still surrounding the army.

"This would so be the wrong time to say I *told you so*," Shari said drily.

Brinley coughed. "I have a suggestion."

Everyone turned to the white-robed Linked. Tania marvelled how her robe was so clean even after everything they'd gone through. Even grass knew not to stain the hem.

"The dead of the Weavers are entombed in stone, and their spirits preserved in order to protect Vannali if needed. The stone statues line the island, and the only exception to them are the Linked, whose spirit is passed into the island. Now, I believe, counts as a time of need." Brinley had the same serenity as Zana, her hands clasped, speaking as if the subject was as mundane as the weather.

"I have to agree," Zana said. She looked over Ronah's expanded grounds and sighed. "Rakemyst is not responding. Innarn is unreliable and our defenders are battered or littering the halls of the Healers Centre. Call the spirits."

Tania felt a chill go down her spine. "I don't think we should..."

It was too late.

Brinley nodded at Zana and shifted away.

Glancing around, Tania caught Shari's gaze and shivered.

'*Spirit's preserve.*' The whisper filled her mind.

'*Spirit's preserve.*' Louder this time.

'*Spirit's preserve.*' The ground beneath her feet rumbled, and for a wild moment, Tania thought Ronah was protesting.

Shari turned, sword in hand. "By the Life of Lissae," she breathed.

Straightening, Tania spun around. Marching towards them in perfect synchronisation were hundreds upon hundreds of white-robed beings. All of whom looked in perfect health for those who were supposed to be dead.

"Step aside," Zana murmured, tugging on Tania's arm.

The spirits-turned-flesh surrounded the wall, and weapons snapped into hands, pointing at their clamouring foe.

Brinley, looking even more worn, shifted back to Tania's side. "Lower the wall," she said. Tania felt Fenix wrap their Innarn around the Weaver to hold her upright.

"Incapacitate—don't kill." Shari's voice rang out over the eerily silent spirit army.

As one, they snapped their heels together, gaze never leaving the wall.

"Here we go," Tania said. Waving a hand, she lowered the walls of the makeshift enclosure.

Mainlanders yelled, ready to charge, but froze when they realised they were surrounded.

Shari shivered. The spirits felt entirely too solid to her. It was stirring up memories of the Hantra, but a quick scan of the white-robed army showed none of the corruption. Every spirit that had been raised was there because they wanted to be. They had protected their Realm during life and vowed to continue in death.

Watching, Shari let her Innarn swirl around her in case she had to intervene.

Moving as one entity, the spirit army tore through their ranks. White robes flashed through dropping oily black uniforms, and the mainland defeat was more of a whisper than a yell.

The Altoriae wasn't sure if she should be glad there had been a battle she hadn't had to fight, or worried that the spirits remained as the last of their foes met the ground.

Wolf sat slumped at Arilla and Calem's kitchen table, his head in his hands.

Belfar swallowed heavily as he sat opposite his mate.

They had spent the night searching for Calem and Arilla, to no avail. Wolf had shared the memory of the final moments of the battle–the struggle to get to his brother's side, the moment the minotaur tripped. How the Realm went white before they were flying through the air in a place they'd never been before but was somehow the same.

The endless night winging around the newly expanded islands, trying to find a brother whose Innarn signature was everywhere and nowhere at the same time.

"I love you," Wolf said, his normally gravelly voice even more hoarse. "You need to be sure of that."

Heart sinking, Belfar reached across the table and took one of Wolf's hands. "What are you planning?"

"I made a vow." Wolf raised his head, tearstained cheeks flushed from crying. "And I broke it."

"A vow?" Belfar thought back, and his heart sunk even further. "The Allegiance Ceremony on Rakemyst."

"I promised her, Belfar."

"I doubt that she would hold you at fault." Belfar ran his thumb over Wolf's knuckles.

"What if she does?"

Belfar fell silent. A life without Wolf wasn't worth contemplating.

The remains of the mainland army stood four abreast in lines guarded by the Weaver Spirits.

Shari looked at them. Bruised and bloody, most seemed to take their defeat in hand. Although a few looked angry enough to continue the fight.

"Where to?" Brinley asked.

"Let's get them back to Lissae," Jonathan suggested.

Nodding, Shari led the snaking line towards the doorway, Wisp appearing in a puff of white by her side. Jonathan was on her right, Samuel on her left. Prickles ran up and down her back. Clearly, not all of the mainlanders were happy. Reinforcing her shields made Wisp huff and rub against her for a few steps. Shari could feel the dense Innarn of the Linked, who walked in a row behind the end of their prisoners, ensuring none escaped.

Finally, after more distance than she remembered from the night before, they were at the doorway.

Jonathan gestured for her to do the honours.

She reached for the handle and expected something like the pleasant tingling she got each time she'd opened Lissae's double doors.

Nothing.

Shooting Jonathan a look, she raised her brows.

He shrugged.

With nothing else to do, Shari opened the door. Only to see a smooth grey wall. "We're sealed in." Something Mitch had said to her before made sense. "New Realms need time to settle," she repeated dully.

"How much time?"

Running her fingertips over the carved feather inlay, Shari sighed and gently closed the door. "As much as it takes."

"And what do we do with this lot in the meantime?" Brinley asked.

Shari wanted to shrug and say she didn't have a clue. That maybe, it wasn't up to her. She tried to shift off-Realm and shuddered, forced back into her body by a wall as smooth as the one behind the door.

Jonathan brushed against her arm. "Perhaps see if one of Rakemyst's fallen islands would be big enough to hold them."

"You're going to abandon us?" a mainlander yelled.

"You tried to kill us, even on a new Realm. Prove that you can play nice, and maybe you can rejoin civilisation," Shari snarled.

"In a lifetime or two," Samuel added.

The mainlander paled.

"Sooner for good behaviour. We'll be by to check up and make sure that you are alright. I promise we won't forget about you." Jonathan's words were nice, yet his tone was anything but.

The soldiers around them gulped.

After eyeing the outspoken man, Shari asked, "Zana?"

The Linked appeared next to Jonathan in the smoothest shift Shari had ever witnessed.

"There are a few islands which would do nicely. Two already have established gardens. With your help, we can ensure everyone gets a roof over their heads." Rakemyst's Linked was as serene as ever.

"The Returned would be grateful to help," Tania said. 'This excess of Innarn is proving to be dangerous. If they don't get to use it, I'm not sure what is going to happen,' she admitted to Shari.

"They are quite brilliant," Shari said.

Zana and Tania dipped their heads. Together, they closed their eyes.

A few breaths later, and Zana smiled. "It is done."

Shari smirked. "Maybe Collis should shift them in."

Samuel shuddered beside her. 'Every shift that boy does is like having your atoms rearranged in a blender.'

'Why do you think I suggested it?' Shari said.

'Evil.' He looked at her from the corner of his eye. 'I love it.'

Shari grinned.

The mainlander who'd been glaring at her only had enough time to draw a breath to protest before his entire party disappeared.

Chapter Four

Samuel glanced at Tormorylth, who was doing her best to appear unaffected.

She had not had as much practice as him and wasn't quite as successful as hoped.

Temira's body was laid out on a stone slab, and the three hatchlings gathered around her, glancing at the small crowd.

With a shake of his shoulders, Samuel changed form, and Sanithane joined them, Sneeze perched on his head.

Holding her head high, Tormorylth only wavered a little as she started her send. *'We gather today to honour the last of the Ulnan, Temira of Talhan. Despite her dislike of the title, Temira was known fondly as the technomancer of Lissae. She helped to improve the health of many beings, and she will be sorely missed.'*

Sanithane wasn't entirely sure who would miss the prickly healer, but there would be some.

'In the tradition of the Ulnan, Temira's flesh will be consumed so her knowledge will be gained.' Tormorylth flicked a glance at him, and

Sanithane nodded in encouragement. *'Please leave if you do not wish to watch.'*

A glance showed Tania gripping Cyrus's hand hard enough that he worried the man might have a few broken bones by the end of the morning.

Tormorylth waited a moment longer and lowered her maw.

Gritting his teeth, Sanithane forced himself to watch every bite.

It was enough that he'd destroyed Temira's Realm and had hesitated to complete her last wish. He would not dishonour her by looking away now.

Stepping outside Books 'n' More, with Jonathan and Samuel, Shari turned around when someone coughed behind her. Her uncle and his mate were gazing at her with solemn faces.

"Have you seen your parents?" Wolf asked.

Shari looked away from his red-rimmed eyes. It hadn't occurred to her that others might not know what had happened to them. She cleared her throat. "They, ah, they became the Realm."

Belfar's jaw dropped open.

Wolf frowned at her, then studied at the ground. "How?"

She didn't have to look to know that Jonathan was running a hand down his face, or that Samuel was clenching his jaw, staring straight ahead as if he could see through to the fabric that made up their new Realm.

"I'm not really sure," Shari answered honestly. "Just that their bodies aren't with us anymore, and their souls combined to give us this." She waved her arm to encompass everything around them.

Wolf silently handed the Altoriae the hilt of his sword. Beside him, Belfar groaned and hid his expression behind his feathered wing.

"What are you doing?" Shari asked, taking the blade automatically.

"I've failed to uphold the vows I promised you," Wolf said, his gravelly voice shaking as he sank to his knees.

"Vows?" Shari thought back. And she hissed. "If you think, for one single moment, that I'm going to do–what? Strike you down with your own Vebnah-damned sword? For failing to do what I–" Her breath hitched, and Samuel and Jonathan stepped forward, each laying a hand on her shoulders. "For failing to do what I could not prevent either, then you are out of your mind."

Dropping the sword and falling beside him, Shari grabbed his face in her hands. "You are the last remaining family from my father's side. And the only family member who doesn't try to kill me on a daily basis. Besides, you vowed to protect my family when I couldn't be there to do so. I was there–" Shari choked off her words. "I was right there. And I couldn't stop it." She looked away, unable to meet the man with the same eyes as her father. Swallowing, she blinked rapidly. "You aren't going to the Spirit Realm until you're old and grey, Wolf Dawn. And I certainly won't be the one to send you there."

"It is your right–" Wolf started to say.

Reaching out, Shari gripped the front of his tunic. "If you say I have the right to choose your punishment, then so be it," she snarled. "You have to *live*. To spend each day finding joy and love, the way my father would have wanted you to." Roughly, she pushed away from him and got to her feet.

Wolf remained on his knees. "As you will it."

Belfar, tears in his eyes, lowered his head.

'Don't you dare let him succumb to pity,' Shari sent to him.

Looking up, Belfar met her gaze and nodded.

'And if he tries, find me. I'll make sure he doesn't.' Abruptly, Shari shifted away, landing in the back room of her parents' tavern.

Stumbling backwards until she hit the wall, Shari slid down and wrapped her arms around her bent legs, resting her head on her knees. She wondered when it would stop hurting. Flashes of her parents passed behind her eyes.

Arilla in the kitchen, laughing as she tried to swipe frost from a cake and Calem chasing her away. Both of them humming as they worked in the garden, bumping shoulders and occasionally bursting into song. Warm hands and a soft voice soothing aches without questioning where they came from. Vallan pie served fresh after a nightmarish patrol. The empty house. A dull, thudding memory of watching her parents wrap their arms around Grace...

Shari lifted her head and frowned.

What happened to Grace?

Zoeday
Seventh day of the first week of Waeghost

It felt like tear tracks were permanently carved into her face. Shari stood between Samuel and Jonathan, listening to another list of the dead. For the last five days, all the remaining elders, the dignitaries, and anyone deemed important—apparently that included her—attended each and every mass funeral.

Even when her heart was numb.

Ronah, the heart of the invasion and the spot where her parents had... gone, had been the first and hardest. The rest had been a blur of names, tears, and grief thick enough to slice.

Today marked the final mourning. The Weavers had suffered the least, but even they had casualties. Ronah, of course, being the centre of the fight, had lost more than any other Shifting Island, and she had broken when their names had been read out.

Now, as the stars started to decorate the sky, the head of the Weavers called out the last name. Their elders moved as one, encasing their fallen in stone skin as the head Weaver chanted "Spirits preserve" until the final, spooky statue was complete.

Scrubbing at her face, Shari decided that enough tears had been shed. There had to be better ways to honour the dead, even if she couldn't stop crying at the moment.

As the Weavers dispersed, she nudged Samuel's arm.

Perched on his shoulder, Sneeze grumbled at her.

She laughed, a watery sound, and blindly reached out. Shari grabbed Samuel's hand. *'What's the song for when your parents turn into a Realm?'* Shari sent, her throat too thick with tears to talk.

Samuel gripped her fingers tighter and turned to face her. She stared in awe at the remnants of grief she hadn't expected to see.

'I don't know, but we'll make one. Just for them.'

CHAPTER FIVE

Adonday

First day of the second week of Waeghost

Shari waved to Edward as she walked past his garden. "Well met."

"Well met, Altoriae." Edward smiled at her, the same as he always had.

It was nice to have someone not scared to meet her gaze.

"Gardening today?" he asked, nodding at the bucket with the hand trowel in it.

"Wolf asked for some help. Said the garden needs a bit of a tidy. And I could use the distraction," Shari admitted.

Edward lowered his gaze, and too late, Shari remembered that his wife, Harmony, had been amongst the fallen. "Edward, I'm sorry," she said. *Sorry for not being quick enough, for letting them get close. So very sorry your soul is aching.*

"Bah," Edward said, swiping a sheen of tears away with a dirt-stained hand. "She was defending our land. Our Altoriae. Harmony kept to our vows. And I'll join her soon enough."

"Can I be selfish and say not too soon?" Shari asked, hating how small her voice sounded.

"Oh, Shari. You won't get rid of me that easily," Edward chuckled. "Everything else might be fluctuating, but the carrots are still going strong. Who else would help me eat them all?"

Laughing, even if it was a little watery, Shari nodded. "Carrot stew at the castle tonight?"

"With all the Thornes?" Edward asked, then winced.

Years of practice meant Shari's grin remained steady. She wasn't about to mention Terrance if Edward didn't bring him up. "Of course! The more the merrier." No doubt she'd regret that decision when she was aching for silence at the end of the day, but if it made Edward smile, she was hard pressed to say no. Dipping her head, Shari said, "I'll see you tonight. Until then, I bid thee well."

As she walked on, Shari took note of the land around her. Plants that should have been struggling were flourishing, while those that were in bloom just over a week ago were dying by the barrow full. Bereni houses were standing firm and unchanged, but rezems looked bigger from the outside, and plasma houses were cracking quicker than their owners could repair them.

Curious, Shari crafted a little plasma ball to hold in her hand. Innarn whooshed out of her fingers more like a waterfall than a running tap, and the ball was big enough for her to walk through. Plasma had always been her element, the one that came easiest. Right now, the ball flickered and died before she recalled it.

Frowning, Shari continued on her way, wondering if Innarn was going to be different here. Each Realm she visited, her Innarn had been slightly changed, but she had still been linked to Lissae. Now, if Shari prodded that link, it was gone. Severed.

Unnerved, Shari shifted, not wanting to walk the rest of the way. Hopefully working in the garden would clear her mind.

Wolf and Belfar were already in the yard, trimming back branches of a tree which seemed to have doubled in size in the last week. They waved in greeting.

"Well met," Shari said. After setting down the bucket of tools, she got to work.

Hours later, Shari used her arm to wipe away the sweat on her forehead before rolling her sleeves up.

Placing the last of the dead buta plants to the side, she looked at the garden in her parents' backyard.

Wolf's backyard now, she supposed.

Wolf and Belfar were both working on a different section and were trying to curtail the new growth they had encouraged. Carrots weren't the only thing excited to be on the new Realm.

A new Realm.

Shifting to sit on the ground properly, Shari tentatively buried her hand in the freshly dug soil. '*Mum? Dad?*'

No answer.

Ducking her head, Shari took a shuddering breath. As she pulled her hand away, a tiny tendril of a vine attached itself to her finger and wound, unbidden, around her hand.

"What are you doing, little one?" Shari asked, using her other hand to gently stroke the vine.

Wisp appeared by her side and snuffled at the plant, huffing as leaves unfurled.

"We should get you in the soil," Shari murmured. Carefully transplanting the clingy little vine, Shari grinned when it finally sank into the ground. "Stay there. You'll be happier," she said when it reached for her again.

Pulling her hand back, Shari looked down.

The scars on her hands—the ones she'd incurred during her failed attempt to change her form—were gone in the places the vine had touched her skin.

After shoving her sleeve up, Shari traced the ones on her arm with a shaking finger. Arilla had hated her scars—had seen them as failing to keep her child safe.

Somehow, from beyond the portal, she'd managed to create a plant to heal the scars Shari had learned to live with.

Releasing a shuddering breath, she patted the little vine. *'Thanks, Mum.'*

The hatchlings were sleeping, finally.

Samuel eased the hidden door to the castle open and slipped through. He'd been wanting to check on Lizbeth since the start of the mourning, and the want had become a need.

The castle was all but deserted now, the guild busy trying to help everyone settle in. Trying to find their place in the new Realm.

Sneeze, nestled on his shoulder, rubbed his scaled head against Samuel's scratchy cheek, warbling gently.

Hands in his pockets, Samuel chuckled as he hit Ronah's streets. He was rather adept at finding his purpose in new places.

Or, at least, he hoped so.

Samuel had lost count of the number of Realms he'd visited and had to learn to blend in—or die trying. Really, only one... now two, counted.

Lissae.

And Carilla.

'Thank you,' he sent to the ground below his feet, below Ronah's belly. *'For every sacrifice you made for your daughter. And for the sake of those around her.'*

There was an annoyed grumbling in his head, which reminded him so much of Shari's father, he couldn't help but grin.

Humming, he wandered down the street, trying to find the right tune to honour both the older Dawns. It was a challenge, as it wasn't quite the same as the usual acknowledgement of a warrior. This was more of a celebration as well. The right sound hadn't reached him yet, but he was sure it would before long.

Arriving at Lizbeth's house, he was delighted to smell fresh baking. With the return of Innarn, he'd forgotten that there would be the return of cookies as well.

Sneeze grumbled. 'Not *just cookies*,' the tiny draci sent.

Reaching under the draci's chin, Samuel scratched until Sneeze snorted at him. 'No, *not just cookies*.'

Through the window, Lizbeth was walking confidently towards her door, no more of the slow, hesitant steps from when the Innarn had faded on Lissae.

"I promised I'd fix the fading Innarn," he said with a smirk as the door opened.

There was a *boom* and a rush of wind that blew him backwards. Sneeze chittered angrily in his ear and there was a soft body on top of his.

Groaning as something bony jabbed into his stomach, Samuel used Innarn to help Lizbeth to her feet before she could hit something vital.

Out of the corner of his eye, he caught the tail end of a white robe whipping around a house down the road. Gawkers were the same in all the Realms—ready to look but rarely prepared to help.

"What happened?" he asked, slowing getting his aching bones to stand. This whole squishy flesh suit was going to be the death of him one day.

"We've gone from no Innarn to too much," Lizbeth said, staring unseeingly at her house.

Turning to look, Samuel gaped as the structure knitted itself back together. The blasted door was pulling back onto its hinges, debris from inside was righting itself, and knickknacks and memories were slotting into the correct spots. The smell of burning was replaced with fresh cookies.

Samuel glanced at her. "Perhaps I fixed it a little too much?"

She laughed. "Or perhaps the fix wasn't yours to claim." Lizbeth headed back into the repaired house, beckoning him to follow.

"Why must you know me so well?" he grumbled, accepting the plate of steaming cookies from her.

"Because I'm your friend."

The words were sweeter than any of the baked goods she'd shared.

"Bored!" Nerina threw her head back and sighed.

Yessna wondered if it was frowned upon to stab the healer a few hundred times. Once for each utterance of...

"Bored," Nerina said again.

"Well, do something," Yessna snarled.

Their small clearing had become significantly larger. Yessna couldn't even see the tree line on the other side of it now.

"What do you want me to do?" Nerina snapped.

"Patrol," Yessna snapped back. The healer had been inconsolable at the loss of Drah during the battle with the mainlanders. Personally, Yessna thought it a minor miracle that he had lasted as long as he had without his twin.

Nerina stormed off, muttering and kicking at things as she went.

Smoothing her fur down, Yessna growled and sent a wave of Innarn to tidy up. A long-forgotten memory of a tiny wooden shack, filled with colourful cushions, laughter, and hugs, came to mind. A yearning so visceral filled the Ferah that she wasn't surprised to see the shack before her.

A low whistle filled the clearing. "How'd you do that?" Wubi asked.

Yessna blinked. "You can see it too?"

Wubi walked up to where she could see the shack and rapped knuckles on very real-sounding wood. "Bet if we all had a place like this, Nerina would get her healer's kit untwisted."

Narrowing her eyes, Yessna glared at the clearing. A few years ago, they'd come across a little village and they'd spoken about it for months after, saying that if they could, the whole U'sala crew would go back there to retire.

Of course, the next time they'd stepped foot on the Realm, the village had been decimated, and the villagers in the surrounding area were distrustful of anyone not born with leaf-coloured skin.

Picturing the village in her mind, Yessna tried to imagine it in their not-so-little clearing. There had been a blacksmith and a bakery, a tannery, and a library. A tiny store that traded for bits and bobs, and a bigger stable for even the heftiest of beasts. Small cabins had lined the streets as well—things big enough for only a couple, with thatched rooftops and glass panes for windows.

Faster than she had been expecting, the village took place, springing up around them like a mirage come to life.

"Looks like we're calling Ronah home. At least for now," Wubi said. "I'll tell the others, shall I?"

Yessna nodded mutely. That much Innarn use should have wiped her out for a week, if not more. Now, it just felt like a quick nap and she'd be right to do it all over again.

The thought of that much Innarn was rather scary.

Not quite as scary as a white-robed figure who entered the clearing on silent feet only a dozen lengths away. The being paused, and the oversized hood moved as if it were looking around. Innarn dense enough to taste was lashing around the being. Catching sight of her, he disappeared back into the trees.

Shivering, Yessna smacked her tongue against the roof of her mouth.

A nap was definitely in order.

But maybe she'd set the wards first.

Brinley stood solemnly amongst the green resting spot of their spirits. Hands clasped, Vannali's Linked looked over the gathered elders and sighed.

The Innarn flowing through her was reaching dangerous levels, but she had the feeling that it would all be required to call the spirits back to their resting places. The elders were... old. Weavers lived longer than the other races of Lissae, and the elders who remained were wizened and wispy haired. It had been quite astonishing that they'd been able to enact the preserved Innarn without combusting on the spot.

Brinley wasn't willing to risk their lives, and the knowledge they held, with a second mammoth use of Innarn so close to the first.

Stretching her arms out and rolling her head to loosen up neck muscles that were far too tight, Brinley took a deep breath and held it.

"Spirits return," she breathed out, starting the chant softly, and slowly growing in volume. Her Innarn was spilling out from her in silver, seeking tendrils.

Figures in ancient cuts of white robes surrounded them in a spiralling line, heading right for Vannali's Linked.

It's *working*. Relief made her stumble over the next word.

The robed beings stopped. Hooded faces turned towards her. As one, their hands rose, and they slowly pulled the material away from their heads.

Heart sinking somewhere in the vicinity of her ankles, Brinley caught sight of the last being she would have expected and passed away in a dead faint.

Hours later, when she woke up on the dew-soaked ground, Brinley moaned. Cupping her shoulder, she rolled over and groaned at the popping noise it made as it slid back into the socket.

Cautiously getting to her feet, Brinley glanced at the elders who had been kind enough to pass out alongside her. There was a distinct lack of stone sculptures around.

Shivering, Brinley had the horrid feeling it would be up to her to let the Altoriae know that the spirits were still walking amongst them.

CHAPTER SIX

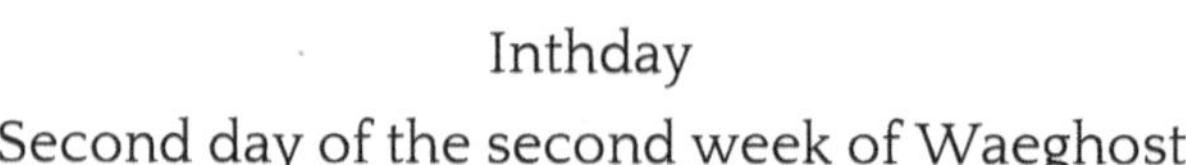

Inthday
Second day of the second week of Waeghost

Therion shaded his eyes against the glare of the too bright sun.

The Innarnians had dumped them on the island with nary a word, not that he could really blame them. Now they'd set the white-robed ones along the opposite shore, the light blinding as it reflected off their robes.

All he wanted to do was go home. There wasn't much there for him, a few chickens and a crop of wheat which needed harvesting. He had planned on trading it for some lumber to make a better bed for his ageing parents.

That was before he'd been drafted. All the able-bodied had been rounded up from the villages of Jinkor, shown how to swing a sword, and herded onto boats so quickly he barely had time to blink.

If what the Altoriae was saying was true, going home was no longer an option. Therion scowled. It was alright for *them*, with their Innarn and their powers. It was probably easy to make a new life when you could craft one straight out of the air. He could feel a rush of heat in his chest. Throwing his head back, Therion screamed. Heat surrounded him as jets of fire poured from his fingers.

An aborted scream doused the fire running through his veins.

Ishta, who'd been on his ship, peered around a tree trunk, staring at him with wide eyes. "I didn't know you were one of them," she whispered.

Therion looked at his shaking, soot-covered hands. "I didn't know either." He glanced over to where the white-robed figures had stood. The shoreline was devoid of life. Had they left before or after his spontaneous combustion? Either way, Therion had a feeling the answer wasn't going to be good for them.

Shari ran her finger down the list of the dead for the fifth time.

Grace still wasn't on it.

As much as her cousin annoyed her, Grace was the only cousin she had. Shari wasn't sure what it said about her that Grace insisted on trying to make her a pincushion whenever possible, but she'd happily deal with dodging blades if it meant seeing family that was closer to her age again.

Wolf and Belfar were great but so often lost in each other, and they had a life outside of hers. And Grace... she'd never have her parents again, but her prickly cousin reminded Shari of home.

Maybe she needed to talk to Skye? A quick scan showed Grace's roommate was in the castle kitchen. Shifting there, Shari smiled as Skye guiltily shoved the last of a muffin into her mouth.

"Oh, I don't blame you," Shari said. "Dealon's muffins are amazing. I was wondering if you'd seen Grace at all?"

Skye swallowed heavily and shook her head. "Not since the final battle on Lissae," she said. "I keep thinking she's going to pop up and scare the life out of me, but nothing yet."

Shari frowned.

"She hasn't tried to stab you again?" Skye asked hopefully.

Laughing, Shari shook her head. "Not since we crossed over." She admitted. "Maybe she got lost? She was up high. Maybe Grace ended up on a different island." The words rang hollow even as they left her mouth.

"Maybe," Skye said. She looked about as convinced as Shari felt. Snagging another muffin, Skye gave her a half-hearted wave and left the kitchen.

Shari slumped at the bench. Ronah didn't quite feel the same. A slumbering, lumbering beast, who felt so much more than the cheeky island she'd grown up with.

Reaching out with her Innarn, she prodded the island, sighing when there was no response.

She let her Innarn flow, poking and digging around the Shifting Islands, before coming back with readings she hadn't expected.

Innarn was at an all-time high, with a significant amount of the mainlanders they'd banished showing signs of abilities they probably weren't aware they had. There were more beings on the islands than Shari had thought arrived, and unless there had been a sudden spate of births, she should probably talk to Jonathan about it.

The one thing that was missing was her stabby cousin.

Somehow, Shari had the feeling Grace was still on Lissae.

Tania rubbed at her tired eyes and leaned against Collis. She missed Ronah's constant mental prattle. There had been an exhilarating moment when Ronah grew beyond her comprehension, when her head had once again been filled with her island's chatter. After the growth spurt, things had been depressingly quiet. It was making it hard to sleep.

"Did you... is it normal, to hear Ronah?" she asked her soul-match.

Collis offered a nod. "It's normal for the Linked to. My mother often commented on it," he said, wrapping an arm around her to rub her shoulder. "Most of us are not so fortunate, although Muran was able to hear the island as well."

"I miss it," she said.

"Do the other Linked hear their islands?" Collis asked.

Tania lifted her head. "I hadn't thought of that," she said. *'Zana, can you hear Rakemyst?'*

'Not since he grew.' There was a weariness to Zana's reply that Tania hadn't expected.

'Cyrus? Is Talhan speaking to you?' Tania included all the Linked in the send.

'No. I figure that he's regrowing crystal.' Talhan's Linked sounded as tired as she felt.

'Fenix?'

'Cantash has been quiet. I think zir is recovering after the growth spurt. I know I needed to when I grew a whole hands-width overnight.' Fenix, too, felt exhausted.

'You can remember being a baby?' Oakley teased. Over the top of Fenix's spluttering, Ginorti's Linked added, *'Island has been as quiet as the leaves.'*

'So long as it's not as silent as before, I'll take quiet,' Domic sent. *'I do believe Fenix is right, and our isles are recovering. If I reach out, I can still feel Akoren.'*

'I can feel Vannali too. She is mourning for her released spirits.' Out of all the Linked, Brinley was the best at hiding her weariness. *'She does, however, remain silent.'*

Tania flinched. If she never heard silence again, it would be too soon. Collis held her tighter and kissed the crown of her head.

'What do we do?' she asked.

'Wait,' Zana sent. *'All we can do is wait.'*

Anika sniffed and lifted her chin as she looked at the door of her childhood home.

"If you aren't ready, we don't have to do this today," Edward, her grandfather, said gently.

"If not today, then when?" Anika asked.

Edward grinned. "True."

Still, she paused a moment longer before reaching out and opening the door.

The silence inside was deafening. Dust drifted through the air, sparkling in the sunlight streaming through the uncovered windows. Anika sneeze twice.

With a whispered word from Edward, the dust disappeared, along with the wilted flowers in dry vases.

Her mother always had flowers in the house.

Sniffing again, Anika stepped through the door. "I'm not sure what you want me to do," she said. "Dad packed everything when he kicked me out."

Hanging his head, Edward rubbed a wrinkled hand over his face. "I should have stopped him," he said, his voice breaking.

"And then I would have spent the last weeks of their lives..." Anika gulped back the tears. "Fighting with them. I would have hated myself afterwards. It worked out for the best." She just had to keep telling herself that.

Arms wrapped around her, strong and sure, and Anika sank into the hug, grateful that her grandfather was still around. Her extended family was huge, and if she wanted, she'd never be alone again.

Samuel glared at Jetonyx, who was winging through the sky, light glinting off his new, golden scales. It was somewhat disconcerting to go from being the only golden Q'Aralide for the last four thousand years to having three others fly rings around him.

Shadow leaned harder against his leg, and Samuel buried his hand into the palon's thick fur. Ever since Shari had named Wisp, Shadow had all but glued himself to Samuel's side.

Not that he was complaining.

Annoyed chittering in his ear made him raise a hand automatically to the draci, who was demanding his own scratches as well. Sneeze had trained him without Samuel even realising.

"Clever, aren't you?" he asked.

'Yes,' Sneeze answered. One of his favourite things about the little draci was his absolute lack of pretence.

If only more beings could take a scale from Sneeze's book, the Realm would be a better place.

"You sulking?" Shari said, nudging his shoulder with her own.

No matter what the Altoriae said, he definitely didn't jump.

"No," he grumbled. He really did sound like a sulking teen.

Shari laughed. "You could go fly," she suggested. "I can hang out down here. Keep an eye on these two."

'I keep eyes on you,' Sneeze retorted.

'Of course you will, but she needs to feel needed,' Samuel soothed.

Huffing, Shari crossed her arms and looked away.

Sneeze nodded and flew to rest on Shari's shoulder. Shadow moved more slowly to her, taking a long look at Samuel as if to check he was alright.

"He prefers your company now," Shari said.

"I didn't mean to..."

"It's fine." She broke in. "I'm glad he has someone he feels safe with."

Sucking in a startled breath, Samuel changed form before he could say anything in reply.

Since when did beings feel *safe* around him?

CHAPTER SEVEN

Kerday

Third day of the second week of Waeghost

Vannali's Linked was sitting at the kitchen bench of Ronah's castle like she was there every day, casually carving off slices of a silvery fruit with her Innarn and eating them with dainty bites.

Shari paused in the doorway, taking in Brinley's profile. With the white hood thrown back, the dark bags under her eyes, the pallor of her skin, and the lines worn deep between her brows indicated that all had not gone smoothly for Vannali during the... change. Birth? Process of creating a new Realm?

The ground seemed to pulse under Shari's feet, and before she could contemplate the phrasing, Brinley turned to face her.

"Well met, Altoriae."

"Just Shari, please," she said.

Brinley nodded and wiped crumbs from her lips. The remains of one of Dealon's creations littered the plate on the counter before her. "Shari. I thought you might enjoy a tour of Vannali, now the worst of the change is over."

Change felt like too simple a word to encompass everything they had gone through, but maybe simple was best.

"A tour sounds great," Shari said. A glow by her side announced Wisp's arrival before the beast materialised. Almost without thought, Shari's hand dropped down and sank into his fur. He leaned against her, his weight comforting.

Between one heartbeat and the next, Jonathan and Samuel shifted in. The former looking decidedly rumpled, and the latter with a draci on one shoulder and a jet-black palon leaning on his other hip.

"Excellent. I did hope you'd all come," Brinley said. "Shall we?" The Weaver shifted away before the others could comment.

"What is it with the Linked and thinking we'll drop everything for them?" Samuel grumbled. "I was just about to eat."

Shari snagged a rutenberry muffin from the counter and tossed it at him. "Here."

After sniffing it cautiously, Samuel took a bite. He reached out and snagged three more as Shari shifted them to the location Brinley sent through.

Grinning, Shari bumped her shoulder against his arm and pilfered a muffin from his stash. "I haven't eaten either," she said as she walked towards the waiting Linked.

There was a brief scuffle behind her before Jonathan, holding half a muffin, appeared on her right.

Brinley was waiting for them, hood up, appearing serene as the Guardian and his apprentice fought over a muffin.

'*Are they always like this?*' Brinley sent to her on a tight band.

'*Only if there are rutenberries involved. Samuel would do pretty much anything for them,*' Shari replied. She took a bite of her own breakfast snack and shifted another into Samuel's hand before he became grumpy. They were standing on Vannali's side of the frost-covered bridge to Ronah.

Shari's breath was visible in the frigid air, and bumps littered her uncovered skin. Despite the early hour, there were still beings moving about in the chill of the fog, some lugging carts of goods towards the other bridges, some walking alone, white hoods visible in snatches through the mist.

'*Come,*' Brinley sent to the group.

Ignoring the twinge that reminded Shari of the last island she'd toured and catching her parents' gaze over the crowded chamber in the waters below Akoren, Shari followed the swishing white robe.

Without proper reference to how big Vannali was before, it seemed massive now. They walked for an age, both getting nowhere and travelling great distances. Shari could sense the forest they were heading towards, and it had been over four leagues away when they'd started. A mere ten minutes later, they were on the outskirts of it. The most noticeable feature wasn't the piles of broken stone that littered the sides of the wide path, but Brinley's flinch every time they passed another lot of rubble.

Entering the forest felt like stepping into another Realm. There was a quiet in these woods that was similar to the hush that fell over all beings who entered a forest, but this one was deeper. Denser.

'*The spirits here are restless,*' Samuel sent, stepping closer to her. It felt wrong to talk in the face of such silence.

'*I can feel it too.*' Shari didn't move away when Jonathan closed in on her other side. Spirits *could* be friendly. These felt strong enough to forcibly remove them if they so wished. A ghostly form slipped by, a robe brushing against the toes of Shari's boots, and tension seeped out of her shoulders.

'*I know these ones,*' she sent.

The spirit turned, and Shari felt it dip into her mind, sharing—not a scene from zir's untimely demise—but a snippet from when she'd used a spirit shield during the testing for the Guardian's apprentice.

'*I thank you for your help*,' she sent, tipping her head. The spirit bowed back and continued on.

Brinley weaved through the trees until they abruptly parted, and the group found themselves in a small clearing. Mossy logs appeared, large enough for them to lie on.

'*The easiest way to cover Vannali's... new expanse is to astral travel. Would you be willing to join me?*' Brinley sent.

With Jonathan and Samuel so close to her, Shari didn't even have to try to slip into their minds. The thoughts of *protectors, Shadow, Wisp*, filled her thoughts.

'*Of course*,' Shari sent, nudging Samuel in the ribs when he growled.

Rolling his eyes, Jonathan walked over to the log on her right, Samuel taking the one on her left. Shari laid on the log opposite Brinley, and Wisp's heavy weight settled across her chest. An *oof* from the left said Zoom... Shadow was doing the same to Samuel.

'*Ready?*'

Shari had to grin. Anyone else would have questioned Wisp laying on her, and the dangers of astral projecting with a creature so close, but it appeared that Brinley trusted them enough to know their limits.

'*Let's go*,' Shari sent.

Brinley's soul rose above her body and waited for the others to join her. Wisp let out a discontented whine, his eyes tracking Shari's astral form as she moved to the centre of the four logs.

Rising out of the clearing, Brinley beckoned to them, and Shari followed, Jonathan and Samuel close behind. Vannali's Linked shot upwards, out of the fog, and Shari grinned as she zoomed after her.

Vannali spread out below them, the white-tipped mountain peaks glowing orange in the morning light.

The forest ringed around the island, with gaps left for the roads that led to the centre city. A huge, round structure with concentric circular roads led to a tower in the middle.

'That's our library,' Brinley sent. 'A repository for our collective knowledge.'

'Was it damaged in the change?' Jonathan asked.

'Our scribes are checking at the moment.'

Something in the way Brinley answered caught Shari's attention. 'Not the elders?'

'They are otherwise engaged.'

Images of beings stepping out of stone, leaving behind the piles of rubble she'd seen on the journey to the forest flashed across the Linked's mind.

Shari shivered. She had the strong feeling that she was not going to like what the elders were checking out. She chanced a glance at Jonathan's astral form, which was scowling just as fiercely as she expected. A large part of Shari wanted to ignore the problem. To push it behind her where she had the luxury to worry about it later.

Heaving a sigh, Shari shook her head. Ignoring the issues hadn't worked so far, and there was no indicator that it was going to work this time.

'What has them worried?'

Brinley was looking over the mountain pass on the far side of the forest. Between the circular city and the lofty peaks, smoke rose in lazy spirals, showing smaller towns dotted here and there.

'The spirits should have returned to their rest. I have found that they are disinclined to do so.'

Shari blinked. 'The spirits that were called to help with the mainlanders?'

'Yes.'

'How do we return them to their rest?' Jonathan asked.

Astral form shivering, Brinley shook her head. '*We have tried. Said all the right words. Completed the motus and the ritual thrice, and still, they walk amongst us.*'

'*That's why I saw Kerk?*' Jonathan sent. Shari gave his astral form a sharp look. Her Guardian had forgotten to mention a previously deceased being walking amongst the living.

'*Were they a Weaver?*' Brinley asked.

'*No. He was one of the U'sala.*'

'*Then the problem may be bigger than I first expected.*'

Looking out over the snow blanketing Vannali, Shari shivered with more than just the cold.

'*Perhaps there is something in the caves.*' Brinley's thought was soft, but not enough to escape Shari's notice.

'*The caves?*' Shari asked.

Brinley startled. '*Yes, but you can't astral project there. We'd have to use physical forms.*'

'*If it stops the influx of beings who shouldn't be here, it's worth trying, right?*' Samuel asked.

'*Let us return to our bodies and see what the caves will show us then.*' Brinley seemed almost resigned to the idea.

Shari looked at Jonathan, who shrugged.

'*Worth a shot,*' Shari sent, and blinked, opening her eyes to see only white. For a moment, she thought she was somewhere else, but the weight on top of her and the huff of bad breath in her face made her realise she was staring at Wisp, who had moved since she'd left, laying his head next to hers so all she could see was his fur.

She pushed at him, groaning, until the Shadow Bringer moved. "Lump," Shari said as she got up.

"Almost as bad as Shadow," Samuel grumbled.

Grinning, Jonathan jumped to his feet. "Poor you," he said to them both.

Rolling her eyes, Shari looked at Brinley, who seemed to be fighting a smile.

"Shall we?" the Weaver asked. "The entrance isn't far." She set off, heading for part of the forest they hadn't seen yet.

After brushing past spirits as they walked, Shari started to smile. Each one was sharing a happy memory from their lifetime: paint splashing across a canvas, a hot meal pulled from the oven to share with friends, huddling under a blanket and watching shooting stars streaming past. Feeling properly happy for the first time in an age, Shari couldn't lose the grin even as the yawning entrance to the caves appeared as they entered another clearing.

"That's not ominous at all," Samuel muttered.

Shari was beginning to wonder if Samuel would have scales permanently indented in his neck with how hard Sneeze was pressed against him. "We'll be fine. The spirits will watch over us," Shari said.

Brinley gave her a sharp look but ducked her head as she entered the cave.

"Onwards," Jonathan said, following after the Linked.

Samuel's feet seemed glued to the forest floor.

"Together?" Shari asked.

"Let's," he said, linking their arms and trudging forward. The entrance was just wide enough for both of them to fit, Shadow and Wisp forced to trail behind them. The cave veered sharply to the right, the walls forcing them to walk sideways, facing each other, until opening out to what sounded like a huge space.

Once her eyesight adjusted, Shari gasped. The cavern was beautiful and reminded her of something she'd almost forgotten.

"The heart of Lissae," Samuel whispered. The sound bounced around the huge cave.

Brinley and Jonathan turned sharply to stare at him. Shari blinked slowly, ignoring everything other than the searing heat of Samuel's hand wrapped around her bicep, keeping her grounded as she took in the rest of the cave.

Throwing a ball of light into the air, she laughed. "It is. It's just like the heart," she said. The pastel walls weren't glowing, and balls of Innarn weren't racing through, but Shari had a feeling it was just a matter of time before that happened.

Something way up high chittered, and Shari craned her head.

There was a mass of something dark moving on the roof.

A tiny part broke away and fell, spiralling out of control. Moving before she even realised it, Shari held out her hands and the thing landed in them.

A creature no bigger than her thumbnail lay in her palm, looking up at her with a tan-coloured face and a tiny, dark brown body.

"What's this?" Samuel asked. He'd moved with her, rather than letting go of her arm.

"One of the pustish," Brinley said. "At least, that's what I think they are." She gestured to the mass above their heads. "They're creatures of myths. Tiny bats who are said to guard Spirit Innarn from misuse."

Looking at Brinley, Shari caught the tail end of a white robe whipping around the corner of the cave and wondered what, exactly, the pustish were protecting them from.

Tania blew into her cupped hands to try to simulate some sort of warmth.

An arm snaked around her, dropping a shawl warm with body heat across her shoulders. Looking up, Tania smiled at Collis. *'Thank you.'*

"Can't have you getting cold," he said. "Where are we going?"

Winding her arm around his, Tania leaned towards Collis, tugging him gently to the right of the main street. "Visiting the refugees. I feel the need to make sure they're settling in properly." She nodded at one of the U'sala cyclops as he walked past, but the twin ignored her, glazed eyes training sluggishly ahead.

Not *a morning person*, she figured with a shrug.

The refugee camp was looking more like a village, with simple rezems making the once flat plain now awash with hills. The occasional chimney stuck out, smoke forming lazy clouds of grey over the bright flowers and foliage that grew on their rooftops. Lines for drying clothing dotted the higher parts but were empty due to the light snow drifting from the sky.

A few kids were outside already, shrieking as they ran around the rezems. One child was taking giant steps in shoes that were clearly borrowed from an adult.

Tania furrowed her brow. Were the too-large shoes for fun or by necessity? She had a sinking feeling it was the latter.

"Where shall we start?" Collis asked.

The children turned, staring at them with wide eyes before disappearing, leaving tiny flurries of snow behind them.

"Oops," Tania muttered.

"Sorry," Collis said.

"That was not your fault. These children have been through a lot." Tania wrinkled her nose and waited for the adults to appear. A curtain twitched to the side in the closest window. Smoothing her features, Tania tried to convey that she was friendly and approachable.

Minutes later, an ancient, leathery skinned woman wrapped in a tatty shawl slowly emerged from the front door of the rezem. Curious faces peered through the slight gap she had left.

"Well met," Tania said.

The woman tipped her head, the closest to a greeting Tania figured she would be willing to make.

"I just thought I'd come by and make sure you were settling in alright, and to see if you need anything?" Tania smiled softly. Smiling too big would come off as insincere, and not smiling at all would not be trusted. Zana seemed to have perfected the balance, but if the scowl on the woman's face was anything to go by, Tania had a way to go yet.

"You are the one who talks to the island?" the woman asked haltingly.

"Yes, I am," Tania said.

"Do you know why we were ripped away?"

That is the question of the week. Tania reached out, seeking the connection that had become so familiar to her. 'Ronah, *what do I say?*'

There was no reply.

The truth had to be better than nothing, right? "Lissae is known as the Mother Realm, but the meaning had been forgotten until it was too late. We're now on a new Realm, and the islands are expanding, trying to settle. I'm so sorry that you were ripped away from everything again, but you will always be welcome here."

The woman scowled at her.

Tania was beginning to think that was just the way her face fell when she wasn't smiling.

"What about my son?"

"Your... your son?" Tania asked, confused.

"He was following us. Hadn't caught up. Is he here?"

Needles and haystacks, Tania thought. "I'm not sure. I can find out, though. What's his name?"

"Yirrisaunder," she said, gripping the crossover of her shawl tighter. The young faces at the door who had been whispering fell silent, as if the answer mattered more to them than it did to the woman.

Tania had the sinking feeling he wasn't just her son, but the children's father as well. "I'll check with the others and see if he arrived."

The lines on the woman's face caved for a moment, and Tania had the horrible feeling that she was thinking the same thing. *What if he hadn't made it?*

No use borrowing trouble. They would have more than enough of that to share around. "Is there anything else we can do for you to make things more comfortable?"

Expression closing off, the woman shook her head.

Tania felt a nudge, which she would have assumed was from Ronah, but her island still wasn't talking to her. Leaning in as if she was sharing a secret, Tania said, "I have a little brother who needs something to do. He's going a bit stir crazy. It would really help me out if you had some jobs for him."

The woman cracked a slight smile. "I have jobs. He strong?"

"Not yet." Tania winked, hoping Alistair would forgive the slight on his physique.

Laughing, she nodded. "Send him to Yirri. I will make him strong."

'*Alistair, do you still want to help out with the refugees?*' Tania sent. She received a sleepy confirmation in return. Grinning, Tania bowed her head. "I'll send him after lunchtime. Feel free to ask him to come back if he's useful."

"I'll make him useful," Yirri chuckled and, still gripping her shawl, disappeared back inside her rezem.

Grinning, Tania glanced at Collis. '*It feels so good to help.*'

'*Or to get others to do it for you.*' His laughter made her mind feel fuzzy and her knees go weak. '*Shall we continue?*'

Another being, this time a middle-aged male, was stepping out of the next rezem while watching them with wary eyes.

Pasting what she hoped was the right smile on, Tania bit back a sigh. It was going to be a long day.

Yessna prodded the fire as Shari sat down next to her. They'd had to set up a bonfire in the centre of the new village to keep Felton happy.

"How are you faring?" the little healer asked.

"Bored outta our skulls," Henot grumbled, the gnome crossing his arms, looking every inch the impatient troublemaker he was.

Shari grinned. "You want something to do?"

"What is there to do?" Nerina asked. "The dream Realm is sealed, as is the doorway. There's no way off this infernal Realm."

The temperature dropped, and the fire spluttered.

"Careful how you talk about my parents," Shari said, her voice low.

Yessna smoothed down her fur, trying to ignore the danger in the little healer's tone. "Nerina means no ill will to them. We aren't used to staying in the one place for so long without there being some sort of job involved."

Heat returned as the fire sparked merrily again. Shari stared into the flames. "I have a job for you, if you want." She glanced around the houses. "Although I can understand if you want to stay."

"We want the job," Kibon said.

Yessna almost fell off her log when Henot nodded vehemently, agreeing with the one with whom he usually fought tooth and nail.

"The mainlanders are having trouble settling in. And honestly, at this stage, I'd rather pound them into the ground than help them adapt."

"Where are they?" Felton asked.

Unnecessarily poking the flames, Yessna was glad Felton asked. She'd have to talk to Shari later about her blood-thirsty tendencies. But considering the Altoriae had just lost her parents and had her entire Realm literally transform beneath her feet, it was fair to say that now was not the right time.

"On an island off Rakemyst. Far enough away not to cause trouble, and with enough room for them all to live healthy, productive lives. It seems that not many of them survived the trip through the portal." Shari stared at the flames. "There has to be a reason for that. I need to believe that there is some good in the ones who made it here."

The fire crackled, the only sound in the silence.

"And you want us to do what?" Nerina asked gently.

"Look after them, guide them, teach them to be decent to others who are different," Shari said.

Henot, who'd been sneaking up to bite Kibon's ankle, sat with a huff. "Suppose we can do that."

"If we can get along, we can teach those mainlanders anything," Kibon laughed.

"So it's settled?"

Yessna looked around the little village she'd created. As nice as it was, they were still bored out of their fur and bickering constantly. "We'll help your mainlanders," Yessna said.

It would be good to be useful again. And if that came with a side of bloodshed, who was she to say no?

Asterion sighed as he slumped back into the padded chair, letting the thick cushions take the weight of his aching limbs.

Something was poking his leg. Leaning to the side, he fished around and pulled the forgotten diary out of his pocket.

"Huh." The innocuous cover did little to give away any information, but the contents could have saved them all a lot of grief.

So would have not tripping over the soldier.

Shoving the guilty thought to the side, Asterion settled deeper into the chair and started reading further than he had before. Perhaps the musings of one of the first settlers of the last Realm would help them figure out their next steps.

Flicking through the pages, Asterion devoured the words of one long gone.

The Realm is different. Bigger now. Xteria has all but quadrupled in size, and my nearest neighbour is no longer just over the fence, but a good five-minute walk before his house is in sight.

Innarn has changed too, becoming volatile and unpredictable. A small spark results in a roaring fire. Many, myself included, are struggling to regulate our output.

The beings here are different, too. There's more of them. Just this morning, I thought I saw Ailan, who has been dead for near on a decade. I must have been seeing things...

Asterion flicked through the pages, frowning until he came to a single line entry.

Ailan is alive. And he's not the only one.

He really needed to talk to the Guardian.

CHAPTER EIGHT

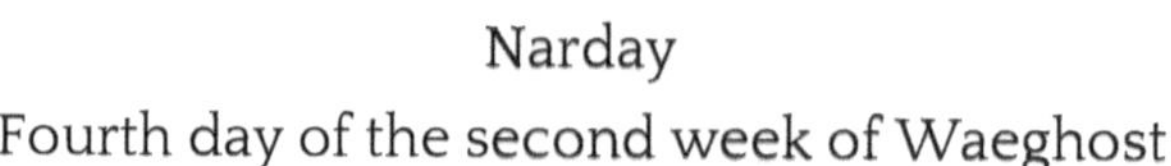

Narday
Fourth day of the second week of Waeghost

Cinorti's forests were alive in a way that Shari found entirely comforting.

Patting the trunk of one of the trees, she paused. The birds and insects had gone quiet. Reaching out, she brushed against a familiar Innarn.

"Well met, General Morrow," she called out.

"This reminds me of a spring long gone," the general said as he came into view.

"Forgive me for not discarding my weapons this time," Shari said. "We're still not sure what came through with us."

"I'll forgive you if you do me the same courtesy." He grinned at her, his mane of silvery hair flowing from the cue he'd tied it in.

"How have you fared? Are all your people safe?" Shari asked.

"Oakley sustained quite a knock to the head, or he would be here to greet you. Our Linked has been through much these last few seasons."

"Hopefully with the new Realm, things will settle down for a while," Shari said.

"We have found the gateway blocked, Altoriae. Is that your doing?"

Shari laughed. "I might, on occasion, beg the Ducibus to close a doorway off, but it's always at their whim. This is standard practice, apparently. Aimed at giving a new Realm time to settle."

The general looked away for a moment and took a breath. "Does our new Realm have a name?"

Feeling her heart sink, Shari wished she could just shift away and avoid the question forever. "Carilla. Named after the first two people through the portal."

Frowning, the general seemed to chew over her words. Shari saw the instant he realised who those two people were. "No," he breathed. "Truly?"

Shari nodded, sniffing in an attempt to hold back the tears she thought were over. Before she could blink, the general wrapped his arms around her, cradling Shari against his chest as he murmured nonsense words into her hair.

After an age, Shari was able to gather herself again, and gently pulled away.

"I am sorry, child, that our old Realm asked so much of you, and the new one took even more." General Morrow's voice was gentler than Shari had ever heard it.

Bobbing an awkward nod, Shari said, "Thank you." She wasn't entirely sure what she was thanking him for. Understanding? Compassion? Allowing her to cry all over his shirt?

"It is not always necessary to be strong," he said. "There is a strength in admitting weakness as well."

Shari felt more wrung out than strong at the moment. "I do thank you, General Morrow." She sniffed, and a quick flick of Innarn set her to rights again. "Will you let me know if anyone on Ginorti requires our aide?"

"Of course, Altoriae."

"I, ah..." *Jonathan's going to kill me.* "I don't think I should use that title. The Altoriae is Lissae's protector, and we're not on Lissae anymore."

The general bowed his head. "As you will it, Shari."

After dipping her head in return, Shari shifted away then realised that, once again, the general was privy to knowledge that Jonathan should have had first.

'*Jonathan, I've been thinking...*' she sent, hoping that immediately was soon enough for her Guardian.

Wait. If she was no longer the Altoriae, was Jonathan still the Guardian?

'*How do you feel about being Guardian of Carilla, instead of the Altoriae?*'

'*Shari,*' Jonathan sighed. There was a hum as Samuel joined the discussion as well. '*What have you done?*'

Explaining her reasoning twice in a row drained any joy Shari had left from Ginorti's forest.

'*It makes sense,*' Samuel said. '*But I still think you're a protector.*'

"What if I don't want to be any more?" Shari whispered to her empty room.

There was no answer.

Samuel stretched and stared unseeingly at the ceiling. Shari wanted to renounce her title of Altoriae.

A small part of him could understand. Shari had carried the burden of protecting Lissae for almost as long as she'd been alive. But without the Altoriae, what was he?

Sneeze bit his ear.

"Ouch!" Samuel slapped a hand to the side of his head. When he pulled it away, it was dotted with blood.

'*You are you. You are not her,*' the draci growled at him.

"Did you have to bite me to get your point across?" Samuel said, rising from his bed.

Jetonyx poked his snout through the doorway. '*Better Sneeze than me. I could snap your mortal form in half.*'

"Do you even know what he was referring to?" Samuel asked, pulling a shirt over his head.

Hatchling and draci had a quick mental conversation.

'Yes.' Jetonyx pouted. '*You are more than an apprentice. You are the Golden Priest, eldest of our kind, and charged to teach us the ways to the Q'Aralide.*'

"Are you making this up as you go?" Samuel laid a hand on the hatchling's snout and pushed him out of the doorway.

'*Yes, but it sounds impressive, and even better. It's true.*'

Three golden Q'Aralides, lined up by size, were gazing at him with huge, pleading eyes. Shadow, the only remaining black spot in his life, sat on his haunches between Tormorylth and Kemanyr and joined in.

"Fine!" Samuel threw his hands in the air. "I'll teach you my ways!" *By Cylanthar's bells, my teachings will be vastly different to what I learned at their age.* A chime sounded in the back of his mind, and pleased laughter rang through his head.

Life in this new Realm would be different for all of them.

"You used to talk to Lissae, didn't you?" Tania blurted.

Shari paused in the act of wiping down the counter of the tavern. She hadn't really known what to do and decided to fall back to her roots and keep her parents' dream going. She wasn't sure how long she could keep it up.

"Yes, she stopped years ago though. I did fall into her heart when I died, and I'm pretty sure that she spoke to me then, but I can't really remember it."

Tania slumped.

"What's wrong?" Shari asked.

"The islands aren't talking to us," Tania said.

It took Shari a moment to figure out what Tania meant. "The Linked?"

Nodding glumly, Tania rested her head on the palm of her hand, her elbow propping her arm up.

Reaching out with her Innarn, Shari prodded at Ronah. There was a feeling of weariness, like someone who'd just fallen asleep and didn't want to be disturbed. "I don't think it's the same thing," Shari said. "Maybe it's just growing pains."

Tania gave her a trembling smile. "I hope you're right."

Shari went back to wiping down the counter. She hoped she was right, too.

Jonathan looked up from his desk, nose twitching. Zac was peering around his office door, a tray of something tantalising held in his hands.

"What do you have there?" he asked.

"Something to celebrate," Zac said, entering the room.

Setting his pen down, Jonathan pushed away from the desk. "And what are we celebrating?"

"I was going to say something trite, like 'survival', but with you around, that would make every day a reason to celebrate." Zac grinned at him.

Laughing, Jonathan stood and made his way to the pair of chairs off to the side. There were definite benefits to working out of the castle library, and quite possibly the best one was the wards which allowed Zac to visit.

"Really though, this is to celebrate the break from fighting every night." He held a hand up as Jonathan opened his mouth. "It's a small break, and one that's not likely to last, but I think it still counts."

"I swear, if I end up in someone else's dreamscape tonight, we're going to have words," Jonathan growled.

Zac grinned at him and lifted the domed lid.

Whatever Jonathan had been expecting, two bowls of pale cake floating in thick yellow sauce was not it. "What's this?"

"Weaver's speciality. Self-saucing lemon pudding." From the proud expression Zac sported, he must have made it himself.

Hiding a grimace at the idea of soggy cake, Jonathan smiled gamely. "It smells amazing." At least that wasn't a lie.

After setting the tray down, Zac handed him a bowl and spoon. "Dig in!"

Perching on the edge of the armchair, Jonathan hesitantly took a bite. Zesty sauce burst over his tongue, followed by cakey pudding so light it just about melted away and made him moan in delight.

"They say it's a perfect dessert for a cold night," Zac said.

Gaze flicking to the still very blue sky on display outside the window, Jonathan raised a single brow.

"Well, I never have been one to play by the rules, have I?" Zac grinned and took another bite.

"Have you had much contact with the Weavers?" Jonathan asked, trying not to appear too eager as he scooped another spoonful up.

"Off and on through the years. Temira would often get them in if someone suffered a brain injury. They're the best at realigning the spirit with the body."

Jonathan hummed, gazing at nothing as he thought about what Brinley had inadvertently said. "What about when they raise the spirits?"

"They'd only do that in the most extreme cases. Weavers firmly believe that spirits need their rest. Quite often, it's the only way for the body to heal," Zac said.

"How do they even return the spirits to rest?"

"You're talking like they already raised them." Zac curled his spoon around the edges of his bowl, chasing the last of the sauce. "Wait. You don't mean the ones that helped with the mainlanders?"

Idly, Jonathan nodded. *How rude would it be to use his finger to get the remaining sauce out of the bowl?*

"Jonathan, do you mean to tell me there are spirits walking around, unchecked?" Zac sat his bowl down.

"Well, the Weavers know who they are. I'm sure they aren't entirely unchecked." The words sounded hollow even to his own ears.

"Forget dreamscapes. It looks like we'll be back to fighting on our own land," Zac muttered.

Jonathan wished he could blame the sinking feeling on the pudding, but he knew that wasn't the case at all. He could only hope that Zac was wrong.

Asterion knocked on the door to the office. "I did not mean to overhear, but that's exactly what I was hoping to talk to you about. Here." He crossed the room and handed Jonathan a small book.

The cover was so old, it was crumbling, the pages yellowed and brittle. And on the first page, there was a hand-written inscription. *Diary of–*

The last word was lost to time, the name rubbed away centuries ago.

"This is a diary of one of the first inhabitants of Rataeo, the last Realm to be born. In it, he talks of the silence before the birth, and after, he talks of spirits walking the lands." Asterion ever so carefully used Innarn to flick to the appropriate passages.

Jonathan bent over the book, skimming the passage until a part jumped out at him.

> *Whilst all care be taken, the Weavers were unable to stop the influx from the Spirit Realm. Just like in life, not all souls are friendly.*

"Maybe we do have something to worry about," he said, sending a warning to Shari to look out for beings who she thought were dead.

Shari was in the middle of sweeping the floor after a long day of tending the tavern, Jonathan's warning ringing through her mind.

Anika slipped through the doors, heels clicking on the floor, and froze. "Oh, it's you."

"Well met to you too," Shari said, trying not to roll her eyes.

"I... forgot." Anika sniffed and turned, grabbing the handle of the door.

"Wait," Shari said, resting the broom against a table. "About my parents?"

"I used to come in and talk to your mum. I suppose I showed up out of habit." Anika sniffed again, and Shari resisted the urge to sigh.

"Do you want to talk about it?"

Anika scoffed. "No."

The tears pooling in her eyes said yes.

"Suppose we have another thing in common," Shari said. "I was sorry to hear about your parents as well."

"I don't know how to be an orphan," Anika said.

"Me either," Shari said softly, her gaze drawn to the bookcases and empty weapon racks.

"Maybe we should start a club," Anika said with a mirthless laugh. "The Lonely Orphan Society."

"Have to invite others, though. A club of two is just sad," Shari said.

"A club of more than two for this topic is worse." Anika's expression fell even further before she gave a hearty sniff and pasted something that barely passed for a smile on her face. "I'll get the word out. Meet here at this time next week?"

"Sure," Shari said lightly. She doubted that many would want to connect over something so morbid.

CHAPTER NINE

Rasshday

Fifth day of the second week of Waeghost

tomping her boots, the snow sizzled, melting as it hit the ground. Shari doubted it was ever cold enough for it to form on Cantash.

Fenix greeted her warmly, and Shari noted the bags under their eyes.

"Is everyone accounted for?" Shari asked Fenix.

Fenix nodded wearily as they led Shari through the winding streets. Like their fellow Linked, Fenix was exhausted. Could it have something to do with the Islands growing so much as they had?

"How did the underground go?" Shari asked.

"Mostly okay," Fenix said. "Although a draci got free, and we've been trying to round him up to keep him safe."

Thoughts immediately turning to Sneeze, Shari looked around as if she could pluck the draci from the air. "Is he in danger above ground?"

"Too many predators, unless he decides a person is his," Fenix said, and pointed right.

Turning down the street Cantash's Link indicated, Shari noted the gutter on one of the houses was a tad loose. A flick of a finger and it righted itself.

Something rattled in the metal as it moved, and Shari froze. "What was that?"

Fenix tilted their head. "Sounds like Hail."

Eyes flicking to the clear sky, Shari shook her head. "Can't be. Sky's clear."

"Not that kind of hail," Fenix said with the grin. They let out a short whistle, and a tiny blue-black head poked over the top of the guttering.

The creature chirruped, claws coming out to grasp the rim before it launched itself off.

Directly at Shari.

Gasping, she spread her hands, and the blue-black draci landed in them with the smallest of grunts. The petite head tilted, and the creature snorted at her, a cloud of steam coming from its nose.

'I *Hail*,' it sent. '*And you mine.*'

Shari blinked. "Sorry?"

The draci blinked and sat up primly, paws neatly placed on the palm of Shari's hand. '*You need draci. You mine now.*'

Fenix grinned and patted Shari on the back. "Looks like you've got a new friend."

A *new friend. Called Hail.* Shari was sure that somewhere, her mother was grinning in encouragement, and her father would be trying to smother an astonished laugh. A friend called Hail when she still had nightmares about clouds? Someone had to be amused somewhere. '*Well, Hail. Do you know Sneeze?*'

Hail's head shimmered blue as it drooped. '*Miss Sneeze.*'

'*Not for much longer. Sneeze has... adopted my friend.*'

Sitting up straight again, Hail smiled and stretched out his paws until he was lying on her hand, head resting on Shari's fingertips. '*See Sneeze?*'

'*We will. I just need to finish making sure Cantash is okay.*'

Yawning, Hail nodded and slumped, the little form going boneless.

Shari looked at Fenix, who was beaming at her. "Hail is from the same clutch as Sneeze but has been constantly escaping. Now we know why."

"Because of me?" Shari asked, gently running a finger along Hail's back.

"Yep. He knew his human was out here somewhere but didn't know where. Cheeky draci."

'Not *cheeky*. *Clever*.' Hail's thoughts were sleepy as he dozed in her hand.

"How am I meant to...?" Shari waved her free hand, trying to encompass everything she normally did. Protect. Fight. Defend.

Fenix's smile changed. "Maybe Hail is a sign that you don't have to anymore."

Still stroking the draci, Shari looked away. Her conversation with General Morrow had been on a whim. Despite wanting to give up the mantle of Altoriae, she was unsure how to feel about having the task she'd been given as a child stripped away from her.

"Shall we continue the tour?"

Shari nodded, her thoughts elsewhere as Fenix showed her how much Cantash had grown. The gaps between the houses were the same in this new Realm, but the amount of land they had was massive once you moved away from them.

"Do you have any plans for what you're going to do with all this?" Shari nodded to the gently rolling hills.

"There's talk of seeing if the eobustus will migrate top-side. We're trialling it in small groups at a time, and most are doing really well. Oakley is coming by later to set up some fencing, as the crystals aren't doing much of a job to keep them contained."

"Will they get enough magma up here?" Shari asked, finger continually stroking Hail's back in a gentle motion.

"Oh yeah, the magma is easy. And there's more room to run than they've ever had before. Which—" Fenix huffed as one of the coal-black horses bolted past them, a blur of speed. "Is part of the problem."

Shari bit her lip so she wouldn't giggle. "I can see how that would be a challenge."

Fenix glared at her, but there wasn't any real heat behind it.

It did, however, make Shari think of the Linked's earlier comment. If the eobustus were able to overcome centuries of living underground, maybe not fighting was a genuine option.

Leaving their little village had been surprisingly hard, but the thrill of a waiting fight was a stronger temptation than the repetitive stability the village had brought.

Yessna sighed as Henot tried to take a chunk out of Kibon's shin. Seeing the two of them fighting made her feel settled. With decades of practice, she plucked Henot up and tossed him to Nerina, careful of his pointy teeth.

"Ready?" she asked. The others, weighed down by their packs, nodded.

It was time to go stir up some mainlanders.

Shifting to the tiny island was anticlimactic. Yessna had half-expected an unfriendly greeting party, but of course, the ones banished to the island had no Innarn at all.

Still, for Blanks, it took a surprisingly short time for one to appear—although he lost all credibility when he dropped the wire pot he was holding and what must have been his dinner scurried away.

"Well met," Yessna purred.

The mainlander continued to gape at them for more time than was polite. Swallowing heavily, he finally found his voice. "Well... met..." he stammered.

Yessna smiled, careful to show her fangs.

They were going to have *fun* here.

Tania reached out, brushing against the sleepy consciousness that was too tired to even grumble at her.

"When are you going to wake up?" she muttered. Being Linked to an island who was almost too big to be called an island any more was a challenge she hadn't expected. Especially when said not-island wasn't answering her pleas for help.

"Talking to yourself again?" Caleb asked.

Tania lifted her head enough to poke her tongue out at her step-brother. "Ronah's not answering."

He knocked his shoulder against hers as he lay down next to her on the only clear patch of grass in the snow-dusted garden. "Do you remember when we first met?"

"How I was so tiny, yada, yada," Tania said. Caleb loved repeating the story any time he thought she was getting too big for her britches.

He clamped a hand over her mouth but withdrew it before she had a chance to lick him. "You were so fierce. You scowled up at me like a white-haired demon, even as you were swaying on your feet. I'd said something to try and make you laugh, but you were unimpressed."

Frowning, Tania turned to look at him, but kept her hands splayed on the ground. "That's not what you usually say."

"What thirteen-year-old wants to admit that a tiny waif intimidated him?"

Tania rolled her eyes.

"Anyway. You were swaying. You raised your finger to poke my chest, took a step forward, and collapsed against me. I was so stunned, I barely thought to catch you. But I did."

"Chivalry isn't dead," Tania said, deadpan.

"Knights are fables. Stop distracting me—I'm trying to comfort you," Caleb grumbled.

"Doing a bang-up job," Tania said, rolling her eyes.

Caleb poked her. "I caught you and took you upstairs. You slept for almost a solid week. Mum told us you'd been sick before you left, that you'd barely slept, and once your body stopped, it needed time to heal. Ronah's gone through a big change. Maybe she just needs time to rest, like you did."

"What did it feel like, for you to have to wait?" Tania asked.

"Agony. This tiny little thing had taken over my bed, and I had to sleep on the lounge room floor."

Tania laughed, but the sound was hollow. "It's not just Ronah being asleep. Innarn is being weird as well. Air is way stronger. Crystals either hold charge or randomly stop working, which, by the way, is not great if it's a fence. Fire Innarn is almost out of control and forget Plasma—a single burst levelled a bereni tree yesterday. Collis spent the afternoon rebuilding it."

Caleb patted her hand. "I can't help you with the Innarn stuff, but I can say that, well..." He lifted his hand so she could see it and clicked his fingers. A steady green flame flickered to life, spinning a hair's breadth above his skin. "I was kinda hoping you could help me."

'Collis,' Tania sent, gaze on the first Innarn her until-then Blank eldest brother had ever produced. 'Have you ever seen green flames?'

Shari jerked as a cold nose touched the side of her neck.

'Sneeze?'

'You want to go see Sneeze now?' Shari asked. They'd just come back from Cantash, and she had thought that Hail would want to see his new home first.

'Sneeze,' Hail confirmed.

'Samuel, are you accepting visitors at the moment?' Shari sent.

'Why are you asking? Usually you just show up.' His send didn't sound aggravated at all, merely curious.

"I can be polite," Shari grumbled. Hail huffed cold air against her neck. Ignoring the chuckling draci, Shari sent, '*I have someone here who would like to see Sneeze.*'

'*Ah, so you don't want to see me at all.*'

She couldn't tell if Sam was joking or not. '*I'm coming over,*' she warned. If Samuel was going to be a tu'zar's arse when she tried to be polite, she wouldn't bother about doing it again.

Laying a careful hand along Hail's back, Shari shifted to the garden in front of Samuel's home.

He was lounging against the door, Sneeze peering blearily at her from Samuel's shoulder.

"Who so desperately wants to meet Sneeze?"

'*Everyone,*' Sneeze sent confidently, sitting up tall.

Shari smothered a smile. Hail was quivering with excitement on her shoulder. '*Hail.*'

Sneeze froze. '*Hail?*'

"Who is Hail?" Samuel sounded exactly like a suspicious father.

A pang of longing lodged somewhere near her heart.

'*I Hail.*' The blue-black draci poked his head out from under her hair.

Sneeze leaped into the air, and Hail followed suit, the two colliding. Shari and Samuel both cast an Air cushion, which sent the two draci spiralling upwards with the combined force. Their wings beat in tandem, even as they grasped paws and chittered at each other.

Samuel's eyes never left the pair. "I didn't realise Sneeze was lonely."

"Sometimes you don't realise you're lonely until someone else points it out," Shari said.

"Speaking from experience?"

"You could say that." Shari felt Samuel's gaze on her but refused to meet his eyes.

"Perhaps we could occasionally be lonely together?"

Shari's gaze snapped to his. "Perhaps," she said with a grin.

The two draci played together for hours, catching up with each other and chittering almost non-stop. Shari was tempted to leave and return, feeling like she was meant to be doing *something*, but every time she made a move, Hail's wings would droop, and Shari couldn't find it in her to deny the draci.

The hatchlings came out to play as well, and Kemanyr looked disappointed.

'*Were you expecting someone else?*' Shari grinned. The tiny golden Q'Aralide had grown even more.

'*Sweet treats.*' Kemanyr's send was so mournful.

Shari looked at Samuel, who flushed red.

"She means Lizbeth."

Biting her tongue, Shari managed to keep a straight face. '*I don't have any rutenberries, but maybe you could grow some?*'

'*How?*' Jetonyx asked.

"Really, you should be asking Edward. He's far better at gardening than anyone else on Ronah," she said.

Tormorylth looked at her with wide eyes.

"Fine," Shari grumbled, and found herself giving an impromptu lesson on gardening to three of the most unlikely beings.

By the end of the afternoon, they had each sowed rows of rutenberries, and were now lazing in the rays of the slowly sinking sun.

Shari looked around. She'd spent a totally unproductive day, and the Realm hadn't ended. Surreptitiously, she reached down and patted the tilled soil. *Thank you.* She could only hope that her parents understood the message.

Cyrus wiped the sweat off his brow. He'd been sweeping out the Techno Centre by hand all day after a failed attempt at Innarn that morning had seen one of his more delicate inventions sparking in an ominous way.

Aching muscles and trembling limbs were making him reconsider the ban he'd put out on using Innarn around the centre.

"Surely it wouldn't cause too much hassle," he muttered. A quick, passive scan showed he was the only one in the building. It would be the work of moments to get all the debris out and ensure that there was no more risk of contamination. After propping the broom up against the wall, Cyrus gathered his Innarn and flicked it through the upper levels first.

Easy.

The first underground level was a little tricker with grime and rubbish hiding in places that he wasn't expecting. Still, his Innarn swept it all together and got rid of it with barely any hassle.

Covering a yawn, Cyrus slumped against the wall. *One last go.* Then he could sleep.

Taking a breath, Talhan's Linked gathered his Innarn and swept it through the last levels of the Techno Centre. A familiar rush of his island adding Innarn to his own filled his veins, and Cyrus swore as careful control spiralled away into mayhem.

Loose items from all over the lower levels slammed into walls and tumbled through doors, with some bouncing off the shield Cyrus hastily raised around him.

But the crystals.

The crystals pierced the shield like a sword slicing unprotected skin. Time seemed to slow as Cyrus turned and tucked his limbs into his torso, curling down to make himself as small as possible.

It didn't stop the sharp shards from shearing through his clothing and striking his spine.

Didn't stop the blackness from creeping in at the edges of his vision.

Stop! The command thundered out of him, and it was the last thing he knew before the Realm faded away.

Chapter Ten

Vebaday

Sixth day of the second week of Waeghost

ollis stretched his arms to the sky and sighed when his shoulders made crunching noises.

"You sound like an old man," Remmy said.

"Not as old as you," Collis shot back.

Remmy laughed and swiped at him with the broom in his hand.

A group of the Returned had been cleaning the streets of Talhan's main city. With the lack of Innarn before the crossing, there were bits of littered tech and crystal everywhere. Cyrus had begged for help first thing in the morning. Apparently, he had discovered that using Innarn resulted in 'unpleasant complications'. The Linked wouldn't expand on the statement, and with the amount of pain leaking through his send, Collis had not been about to ask.

"How are you settling in?" Remmy asked.

Collis glared at the dark-haired man. "I could ask the same of you." This was the third Realm the Returned had shared.

"Ah, but I asked first."

If Remmy poked his tongue out, Collis was going to sever it. He was acting like the sibling Collis had never had. "This one feels..." He paused, searching for the right word.

The Realm itself seemed to hold on to a breath, waiting for his answer.

"... safe."

"Yeah. It's weird, isn't it?" Remmy said. "I keep waiting for something to happen. A nasty to drop from the sky, or a battle to the death."

"I swear, if something happens now, I'm going to blame you." Collis swept with renewed vigour but kept one eye on the sky all the same.

Jonathan looked up as Zac entered the office.

"I've been banished from the Techno Centre for the day. Cyrus is working on something top-secret, so I thought I'd come and annoy you instead," Zac said, making himself at home in the chair opposite Jonathan's desk.

"You're hardly an annoyance," Jonathan said.

Zac flashed him a delighted grin. "Is there anything you need help with?"

"Are you any good at mapping? I'm trying to redo the maps to show the new configuration of the islands."

"I've mapped a few things in my time." Zac grinned.

"Excellent. Do you want to work on Talhan? I'm just finishing up Rakemyst."

"What about Ronah?"

"She was the first, of course." Jonathan smiled.

"Of course," Zac repeated, leaning over the desk to start.

The sound of quill on parchment echoed through the room as the pair worked in tandem. The two Shifting Islands came to life under their hands. Zac and Jonathan took turns in Astral Projecting then coming back to add the details to the maps. Jonathan had to admire Zac's skill as he put the final flourish on the Farm Land area not long before lunch.

He paused when Zac's stomach rumbled. "Hungry?" he asked, lips quirking up in a grin even as his own stomach joined in.

"About as hungry as you. Did you eat breakfast?"

"Ye..." Jonathan stuttered at Zac's raised eyebrow. "Yesterday," he admitted.

"Time to fix that," Zac said. "And possibly get out of this office for a bit. I wonder what the food is like on Vannali?"

"There's a restaurant there I was hoping to try. Shall we?" Jonathan asked.

"Let's."

Swiftly, the two set a ward over their work, ensuring that the ink was dry under a charm. With the maps for both Ronah and Rakemyst finished, and Talhan and Cantash on the way, the islands were almost halfway done.

Holding out his arm, Jonathan grinned when Zac took his hand. He shifted them to the Anima Mundi, an exclusive restaurant which served food meant to feed the body as well as the soul.

"Well met." The Weaver who greeted them was dressed in robes that reminded Jonathan of curls of white smoke. "We have a table ready for you."

"Did you send ahead?" Zac asked as they followed the host.

Jonathan shook his head. "Anima Mundi is famous for knowing exactly when you will arrive and what you are craving."

"Your starters will arrive shortly." Their host, face hidden by ze's hood, bowed and disappeared like the smoke of his robes.

"Impressive," Zac said.

The table they were seated at allowed them to be side-by-side. Silvery curls drifted lazily over the surface, making the material it was made from hard to distinguish. The translucent walls showed shadowy leaves, giving the impression that they were somewhere in a forest, even though the restaurant was nestled in one of the busiest streets of Vannali.

Zac gasped as a grey tuscaro perched on the window they were facing. The bird tilted its head one way, then the other, sizing them up. Opening its white beak, it sang the sweetest song Jonathan had ever heard. He wrapped an arm around Zac, and the two leaned into each other as the tuscaro finished its spontaneous performance and flitted away.

The host returned before either of them could say a word and placed plates covered by a clear dome before them. Under the dome, curls of smoke wafted lazily, obscuring the food inside.

"Lean over and burst the dome, breathing in as you do so," the host instructed, then faded away again.

After raising a brow at Zac, Jonathan picked up his fork and did as the host had told them to. Breathing in, he could smell the sea of Freeson and the wood of the ship from the last voyage he'd taken with his father. The pale, red-veined flesh of the phantom fish sat in a silver broth dotted with flakes the colour of parchment.

His gaze slid to Zac's plate, which held vibrantly coloured vegetables in a blue broth. The expression on Zac's face was just as shocked as Jonathan felt.

"This reminds me of my childhood," Zac said, spearing a purple twig from the plate and glancing at it with awe.

Jonathan gulped, his gaze drawn to the phantom again. "Me too," he said, voice shaking.

Zac popped the twig in his mouth and moaned.

Cautiously, Jonathan speared a bit of the phantom and raised it to his lips.

"*Good eatin', phantom,*" echoed through his memory as the soft flesh dissolved in his mouth. The fish was, by far, the tastiest he'd ever had, but the recollection of the red scales seared into his father's hands meant he'd never dared to try it before.

Lost in thought, the pair ate silently until their host appeared and spirited their plates away. Tiny bowls of rounded ice took their place.

"A palate cleanser," the host said, and stood to the side.

Exchanging a glance, Jonathan and Zac spooned up the ice and dutifully took a bite.

Waves crashed and broke inside his skull, and Jonathan found he could finally breathe freely after the intensity of the first dish. Zac looked almost disappointed but didn't say a word as their host had returned to the table again.

This dish was served on one long oval platter. Blackened chips ringed the perimeter, while chunky diced tomatoes and persea fruit sat under a row of stone-coloured beans, which held a fissure of white in the middle. Picking up the glass spoon on his side of the platter, Jonathan chanced a look at Zac, whose hand was shaking.

"This reminds me of..." Jonathan started.

"Tuklopia," Zac said.

Jonathan glanced up at where their host had been and took a breath to control the shaking of his hand. Tuklopia had been where everything had changed for them. He'd been scared after listening to Joshua's stories about the dangers of caring for others. When the attack during a patrol on Tuklopia had happened, Jonathan had caved and said his eyes had been damaged.

Zac, who had been the one to bring him back to Lissae, had seen it as a personal failing and had withdrawn, seeking a cure for something that didn't need fixing. It had caused them to be apart for years.

Gamely, Jonathan scooped up some of the food. Under a layer of delicious vegetables, it tasted like fear and regret.

Numb, Jonathan ate, the bitterness burning his eyes and making them water.

"Not my favourite thing," Zac murmured, his voice breaking the silence that surrounded them. Jonathan made a noise of agreement.

"Yet it helped shape who you are today," their host said, appearing suddenly once more. The half-empty platter flickered on the table and vanished.

A new set of tiny bowls with ice took its place. They fell on it instantly before sitting back and glancing awkwardly at each other.

"Perhaps this next dish will be to your liking?" the host suggested. A dark-skinned hand appeared and waved over the table, and another oval dish appeared.

This one had two orange translucent towers topped with red metallic dust. Green, the colour of Shari's healing Innarn, melded the two sides in a frozen treat.

Zac gave him a concerned look before he glanced at the host. "I'm not sure if I can eat any more."

The Weaver was unmoved. "You can."

Giving Jonathan another look, Zac picked up his fork and cracked the crystal tower, startling when it shattered with a scream.

"Eat," the host insisted.

Following Zac's lead, Jonathan tensed before he broke the tower so he wouldn't flinch and gamely picked up a piece.

Reaching over, Zac stilled his hand. "Let me try first. If my eyes turn orange, you'll be able to stop me easily."

Jonathan nodded hesitantly. It was not in his nature to let someone else take a risk like that, but for Zac, he could.

Popping a shard into his mouth, Zac locked eyes with Jonathan and chewed. He swallowed and raised a brow.

"No orange," Jonathan said, relieved.

"Your turn," Zac murmured.

With a sigh, Jonathan took a bite. A citrus zing flashed across his tastebuds, harsh almost to the point of pain, before it faded and became sweet relief.

Zac used a shard to scoop up some of the green sorbet from the middle. He chewed for a moment and froze.

Raising a brow, Jonathan reached over and tried the same thing. Tart, sweet, pine and leather, crisp mornings, and a fireplace.

"It reminds me of you," they said simultaneously.

They polished off the plate in record time.

"Last dish," the host announced, and set two sticks of woven silver sugar before them.

"I've heard that this is the dish everyone comes for," Jonathan said to the host.

The Weaver's hood bobbed with a nod.

"Why?" Zac asked.

"It is the future," the host said, and disappeared.

Jonathan blinked a few times, before turning to Zac. "I'm not sure if that was meant to sound ominous or not."

"One way to find out," Zac said, and took a bite.

Following suit, Jonathan bit down and met Zac's gaze, grinning dopily. "Tastes like happiness to me," he said.

Zac grinned back.

As Jonathan finished the last of the dessert, he just hoped that the future wouldn't take too long to arrive.

Cyrus panted as he used his Innarn to pull another chunk of crystal from the ones imbedded in his spine. The next time he thought to take a shortcut, he would remember this moment.

Biting down on the strap the healer had provided, he grunted as they applied the balm and sealed the wound. They had discovered, early in the process, that if the healers tried to remove the crystals, they would simply return to his back as if they'd never left.

Pulling on Talhan to numb the pain had also proven to be a bad idea. Crystals had started randomly sprouting across his body, and only the healer's startled shout had stopped him.

Groaning, Cyrus let his head loll sideways. Pain was a constant friend at the moment, and he wished he could tell it where to go.

"Just a few more," the healer assured him.

Cyrus snorted. The same words had been said on and off for the last few hours. 'Lies,' he sent. Still, he wrapped his Innarn around the next chunk and pulled.

A being more spirit than body shivered into existence. Lost in the folds of a cloak, bones rose as flesh started to form a hand. The being stretched and grinned for the first time in far too long.

'Split the doorway to survive,' the cloaked figure said.

'That, I can do.' He turned and looked at the grave markers littering the cemetery.

Time to wake some old friends.

CHAPTER ELEVEN

Zoeday

Seventh day of the second week of Waeghost

Shari slid neatly to the side as a bunch of children skidded past, shrieking and laughing. Unable to help the grin on her face, she continued on, hoping to find an elder around.

"Come to check on us, have you?"

Shading her eyes, Shari glanced in the direction the voice had come from.

Standing in the shade of the veranda, the man's shock of white hair above sun-darkened skin made Shari pause. The craggy lines on his face confirmed he was one of the elders of the group.

"Just wanting to make sure you have everything you need," she said easily. Wisp leaned against her leg, and Shari buried her hand in his fur. Hail chittered in her ear, hugging as far around her neck as he could with his tail.

The elder smacked together cracked lips. "Could do with some easier access to water," he admitted. "It's hard to get to the well sometimes."

Tilting her head, Shari studied him. These were beings from a desert Realm, and at least two of them were proficient in Water Innarn.

"Things have been a bit, off, since the change," he begrudgingly admitted. "What came easy now comes in abundance. Last time we tried to set the well up closer, we flooded the plain."

By *we* Shari was going to assume he meant *me*. "I can give you a hand with that," she said easily. "Were you after a well, or running water in each home?"

"That's not possible," he scoffed.

Shari grinned. Projecting her thoughts as images into the air, she concentrated on her bathroom—turning the taps on and having both hot and cold water come as needed, being able to fill the bath, turn a shower on, or wash dirt from clothing, and using water to flush away waste. Hail flicked his tail, and the image expanded, with wastewater being recycled for use in the gardens.

The elder's eyes were wide. "This is common?" he asked.

"On Lis... here, it is." Shari's smile became fixed.

He scowled. "We signed up for Lissae. Not sure if we're going to stay."

Opening her mouth to say something along the lines of *Enjoy the comforts of running water while you're here*, Shari found it wasn't her voice that came out at all. "Carilla is far safer than Lissae was." It was her mother's.

Ducking her head, Shari almost missed the sharp look the elder gave her, but it was noticeable even between her tears.

"We can give it a try," the elder said gruffly. Knees creaking as he rose to his feet, the elder shuffled to her side. "Show me what to do."

Sniffing, Shari pulled at the image in the air and focused on the pipes. They would have to raise the well higher up the side of a nearby hill, but the gravity-fed water supply would never run out. She showed him how to connect the taps to the pipes, how to create sinks, baths, toilets, and showers that would hold the water without leaking everywhere. Then how to create the pipes that took the excess water away to be cleaned, so they could use it for their gardens and washing.

Hours later, he turned on a tap in his own home and watched the clear water running for a while. "A miracle, this is," he murmured. "I'm Whitmore, formerly of Ioyitmar."

"Well met, Whitmore. I'm Shari of–" She paused, and the ground beneath her feet seemed to hold its breath. "Of Carilla." One day, many years into the future, she would be able to say that without crying.

Whitmore patted her hand. "That the new name?"

Shari nodded, and Hail rubbed his head against her jaw.

"Guess I'm of Carilla as well."

Grinning, she ducked her head as the ground gave a pleased rumble. "I'll leave you to the rest of your day, Whitmore," she said.

"Bah." The crags in Whitmore's face deepened as he beckoned her before stomping towards the front of his house.

Curious, Shari followed.

Coming to a cramped kitchen, he poked around in a tin on a high shelf. If Shari hadn't seen how steady he was on his feet, she would have been worried.

"We pay our dues," Whitmore said as he turned back to her and shoved a scroll in her direction.

"What's this?" Shari asked.

The elder gave her an impatient wave, and Shari unrolled it, spreading it out on the little counter.

It took a moment for the translation charm to kick in, but when it did, Shari sucked air in between her teeth. "Would your dues be paid if I took a copy?" There was no way she could take such a precious original.

Whitmore glared at her. "You can leave me the copy and take that one." The glare dropped, and he clumsily patted her hand. "My granddaughter Ifera tells me you have more to do with Carilla than anyone else alive. You deserve the original."

After carefully rolling the scroll, Shari waved her hand and made a copy before handing it to him. "Thank you," she choked out.

She got a sharp nod in return. "Don't forget your beast," Whitmore said as she made to shift away.

Shari bowed her head. "I bid thee well," she whispered, and fled out the front door. Putting her free hand on Wisp's head, Shari shifted them both back to Jonathan's office in the castle.

"Shari?" Jonathan asked, looking up from his desk.

Striding over, Shari swept away his paperwork and spread out the scroll again, unable to speak.

Rising, Jonathan came around to lean over her shoulder, and Shari felt the moment he realised what it was. "Oh, Shari," he said.

Unwilling to turn away from the scroll, she accepted the one-armed hug from her Guardian as she greedily poured over the first account of the creation of Carilla over and over again.

Jonathan gently flipped the parchment over, and Shari gasped. She couldn't believe she'd missed it the first time.

An image of her parents, moments before the glowing light of the portal had claimed them.

Shadow bounded towards the door, snarling.

"If you eat Lizbeth, you can deal with the hatchlings," Samuel warned the palon. Shadow calmed instantly, sitting by the door and gazing up at the handle expectantly.

'*Sweet treats?*' Kemanyr sent.

Samuel groaned. '*Lizbeth.*'

'*Sweet treats.*'

Laughter sounded from outside.

'*Lizbeth brings sweet treats—I don't see how she's wrong,*' Tormorylth sent, pushing her maw closer to him as he walked to the door.

'*Beings prefer to be called by their names,*' Samuel sent, and opened the door.

'*As opposed to Golden Priest or Death Bringer?*' Jetonyx asked.

'Yes,' Samuel said, trying not to snarl internally. Still, Jetonyx flinched, and Samuel sighed. '*Names like that have the ability to hurt others. And if you continue to call them by something they don't like, then they might not want to be around you anymore.*'

Jetonyx shrank back. Samuel tried not to roll his eyes. '*Don't look so worried. You can't get rid of me. I meant others, like Lizbeth.*'

'Sweet...'

Tormorylth stepped on Kemanyr's tail. The smallest hatchling yelped then whipped around and attempted to bite Tormorylth, who leaped out of the way.

'*Lizbeth,*' Kemanyr corrected herself.

Samuel opened the door. "I hope you're ready for this," he said.

"Well met, Samuel. I've come prepared," Lizbeth said, holding a basket aloft.

"What's this?"

"Something extra special," she said.

Kemanyr's claws dug into his back. Samuel hissed and pushed his scales out of his skin, forcing her to let go. Sneeze chittered at her angrily, and Shadow regarded the pair of them with utter disdain.

"I think it's right in the nick of time," Lizbeth said.

"Who's stealing time?" Samuel snapped his head towards her, astonished.

Lizbeth blinked, sightless eyes narrowing for a moment as she thought.

If they have messed with her memories, I'll swallow them whole and let them rot alive in my stomach. Samuel prepared to change, wondering how long it would take to track down a time stealer.

"Not nick as in take—nick as in I arrived at the right moment." Lizbeth wore the gentle smile she graced him with when he spectacularly misunderstood something.

"Ah," he said eloquently.

"My Innarn has been a bit wild, and I find the best way to focus is to bake with intent," Lizbeth said. She opened her basket and started handing out loaves of bread. As the hatchling's tails drooped, the bread sliced itself and a thick brown spread smeared across each slice.

"What's this?" Samuel asked.

"Rutenberry spread."

Something about the way she said it made Samuel pause.

Kemanyr, lacking even a modicum of self-control, ate the whole loaf before any of them could blink. She let out a burp of noxious gas which Samuel contained before it could hurt the more fragile of their companions. Then she shrank, her scales disappearing and skin taking their place. An abundance of pale golden hair appeared, flowing over the form of a humanoid child.

"Huh?" Samuel gaped at the tiny being.

The girl turned, frowning fiercely. '*Where did my wings go? My tail disappeared!*'

"Lizbeth?" Samuel asked, unable to look away from the frantically twisting child.

'*If I eat a loaf, will I become wingless too?*' Tormorylth asked.

The mortal version of Kemanyr was growing dizzy, if the outstretched arms and unfocused eyes were anything to go by. Before she could fall, Samuel wrapped a thick layer of Air Innarn around her.

"Oops," Lizbeth said.

"Oops?" Samuel's voice rose an octave. "What does oops mean?"

"I may have put a bit too much in," Lizbeth admitted.

Red was starting to cloud the edges of his vision, and Samuel could feel the ripple of impending change underneath his skin.

"When I bake," Lizbeth said softly, "I can imbue certain things into what I make. Things like relaxation or peace or love. Nothing dangerous, though."

'*Until now*,' Jetonyx sent, and swallowed a loaf in one go. The change in him was just as immediate. A flaxen-haired young adult with an awed expression on his face. He at least was able to change some of his scales to clothing without any help. '*Ugh, why would you prefer this form?*' he asked Samuel.

'To *blend in*,' Samuel snapped, then pinched the bridge of his nose. It did, minorly, help to relieve the headache blooming behind his eyes. Perhaps it only worked when you were worried about the beings you were responsible for? Either way, he was never telling Jonathan.

Tormorylth took the last loaf and nibbled on it. '*Can we change back?*'

"You should be able to," Lizbeth said. "It was just meant to unlock the potential for change, if you wanted it."

Samuel prodded at the statement, and the low bell sounding in the back of his skull meant Lizbeth was telling the truth.

Wearing an expression wiser than her years, Tormorylth nodded and crammed the rest into her maw. Within moments, she too was standing in a mortal body. Unlike the others, her hair was just as dark as Samuel's, but her eyes were the same colour as Shari's.

"I don't know how I feel about having three hormonal Q'Aralides walking around in mortal flesh," Samuel said.

Lizbeth patted his arm. "Try and change back," she suggested to the hatchlings.

The words were barely out of her mouth when all three returned to their natural form.

'It *was fun being little*,' Kemanyr sent.

"Now you should be able to choose if you want to be little or big," Lizbeth said.

One by one, the hatchlings shrank back down to their mortal forms, Samuel scowling the entire time. He shoved away memories of the agony of his first transformation, of how Oalark had wanted to use him, of how his mentor had let her.

These Q'Aralide would never feel like that.

Not so long as he was around.

Wolf cursed as he knocked another frame off a low table. Honestly, how could any Ilutri live in such a place? Picking up the frame, he let out a trembling sigh as his fingertips traced over the image of Calem's robe on the day of his naming ceremony. Arilla was standing off to the side, and he was on the other side of Calem, almost out of the frame. The scowl he wore was a direct contrast to his brother's beaming smile.

The one he'd never see in person again.

Shoving his grief down in a move he was sure his mind healer would call unhealthy, Wolf rubbed the back of his neck. He just wanted to be in his cosy house on Rakemyst with Belfar and ignore this painful new Realm for a month or two.

Even that wasn't going to happen. He couldn't very well let Shari fend for herself after all she'd been through.

"Got everything?" Belfar asked.

"No," Wolf said, sounding even more like he'd gargled with gravel than normal. He took one last look at the photograph and hefted the pack over his shoulder, making sure it nestled securely between his wings. "Let's go."

"We don't have to," Belfar said.

Wolf couldn't reply. He wasn't sure that mindless begging wasn't just going to fall out of his mouth if he opened it again. He strode for the door and ripped it open.

Shari was standing on the other side, the massive white menace leaning against her leg, and a dark scaled draci perched on her shoulder. "Leaving so soon?"

The same words he'd said to Calem after the naming ceremony. The last words he'd said to his brother for a decade. *Wasted time.*

"No," he said, shrugging the pack off his shoulders and letting it drop to the floor with a thump. "Just..."

"We weren't sure which room you'd want to stay in," Belfar said, wrapping an arm around Wolf's waist.

Blinking, Shari looked like she was trying to figure out what they meant. The draci nudged her cheek. "You thought I'd be moving back in?" she asked. She buried a hand in the Shadow Bringer's fur.

"You should," Wolf said. "We'll take... the other bedroom." It would gut him, every moment of every day, but he deserved it.

Eyes wide, Shari looked around the room. "I, ah... I'll think about it."

"You should," Wolf said again. He hated how needy his voice came out.

Shari gave him a tight grin and shifted away before she replied.

Wolf sagged against the door, letting Belfar take his weight, and wondered if he'd done the right thing.

"You have," Belfar said, kissing his temple.

"Mind reader," Wolf grumbled. He could only hope that Belfar was right, and that Shari would come around.

When she did, he'd make sure her bedroom was ready. He knew nothing about being a parent, but he was sure he could...

"She needs a friend, not a parent right now." Belfar broke in before he could let the thought run away.

"Don't know if I know how to do that either," Wolf said.

"You can try."

That he could do.

Collis spread the blanket out on the sand and flopped on top of it. He'd spent the day crafting new rezems on the different islands. Even with the excess Innarn floating around, it had been enough to wear him out. After the long day, he just wanted to lay down and look at the stars for a while.

"Care for some company?" Tania asked.

"If it's yours, always," Collis said.

Despite the dark, he grinned at the fire of Tania's blush dancing across her cheeks.

Folding her skirts, Tania gracefully sank to occupy the space beside him. "What are we looking at?"

"The stars. They're different to those that were in Lissae, and new ones are appearing every night."

"New stars can't just appear, can they?" Tania asked.

"I would have said that new Realms can't be created a week ago, yet here we are," Collis said.

"True." Tania gazed up at the sky and squeezed his hand. She smiled as Collis floated a blanket over them, and she snuggled into his side.

They lay there for hours, gasping and pointing as each new star glittered to life under their watchful gazes.

Stretching up to the night sky with a new body was quite a marvel. She looked around at the stone statues which stood in silent tribute to all those who had come before and smiled.

More of her kin were waiting to return from the Spirit Realm.

And she would be the one to help them.

Chapter Twelve

Adonday

First day of the third week of Waeghost

Hand on the door to Books 'n' More, Shari paused. It felt like the last time she'd entered the shop had been a lifetime ago.

Wisp nudged the door open and trotted in. Shari grinned as the bell sounded, and entered slowly, Hail gently chittering in her ear.

A blue head of hair was all that was visible behind the desk.

Abruptly, Eva shot upright, and Shari locked her knees to prevent herself from stumbling backwards.

"Well met," Eva said, blowing a hunk of hair out of her face. "Wondered when you'd be in."

"Well met. Things got a bit..."

Eva snorted, saving Shari from trying to finish the sentence. "Yeah, they did." She glanced at Shari's shoulder. "Who's this?"

"Hail," Shari said, tickling the draci under his chin. Hail rubbed his head on her fingertips before sitting up and giving Eva the draci equivalent of a smile.

"Cute," Eva said.

Hail preened under her praise.

Wisp put his front paws on the counter, and Eva startled. "You're pretty cute too…"

"Wisp," Shari offered.

Eva raised her brows, the scarring on one side of her face making the expression foreboding. Still, she reached over and scratched Wisp under the chin, causing his tail thump against Shari's leg.

"Is Jonathan in?" Shari asked.

Jerking her thumb towards the door to the back room, Eva gave her a smile that pulled on the burn scars on the side of her face before ducking back under the desk again.

Taking the hint, Shari followed the path her feet knew too well and entered the back room of the store.

Jonathan was, as always, sitting behind a crowded desk. This one had far more mundane books scattered across the surface than Shari was used to. He was so focused pouring over a ledger, he hadn't even looked up when she entered.

"Guardian," she said, making her voice all breathy, "I have a problem that only *you* can help me with." Hail nibbled on her earlobe, and Shari tried not to giggle.

His throat bobbed as he swallowed, and a flicker of annoyance was quickly chased away. "How can I… Shari," he groaned.

She laughed. "Thought I'd come check on you. But I do have a problem."

"Hmm?" Jonathan held out a hand. Wisp sauntered over to lean against the Guardian, the glow in his chest getting brighter as Jonathan patted along the Shadow Bringer's back.

Jonathan's gaze landed on the little draci. "Have a new friend, do you?"

"Yeah, I'm Hail's human."

'*Mine*,' Hail agreed, wrapping his tail as far around her neck as he could.

Jonathan chuckled. "You and Samuel with your matching pets."

Shari scowled at him. "That's not why I—"

Jonathan broke in. "I doubt that Hail is a problem, so what's troubling you?"

"I can't find Grace anywhere. It's been weeks now, and no sight of her. I thought she might have been—" Shari waved her arm, indicating the Realm "—sucked into the same vortex, but I can't feel her Innarn signature at all."

Sitting back in the seat, Jonathan rested his elbows on the desk and steepled his fingers underneath his chin. "She was floating, wasn't she? When the portal opened?"

Flashes of Grace in a white dress, floating above them all flicked through her mind. "Yes, she was."

"Could it be that the portal didn't take her? That she's stuck on Lissae?"

"Alone?" Shari shuddered. Her eyes widened. "There's—we took all the land! What if she's drowned?"

Wisp padded across the room and nudged Shari towards her chair.

"Grace is a survivor," Jonathan said. "She has gone through so much. I refuse to believe that Lissae would allow her to drown after everything else that's happened to her."

Shari hummed as she curled into her chair, tucking her legs up and leaning back. Wisp rested his head on her legs, looking at her with sleepy eyes. "I hope so. She'd only just stopped stabbing me." Hail rubbed his head soothingly along her cheek.

"I think she was trying to make sure you always had your guard up."

Looking at him out of the corner of her eye, she said, "I never thought I'd say it, but I prefer your training methods."

Jonathan laughed, but Shari noted the pleased looked as he ducked his head in an attempt to hide his expression.

"Maybe..." Shari's voice fell away. She wasn't sure that her idle thought wouldn't take away Jonathan's happiness. He glanced at her, waiting. Squirming in the seat, Shari found she couldn't ignore his look for long. "Maybe she could be the Altoriae now."

The good thing about Jonathan was that he always thought before he spoke. Shari could almost see the mental cogs grinding as he turned her suggestion over a few times. "The Altoriae is Lissae's protector," he said finally. "Maybe, if Grace is still on Lissae, she could be."

A wave of relief so strong passed through Shari and made her glad she was sitting down. Hail swapped sides and rubbed his head against her other cheek. Wisp licked at her hand.

"I suppose that means you want to hang up that mantle?" he asked, head decidedly down so she would have the freedom to answer without judgement.

"I think I do," Shari said softly, the words soaking into the book-lined walls.

Jonathan hummed, "If that's what you want to do, I'll support you."

"Thank you, Jonathan." Swiftly, Shari rose to her feet, unable to stay still anymore. "I'll let you know?"

Glancing at her, Jonathan smiled softly. They both knew that she'd already decided.

She just had to be willing to commit to it.

Idly patting Sneeze, who was resting on his shoulder, Samuel stepped outside and immediately shifted to the other end of the building as three rambunctious hatchlings almost rolled right over the top of him.

'*Watch where you're going!*' Samuel roared.

There was a fair bit more snapping and snarling until Kemanyr emerged as the victor, Jetonyx's throat clamped between her baby fangs.

Samuel flicked a sting of Innarn at Jetonyx when the older hatching rolled his eyes. If the tiny one saw, they'd start again, and all Samuel wanted to do was soak up the sun in a Realm that wasn't trying to burn the flesh from his hide for a change.

Jetonyx flicked his tail but conceded. Kemanyr purred happily as she pounced away from him, bouncing around the enlarged yard that was big enough for him to spread out in his natural form at least six times over.

'*There's so much room!*' Tormorylth said. She leaped into the air and, flying low to the ground, did a lap around the yard-turned-paddock.

'*What are we going to do with all this space?*' Jetonyx asked, coming to stand next to him.

"Start a rutenberry farm," Samuel said drily, as he stepped out of the shadow the hatchling cast and looked at the field, wondering who could show them how to till it, and to look after the plants.

'*Treats every day.*' Tormorylth smiled dreamily as she landed beside Jetonyx, a trail of acidic drool hanging from her chin.

Surely looking after plants would be easier than raising three Q'Aralide?

Stepping outside the bookstore, Shari almost ran into Eric Shansky.

"Ree!" Eric said.

"Well met, Eric." Shari grinned. It had been an age since she'd seen him. "Wow, you've become so big!"

Eric grinned at her, then noticed Hail. "Ooooh." Eyes huge, he stretched out his arms and flexed his fingers.

Hail chittered—a different, higher sound to any he had made so far— and pushed against Shari's jaw as if he was trying to meld into her skin.

"He's a bit scared, Eric. I don't know if Hail has seen any kids as big as you before," Shari said. The draci took a chunk of her hair in one paw and pulled, huddling against her as much as he could.

By her side, Wisp rolled his eyes in a move so reminiscent of Mitch, Shari didn't know how she hadn't seen it before.

"I can be gentle," Eric whispered.

'*Full sentences, hey? Eric is doing well,*' Shari sent to his parents, along with a mental image of the front of the bookstore. "What do you think, Hail? Can you be brave?" Shari asked out loud. Silently, she slid a shield over the draci's scales, ensuring no rough touches could get through.

Slowly, Hail let go of her hair and crept down her outstretched arm.

"I know you're going to be super gentle, Eric," Shari said as Eric reached out.

Pulling his hand back, Eric sucked his bottom lip behind his teeth before ever so cautiously patting Hail with two gentle fingertips.

Seeing how careful Eric was being, Shari lowered the strength of the shield around Hail, who was tilting his head to push into the pats.

Shari glanced up as Eric's mum approached.

"Well done, Eric," Louise said softly, kneeling next to her son.

"This Hail," Eric tried to whisper.

"Well met, Shari, Hail," Louise said, offering her fingertip for the draci to inspect.

Leaning forward, Hail delicately rubbed against her fingers before skittering back up to the safety of Shari's shoulder.

Looking at Wisp for the first time, Eric waved goodbye to Hail and hugged his mother's leg as she stood, keeping his gaze on the creature whose head was higher than his own.

Wisp stretched and lay on his belly, dropping his head to his front paws.

"How are you settling in?" Shari asked.

Louise teared up but blinked rapidly. Abruptly, Shari remembered that Andrew, her husband, had been on the list of names of those who had passed into the Spirit Realm.

"I'm sorry," Shari said.

"Don't be, Shari. We've all lost loved ones. It's just... life is difficult, at the moment."

"That is an understatement," Shari said. "If there's anything I can do, let me know."

"You do so much already," Louise said.

Shari gave her a look.

"Well, if you could ask Asterion if he'd mind looking after Eric for a while? I keep reaching out to him, but something is wonky with my sending. I think it's—" Louise broke off again, rapidly blinking.

"I'll ask him to come have a chat," Shari said, flicking Asterion a message.

"Thank you, Shari. You do too much." Louise grasped her hand for a moment, then huffed. "Eric!" she called as the boy scampered away.

Shari bit back a laugh as Eric peered over his shoulder before turning and running faster. For such a little guy, he sure was fast.

Spreading his fingers wide, he marvelled at how *real* it felt. Pinching the soft flesh of his inner arm, he yelped and rubbed at the sting. It was real, then.

Ignoring the white-robed figure leaning over him, he glanced up at the fading blue sky.

The wrong shade to be Lissae, he noted.

Still, he grinned.

It was good to be back.

CHAPTER THIRTEEN

Inthday

Second day of the third week of Waeghost

Jonathan kicked up the sand as he walked along Talhan's beach, shivering in the pre-dawn cold. It was nice not to have to run.

"Fancy meeting you here," Zac said, striding towards him from the other direction.

Grinning, Jonathan turned as Zac reached him, and started ambling back the way he had come. "Someone let slip that you like to take an early morning walk." He glanced at the still-dark sea and grimaced. "Could have waited till the sun graced the sky, at least."

"Gotta get in before the crowds come," Zac laughed.

A shiver ran through Jonathan's frame. "Somehow, I can't see them lining up just yet."

Zac wrapped his arm around Jonathan's waist. "You'd be surprised." They walked in companionable silence for a while. "Last night, I thought I saw the weirdest thing."

The hair on the back of Jonathan's neck stood up. "Weird, how?"

"Xani, walking around hale and whole."

Jonathan froze. "Xani confined to a chair and taken over by the Crystal Intelligence, Xani?"

"Do you know of anyone else by that name? Seriously, I thought I saw her going into the Techno Centre late last night. Maybe it was a trick of the light, or wishful thinking." Zac glanced away and used his free hand to rub the back of his neck.

"Do you really believe that?"

"No," Zac said.

"Then we can check it out. When the sun is actually awake." Jonathan bumped his hip into Zac's.

"As easy as that?"

"Yes," Jonathan said. Xani had died months ago. And the Crystal Intelligence had died with her. If she was back, it could spell more than just trouble. In the back of his mind, he reached out to Shari. *'We may have a slight problem.'*

Anika stood off to the side and watched as beings shifted into the training grounds. A total sense of wrongness was in the air.

Arilla should have been here, welcoming everyone. Grace should have been in the stands, snarling and ready to defend their instructor.

And now, everyone was looking at her.

Silence fell, and Anika had enough sense of Innarn to know the others were sending to each other.

Finally, a huge satyr stepped forward, his flowing silver hair glimmering in the artificial lights of the grounds. He bowed to her, the sword strapped to his hips swinging out behind him.

"Well met, Anika Thorne. I am General Morrow. Since you were the one to request this class, we feel it's only right that you continue to lead it," he said, his words so soft it took a moment for Anika to process that the gentle voice had come out of the body that looked as if it could kill you with a finger.

"Well met, General Morrow. I..." Anika looked at the eager faces peering at them. "I don't know how to lead this class. I..."

"Tell me what you wish to learn, and I will pick one of my satyrs to teach you and the others," the general said.

Anika sucked in a breath. She knew there were a few satyrs who were Blanks as well, and all of them were far more skilled with a blade than she was.

"Innarn has settled now, hasn't it?" she asked.

General Morrow nodded.

She looked out at the crowd again. They had all, as a rule, done exceptionally well to come out as unscathed from the last battle as they had. If there had been some sort of reliable Innarn, it could have been a different story. "Teach us how to fight alongside Innarnians."

He grinned, white teeth flashing. "Excellent idea."

Tania smiled reassuringly at Zana as she poured tea into a delicate cup for Collis. Rakemyst's Linked had insisted on seeing them both today, ostensibly to talk about how they were all settling into the new Realm, but Tania had a feeling it was more than that.

Mostly because Zana's hands were shaking.

The stalwart older Linked rarely lost her composure. As much as she desperately wanted to ask what was going on, Tania had the feeling that if she pushed, Zana would clamp down on whatever she was feeling and would never tell a soul.

Seated next to Collis on a long bench, Tania's Innarn twirled around her, but she hesitated. She wasn't sure about the etiquette—was it polite to use Innarn to help stabilise the cup, or was it considered beyond rude? She felt Collis wrap his Innarn around the base of the cup as Zana lifted it and hid a grin. She supposed when it was your leg that would be scalded, it wasn't impolite.

"My thanks," Collis said, taking the cup. He pressed the length of his thigh against hers, and Tania could feel his concern for Zana flowing through the brief touch.

Zana sank into the seat opposite them and sipped her drink.

Just when Tania thought she would have to say something, Zana blurted, "Is Ronah speaking to you?"

"No," Tania said. "She's resting."

"Resting," Zana said, drawing the word out. She glanced over Tania's shoulder, and her eyes unfocused.

Tania shared a look with Collis, who shrugged.

"Yes, I suppose that could be it." Zana smiled, a brittle thing that looked like it could shatter at any moment.

"How are the Ilutri going?" Collis asked. "I see they are still patrolling."

"Yes." Zana settled back into her chair, topic safely averted for the moment. "The patrols are significantly more difficult, now there is so much more land to cover."

"Do they need help?" Collis asked.

"I'm afraid I don't really deal with the patrollers," Zana admitted. "But you could ask Wolf Dawn. He's scheduled the current groups."

"I will. There is so much excess Innarn at the moment, I feel as though my skin will burn up if I don't use it," Collis said.

Zana hummed and nodded.

"Is that why the snow isn't bothering me?" Tania asked. "It melts when I lay down. I thought it was just body heat."

"It seems that we may need to adjust your training," Zana said, sharing a concerned look with Collis.

"Why?" Tania asked.

"Burnout from too much Innarn is a real thing," Collis said gently. "If it builds in your body to the point where you're feeling hot, well–" He shot Zana a look. "Too much of anything isn't good for you."

Tania sipped her drink, wishing it was cold. Steam was rising from it, almost obscuring her vision.

"Perhaps we can start with Ronah's wards," Zana said, setting her cup aside.

Copying the older Linked, Tania shuddered. The cup wasn't steaming– she was. "Yeah, let's... let's work on the wards."

Asterion shivered as a rush of Innarn swept over him, thick enough that he could almost see it. It swirled through the air and settled in an opalescent dome high above the island before slowly disappearing from sight.

"That's new," he murmured. Tugging his tunic straight, he knocked on the door.

Running footsteps were coming closer to the door. There was a crash, an aborted cry, and the door flung open.

Eric was clinging to Louise, sitting snug on her hip as he sucked his thumb, red blooming along his arm. "Ter! I fell."

"I can see that. Perhaps slowing down is a good thing," Asterion said.

Giving him a cheeky grin, Eric nodded and wriggled until Louise put him down. "Make better, Ter?"

Asterion chanced a glance at Louise, who nodded. "Want to show me how?" he asked. In the dark days inside the pocket-Realm, Eric had come up with all sorts of fantastical ways to cure wounds, big and small. They'd begun to believe that the boy would be a healer, if he ever grew to become an adult.

He was so glad that the vibrant boy would have that chance. Sniffing as quietly as he could, Asterion followed Eric into the house and traced the sound of quiet giggles until he reached an open door at the end of the hallway.

Eric beckoned him through and patted the ground at his side. "Lay down, Ter."

Obediently, Asterion got to the floor and tried to make himself comfortable. Without preamble, Eric placed a well-worn toy on each horn, and lay down next to him.

"Watch," Eric said, pointing to where the ceiling should have been.

There was only sky.

"What did you do, Eric?" Asterion asked, poking the boy ever so carefully in his belly.

Giggling again, Eric waved a chubby hand, and what looked like stardust fell from the ceiling. The red on his arm disappeared as if it had never existed.

There was a muffled gasp, and Asterion raised his head. Louise was leaning with one hip propped against the doorframe.

"It's something Andrew used to say to us," Louise said, her voice breaking on her dead husband's name. "I'll love you so long as there are stars in the sky."

"And Andrew—" Asterion broke off. There was no polite way to ask how he had passed on.

"Mainlander," Louise said shortly, her gaze cutting to Eric for a brief moment.

Asterion nodded and lay back down as Eric started fussing over the toys. "Looks like he's still watching over you," Asterion said softly.

Louise, a hand pressed to her mouth and tears welling, nodded and stepped away.

Asterion had to stop himself from growling. The mainlanders of Lissae had quite a bit to answer for. How many families had been split on the Shifting Islands because of a war no one wanted to fight in?

Groaning, he held a hand to the small of his back as it cracked into place. "It's been centuries since I was able to stretch," he said.

The white-robed figure ignored his theatrics. '*Wake the others. We are running out of time.*' Plasma so light it was almost silver was curling around the being.

He grinned. "Time? I can help with that."

Flexing his fingers, he reached out with his Innarn to get a sense of when he was. "Oh..." he breathed. "This is going to be fun."

CHAPTER FOURTEEN

Kerday

Third day of the third week of Waeghost

Jetonyx grumbled as he squashed another rutenberry between claws too large to do the delicate job of shelling them.

Kemanyr laughed at him. '*Change!*' she sent.

He scowled but managed to keep the pooling acid behind his fangs. '*If we are to be farmers, we need to be able to do everything in both forms.*'

'*Or we could use the form most suited to the task,*' Tormorylth sent.

Sighing, Jetonyx made a show of rolling his eyes. He wasn't about to admit that the younger hatchling was right.

"Don't be rude to your nest mates," Samuel snapped as he joined them.

The girls giggled, and Jetonyx huffed. At least if they were in their natural form, he wouldn't have known they were laughing at him.

"That goes for all of you." Samuel scowled. The girls ducked their heads, fingers flying as they shelled more of the berries to expose the seed hidden within.

I need to learn how to be intimidating in both forms. Jetonyx sighed.

"How goes the planting?" Samuel asked.

'We ran out of seeds,' Jetonyx sent. 'Someone kept eating them.' Carefully, he looked at Samuel, not allowing his gaze to slip to Kemanyr unless it gave her away. While he knew punishment was unlikely, it was still a possibility.

Samuel sighed. "I know they're tasty but do try to leave some for planting."

The original crop had succumbed to the snow, so they were trying again. Assuming they'd have enough left to put in the ground, that was.

Guiltily, Kemanyr nodded. As soon as Samuel turned away, she popped another berry into her mouth.

Jetonyx sighed. He couldn't remember having nest mates who were so brazenly disrespectful.

Although he would only admit it on pain of death, he kind of, sort of, maybe liked it.

Just a little.

Yessna wrapped her paws around a mug of daborang and growled low in her throat. If another mainlander tried to pull her tail, she'd pluck their finger bones out and wear them as a necklace.

One of the females came up next to her, brows low as she tried her best to scowl. It was hard to put into words exactly how unimpressive it was after facing down three hungry Q'Aralide hatchlings.

"We just want to go home," she said.

Tail lashing, Yessna took a long drink of the spiced tea. "You came here to fight. To kill those different from you, knowing that you might never return. And now, you won't." She'd had variations of the same conversation with many of the mainlanders on the island. At this stage, the Ferah would prefer it if they picked a fight than started to talk.

Of course, few were so obliging.

"Can't you just"–the female wriggled her fingers in the air–"make us disappear?"

"Oh, that I can do," Yessna purred, carefully placing her cup on top of a tree stump and going for the handle of her blade.

"Not what she meant." Wubi was by her side in an instant, his hand over her paw.

Yessna scowled and was pleased when he flinched. "She meant shift them back to Lissae."

"For the love of Dark," Yessna muttered. "Go get everyone together," she snapped at the female, making sure to show some fang.

The mainlander scampered.

"What are you planning?"

"Telling them once and for all," Yessna snarled, stalking towards the largest clearing on the island. She could feel Wubi sending to the others, and boot steps hurried to fall in line with her.

Within a few minutes, a sizable crowd had gathered, all sneering at her.

Slamming a fist into the ground, she forced a small plateau to raise the U'sala above the bulk of the crowd. "Do you understand how a door works?" she barked.

Blank faces peered up at her.

"You open it, walk through, and it closes after you. The door to Lissae is locked and the key melted down. There is no going back."

The crowd scowled and jeered up at her.

"You have a choice. You can work with us to make this new Realm bearable, or we can end this right now."

"And how are you going to take all of us?" a male up the back shouted. He probably thought the crowd offered him some anonymity, but Yessna's hearing and eyesight were far superior to what Lissaens had to work with.

Henot tapped her on the back of her calf, and Yessna let the claws of her back paws out enough so that he could see them. Henot tapped twice more. One of her ears flicked as she followed the sound of tiny boot steps clambering down the plateau and through the crowd.

"I've taken on bigger armies myself, and with my team, you don't stand a chance."

"Who do you think you are?" he sneered, spitting on the ground. "Some furry Innarnian aberration come to tell us what to do?"

The female next to him was nudging him, gaze flying between the pair with worry lines heavy on her face.

Yessna drew herself up taller. "We are the U'sala," she said.

Gasps whirled through the crowd. Even the Blanks of Lissae knew of their prowess. And if it helped their small group to take credit for everything the U'sala did, Yessna wasn't above using the fear and awe the name evoked.

"So what? A bunch of aberrations aren't—" He broke off, eyes going wide as he sucked in a bubbling breath.

Yessna raised a paw and extended a razor-tipped talon.

On the signal, Henot, his grisly task complete, could be heard making his way back to the plateau.

Blood dripped from the mainlander's mouth and soaked into his beard as the female next to him screamed. He dropped like a felled tree, the spreading bloom of red on the back of his shirt the only indication that his death wasn't due to Innarn.

"We work together," Yessna said. "Or you won't survive."

There was the expected grumbling, and a bout of mild panic from those who weren't trained soldiers.

"And what are we meant to do about this?" a female off to the side asked. She prodded the man next to her, and he gave the best attempt at a scowl Yessna had seen all day.

"Therion, show them," she hissed, prodding him again.

"Ishta," he groaned. Reluctantly, Therion raised his hand and a ball of fire sprang to life above his palm. "Since we got here, I can do this," he said, loud enough for the others to hear.

Others around him weren't gasping.

"And who else has newfound powers?" Nerina asked.

Hands all through the crowd raised, with only a few who were left shaking their heads.

"Well," Yessna purred. "This just got interesting."

The tavern was bustling, and Shari was meant to be delivering meals to a few waiting patrons, but she was slumped in a chair at Jonathan and Zac's table, flicking Innarn to deliver the dishes as they were ready. Wisp was resting under her seat, unwilling to leave her in such a crowded space.

"Do you think Xani is a real problem?" Shari asked.

"I think there's the potential she could be, but I've scanned the islands and I can't find her anywhere. Maybe she was an echo? Or wishful thinking?" Jonathan said.

"Cyrus isn't the type to go for wishful thinking, and if she was an echo, wouldn't she have been in her chair?" Zac shot back.

Shari hid her grin behind a cup. It was good to know that Zac was going to challenge Jonathan and not just agree blindly with everything he said.

"There has to be more to this," Jonathan said. "There have been other reports of the dead walking around, but any time I show up to check it out, they disappear, and any scans I run aren't working." He rubbed a hand across his face and sighed.

Zac rose. "We aren't going to solve the problems of the Realm by stressing about them. Come on. Let's get you to bed."

"But—" Jonathan broke off at the look that Zac gave him and reluctantly stood.

"Heading out?" Shari asked, hiding a smirk.

"We'll try to get an early night. Tackle this dead problem tomorrow," Zac said, fingers firmly entwined with Jonathan's.

"Sleep well," she said.

"Are you heading home soon?" Jonathan asked.

Home.

She wasn't sure where that was anymore. Hail, perched on her shoulder, chittered comfortingly into her ear. "Gotta tidy up here," Shari said, indicating the tables laden with dirty plates and the floor that needed sweeping. Dealon had kindly taken over cooking detail, and Mu had joined Collis in waiting on the tables. Now, with most of the diners on the way out the door, it was time to clean up.

"Don't be too long," Jonathan said as Zac tugged him through the door.

Shari waved half-heartedly. She glanced around quickly and didn't spot anyone. Flicking a finger, she set the tavern back to rights in a single moment.

"Impressive," said a voice from the reading corner.

Wisp growled as he came out from under her chair.

Blade at the ready, Shari was by their side in an instant. It took a moment for her to place the Returned woman who had been tortured by Chamele, but when she did, Shari lowered her weapon.

Joana smirked at her before looking around the room. "My parents started this tavern. I'd just taken it over and was showing Toby the ropes when Anriluka took us." She ran a fingertip over a row of book spines. "Wish I'd thought of a library. It's rather clever."

"That was my dad," Shari said. "Food for the body and the soul." Resting his weight against her, Wisp glanced up. Shari tousled his fur.

Hail rubbed against her jaw, and she raised a finger to stroke it gently along his back.

"Sounds like a clever man," Joana said.

"Did you want to take over the tavern again?" Shari blurted. "It was their dream, not mine. And I've no idea what I'm doing. Not really," she admitted.

Joana blinked a few times. "What about you—don't you want to...?" She waved a hand.

"Never in my wildest dreams did I think I'd be working here, let alone managing it," Shari conceded. "I... I don't know what I want to do yet, but this isn't it."

"I'd be honoured," Joana said.

"Brilliant! Collis has been waiting tables, Dealon would love to keep cooking, but if you have someone else, then, well, it's all yours now."

"Just like that?" Joana asked.

"Just like that," Shari confirmed. "Although I'd like one last chance to close up."

"Of course!" Joana said.

Shari grinned as Joana slipped through the room in a daze, her hand lingering on the doorframe as she left.

"I'll add you to the wards, and you can change them tomorrow," Shari called after her.

Wisp padded towards the door, ready to go too.

Hail leaned against her neck, knowing the night was almost over.

As Joana waved in acknowledgement and the door closed behind her, time seemed to flicker and slow down. Shari frowned. Slapping the palm of her hand against her thigh, she sped it up again. *'Just because you want to spend more time with Zac, doesn't mean you get to slow things down.'*

Jonathan's send was a sleepy brown. *'Wassant me.'*

Shari frowned. Who else had the ability to mess with Time then?

The Time Innarnian cracked his fingers and frowned.

The weight of the white-robed being's gaze was heavy. *'Why has it not worked?'*

"I'm not sure. Maybe Time Innarn doesn't work properly here."

The white hood bowed. *'Then you have outlived your usefulness.'* Smoke climbed up from the ground, snaking around the figure before solidifying into a scythe, plasma dancing along the blade.

Before the failed Time Innarnian could utter a sound, the scythe swung, cutting through flesh and bone neatly. The soul was sent back to the Spirit Realm, and the body disappeared in a bright flash as if it had never existed.

Heaving a silent sigh, the white-robed figure turned and looked at the final statue. She was the one he was fearful to wake. She had resided in the Spirit Realm for longer than any other. Some said that the Realm had started with her, and now, if they wanted a chance to stay, she would have to be the one to lead them all.

Approaching slowly, the being crossed the small clearing and ever so carefully tapped the tip of the scythe to the statue's chest. Plasma arced and raced along the figure, and the last of the stone fell away from the final trapped spirit. Elaborate white robes fell back from a very recognisable face.

"Why have I been summoned?" Kay'imi, the first Altoriae asked.

'We must wake the others. We are running out of time,' the being in the white robe said.

Kay'imi looked at the other Weaver, peering into the depths of his soul. "Very well," she said. "We must move swiftly then."

She strode forward, the crowd parting before her. As she went, the blood in her veins started to tingle, pulling her to one side. Pausing before one of the men, she raised a perfectly sculpted brow. *Altoriae,* her blood sang. "What are you doing here?" she asked.

"Same as you—I was summoned." Muran shrugged, the ink on his skin rippling with the movement.

"You desecrated your body?" She sniffed.

"It was that or be eaten," he said, gaze hardening. "What would you choose?"

Reaching out, Kay'imi cupped Muran's cheek. "I am sorry for all you went through when I couldn't reach you."

Muran shrugged, like the constant pain and suffering he had endured was no big deal. He gestured to the crowd of familiar faces around him. "Now we're back, we can help."

"And how do we do that?" she asked.

"Make sure no one else has to go through what we did," he said, like it was the most obvious thing in the Realms. The others nodded.

Kay'imi's mind flashed back to all the battles, the backstabbing, the regrets, and she nodded.

No one else would suffer. Not while she was alive again.

CHAPTER FIFTEEN

Narday
Fourth day of the third week of Waeghost

Shari contemplated wading through the crowd gathered in the tavern, but Wisp stalked in, head low, and cleared the way for her. Following, Shari waved at Joana, who was staring at her with wide, worried eyes.

Making her way through the packed bodies to the bar, she grinned at the other woman. "Looks like a pretty good first day," Shari said.

Worry faded away, and Joana laughed. "I've never seen it so busy," she said.

"I may have had something to do with that. Anika wanted to start a club, and I kind of offered the tavern up as a space to meet." Shari winced. Hail chittered soothingly in her ear.

"The more the merrier. Maybe entry fee into the club is a meal?" Joana winked and whirled away to take the next person's order.

Shari grinned. She'd have to let Anika know.

Anika, dressed in red, opened the doors and began stomping the snow off her boots, freezing upon seeing the swarm of bodies in the room.

Think of her and she appears. Shari stood on the rungs of one of the bar stools and raised a glass in Anika's direction. Wisp huffed and pulled at the hem of her top. She sank onto the stool again and rubbed his head.

Watching Anika make her way through the crowd was like seeing an artist at work. She stopped and spoke to individuals and groups with a smile and a wave, careful not to get into their personal space, but enough for them to know she cared. And Shari, after spending a lifetime observing Anika, knew that the shallow, vapid girl from only a year or so was gone.

"Well met," Shari said, sliding a glassful of swirling silver liquid from Joana her way. The Returned was making her mark on the tavern and had reintroduced xin, the pale mauve liquid the Weavers favoured. The heated drink gave off steam and helped to ward away the chill of the night.

Hail raised his head to peer at Anika but didn't make a sound as she grabbed the drink and took a swig.

"Well met," Anika said, glancing at the sizable group. "I didn't think this many would be able to make it."

"I mean, you are an inspiration," Shari said drily. She caught sight of a flash of white hair and the pointed ears of a certain reporter and made a note to seem as enthralled as possible.

Shari grinned, bemused, as Anika turned to the crowd and cleared her throat.

"Thank you for coming," Anika said. "Welcome to the first meeting of The Lonely Orphan Society."

There were a few cheers and even more winces.

"Yes," Anika laughed. "The name needs *serious* work. Even the acronym is a bit on the nose. But we're here today not just to figure out a better name, but to support each other through a time when we should have our family close by but aren't able to." An artful tear escaped her lower lashes and hung there for a moment before falling.

Shari gritted her teeth so she wouldn't roll her eyes. *Trust Anika to be able to cry and still look pretty.* Hail chittered at her, and Shari could feel the thoughts of *don't be petty* rolling off the little draci.

Wisp offered more support by grumbling slightly as he settled.

Sitting to the side, Shari sipped her drink as others slowly shared their stories. By the end of the meeting, they had all laughed, cried, and snacked on something new Joana had added to the menu that made Shari want more. Still, after everything, she felt more alone than ever.

Hail nipped at her ear, and Shari grinned. *Maybe not as alone as I thought.*

Ginna, the reporter for *The Shifting Island Sentinel*, slid up to her. "Well met, Altoriae," she said. "I'm sorry to see you here."

For a moment, Shari couldn't figure out what Ginna meant. "Without my parents' sacrifice, LOS wouldn't be here today. None of us would be."

"Still, being unexpectedly orphaned isn't the most fun thing in the Realms." Ginna accepted a drink from Joana and knocked the whole thing back in one gulp.

"Speaking from experience?" Shari asked. Hail nudged his head into her jaw.

"Decade's old," Ginna confirmed.

Shari didn't know what to say. "I..."

"That bit," Ginna said, tipping her empty glass in Shari's direction, "never gets any easier. The sudden halt to a conversation as people struggle with how best to word their next response. Grief is a process that is different for all of us, but it's one that shouldn't be endured alone." Ginna squinted at her. "You aren't alone, are you?"

"I have my guild, and my uncle and his mate," Shari said stiffly, hand tangled in Wisp's fur and Hail's scales pressing into her neck—the creatures who had adopted her keeping her grounded.

"Lean on them. Let them help. If that's one thing losing someone is good for, it's learning who you can count on." Ginna got to her feet. "I'll never try to interview someone at a meeting like this. Emotions run too high, and I know very well that there are things better left unsaid. But I'll reach out soon, alright?"

She was gone before Shari could respond.

Tania smiled nervously at the others. They were meeting in the underground chambers of Cantash, to pretend like the world above wasn't freezing over.

To be fair, Cantash was as toasty as ever, but they were the only ones. All the other islands were feeling the cold. Fenix, ever the host, had laid out a spread Cantash would be proud of. If their islands were currently aware, that is.

As if Brinley had heard Tania's thoughts, she cleared her throat.

"So," Brinley said. "Are your islands talking yet? Vannali is still silent."

"Straight to the heart of it," Oakley said bitterly. Ginorti's Linked scowled at Brinley, who shifted in her seat but made no apology.

"No," Tania said, dropping the smile she'd tried so hard to keep up. "Ronah hasn't said a peep."

"Nor Rakemyst," Zana added.

One by one, the others all shook their heads.

Brinley slumped. "I was hoping I was the only one," she admitted.

Oakley's scowl didn't abate.

"Well, what are we going to do about it?" Domic said. "It doesn't feel right, not talking to Akoren."

"I know what you mean. I never realised how much mental space Talhan took up. He was always just *there*. I don't think we can do anything," Cyrus said. "Other than wait."

"I don't like waiting." Fenix scowled.

"Me either," Tania said. From the expressions the others wore, no one in the room was happy with it.

But it wasn't like they had a choice. Eventually, their islands would talk again.

Eventually.

Tania shared a look with Brinley. If they all wished hard enough, would her wishful thinking come true?

"You had a meeting today," Yessna said, slumping next to Shari at the castle table and retrieving a dagger from a hidden sheath. After grabbing an apple, she started to carve a slice off.

"How did you know?" Shari asked.

"Little draci told me," she said, pointing the tip of her dagger at Hail.

Said draci huffed and turned to show the Ferah his tail. Wisp growled at Hail but halted the moment Shari laid a gentle hand on his fur.

Yessna laughed and sliced off another bit of apple. "How did it go?" she asked.

"Good. Busy. Felt like half the island was there," Shari said.

"Did you talk to anyone?" Yessna asked.

There was a studied nonchalance to her that made Shari stiffen. "Yes. I spoke to a few beings."

The Ferah kept her eyes on the blade as she took another slice. "About your parents?"

Shari's chair made a horrid screeching sound on the tiles as she got to her feet. "No." She went to storm off, but Yessna grabbed her wrist.

"Sit," the Ferah commanded.

Glaring, Shari tried to tug her hand free.

"What, you think mind healing is going to be all sappy and pretty? Sit," Yessna growled.

Heaving a sigh, Shari sat. "No. But I'm not ready to–"

"Then you say that. And we tackle something you are ready to deal with. But you don't get to walk out when it gets hard. Now tell me something true."

Shari narrowed her eyes at the Ferah. "I'm not liking you much at the moment."

Yessna threw her head back and laughed. "Good! We don't have to be friends to get your mental health better." She sobered quickly. "It helps though, little healer."

Despite wanting to huff, Shari nodded. "Yeah, I know," she said. "But sometimes..."

"Sometimes talking is harder than swinging a blade, and yet, I get the feeling that you don't want to do either."

Shari scowled. "Why are you so perceptive?"

Yessna just laughed at her again and tossed her a hunk of apple.

When Samuel agreed to walk with Jonathan along the elongated main street, he hadn't expected to be accosted.

He really should have known better.

Samuel glanced at the dark head level with the bottom of his ribs and sighed, sheathing the dagger that had flown into his hand. Sneeze huffed into his ear, and Jonathan, off to the side, was covering his mouth in a vain attempt to hide the snigger which was threatening to break free.

Getting tackled by this student was becoming the norm. Samuel couldn't decide if he liked it or not.

"I thought you'd been hurt. Mum wouldn't tell me *anything*," Laura said.

"Do you honestly think that there's something on this Realm capable of causing me pain?" he asked, arms held out like one of the crow-scaring devices farmers used.

Laura laughed at him. "Course not. But if something hurt the Altoriae then you'd go after them, and then they'd try to hurt you."

It was a tad disconcerting when a hatchling was able to read you so well. "Try is the most appropriate word. I could rend them in two with a mere thought."

"And that's why I'm glad you're okay," Laura said, finally releasing him.

He dropped his arms. "I'm touched," he said drily. Laura beamed at him.

"How are you settling in?" Jonathan asked.

It was as if the child had two settings. Gloomy as the grave or beaming like the sun. "It feels nicer here, like I'm not burning all the time."

Samuel glanced down at the child and nodded mutely. He should have figured it out before this human-shaped hatchling did. This new Realm of theirs was darker. Not by much—maybe two levels down from Lissae—but it was a welcome change indeed.

"It's good not to be in constant pain," he agreed.

Jonathan looked at the pair sharply but said nothing.

"Oh, still constant, but just not as much." Laura looked cheerful about the situation.

Only a hatchling. He sighed but smiled at her.

"Thank you," she said, "for letting me be me." She gave him one last squeeze around the middle and raced off.

"What was that about?" Jonathan asked.

Gazing after the hatchling, Samuel smirked. "Sometimes, being dark has its advantages." Sneeze huffed in agreement.

Jonathan scratched at the skin of his arm. "Like not wanting to rip your skin from your flesh when your old Realm decides it's had enough and births a new one?"

Samuel's smirk grew. "Exactly."

"Is that what Lissae was like for you?" Jonathan asked.

"Worse," Samuel said shortly.

"And yet, you came when I asked." Jonathan clapped his shoulder.

"We're going with 'asked', are we?" Samuel raised a brow.

"What? Like you'd ever let a mere mortal like me command you," Jonathan said. "Well, maybe if the mortal was Shari..."

He laughed as a bolt of Innarn flew from Samuel's fingertips into his unprotected side.

The ripples in the water grew wilder as a figure emerged from the depths at the whim of a being in a white robe.

'*Split the doorway before we run out of time,*' the white-robed being ordered. A mass of Spirits turned solid, nodded as one, and stepped forward onto the land.

They had work to do.

Chapter Sixteen

Rasshday
Fifth day of the third week of Waeghost

hari froze. On the other side of the hallway, Remmy, one of the Returned, stood. He gave her a cheeky grin and touched his finger to the side of his nose.

Wincing at the reminder of punching his nose, Shari said, "Well met, Remmy. How are you?"

Wisp grumbled at the man, but Shari ignored it. The Shadow Bringer was decidedly not a morning creature.

"Good, and you?" He barrelled on, as so many of the Returned did, without waiting for her to answer. "I was wondering how you do it."

"Sorry?" she asked. "Do what?"

"Well, Collis has a stupid amount of Innarn. Always has. The rest of us learned, over the years, and figured out how to gather and keep more. We'd be about the same as your level now."

Shari didn't know if she should be insulted or honoured by the comparison. "Yes?" she settled for.

"And it *burns* if we don't use it. Don't you have the same issue?" he said.

"Oh. Well." She paused to think. "I had to hide for a long time, and I configured a shield that would contain my Innarn, stop it from leaking and others figuring out who I was before the test. I wonder..." Shari glanced at Remmy and weighed the odds of him stabbing her if she lowered her shield. Hail chittered at her.

'*Protect you,*' the little draci sent.

The glow in Wisp's chest grew brighter and he stepped away slightly, muscles coiled.

'*Thank you, Hail,*' Shari sent back. If he'd kept her secret for this long, she doubted he was about to stab her now.

Closing her eyes, Shari allowed her mirror shield to drop slowly.

Innarn lashed out of her, slamming into the walls and creating great fissures in the ground. Remmy's yell made Shari snap the shield back up.

The Returned was clinging to the wall as the floor beneath him had crumbled away. Wisp was standing on the only other bit of intact ground.

"Huh," Shari said. "Maybe that shield is good for more than one thing." She smoothed over the floor, and Remmy dropped back down.

"I'd appreciate it if you could teach us that one," Remmy said, panting lightly. He looked at the spot that had gaped open just a moment ago. "Looks like it might come in handy."

"Sure." Shari smiled.

At least someone wasn't asking me to fight.

Samuel stared at the pile of torn pages scattered across Jonathan's desk in the back room of Books 'n' More and wondered where to start.

Terrance, may the tu'zar rot in the bowels of Altum, had managed to destroy a good three-quarters of *The Altoriae's Handbook* before Samuel had stopped him.

He'd asked Jonathan if he could borrow the office to 'work on a project undisturbed' and then left the Guardian with the bickering hatchlings before he was tempted to take another layer of scales from the lot of them.

The book had been burning a metaphorical hole in his pocket-Realm, and Samuel found the idea of being able to repair something instead of being forced to take it apart was quite appealing, not to mention getting the chance to write in peace again.

Now it was all laid out before him, he didn't know where to start.

'At *the beginning*,' Sneeze sent unhelpfully.

"I never got a chance to read the book," Samuel groused. "I don't know where the beginning *is*."

Sneeze heaved a sigh worthy of one of the hatchlings and climbed down Samuel's arm, leaving pinpricks of pain on the way. Clamping his jaw shut, he used his paws to go through the pile of papers until one with a fancy inscription of the title stood out.

'*Here*,' Sneeze sent, and leaned his head over the side of the table to breathe out. Sparks flew harmlessly to the ground. '*Check the back*,' the draci suggested.

Samuel was going to take it as a suggestion rather than the order it sounded like.

The back of the title page held the start of a list of other pages and the order they went in.

"You are far too clever," Samuel said to the draci.

Sneeze purred and went to curl up in the corner of the desk.

Hours later, Samuel stretched his back out and groaned when it creaked. "I think I'm done," he rasped.

"Done what?" Jonathan asked from the doorway.

Samuel absolutely did not shriek or send a jolt of Dark Innarn to destroy the door, no matter what the lying Guardian might say.

After a quick flick of his hand to fix the door, Samuel held out the repaired *Handbook*.

It was quite satisfying to see the Guardian's jaw drop.

"You restored it," Jonathan breathed.

"As good as new," Samuel said. It had taken a fair amount of concentration, and the lightest Innarn he could produce, but to look at the book now, you'd never know that it had been torn to shreds in a fit of rage by someone not even worthy of glancing at it.

"You are worth your weight in gold." Jonathan took the book with careful hands.

Samuel frowned. "Why would I want that much gold? My scales are worth more, at any rate."

Jonathan laughed. "I mean, you're brilliant. Thank you, Samuel." He gazed straight into Samuel's eyes. "I'm glad you let yourself be trapped."

Huffing fit to match Sneeze, Samuel ducked his head to hide a smile. "I'm glad too," he said gruffly.

Wolf and Belfar were winging through the air. Even though there was an excess of Innarn around, Wolf was aware that he was not the only one keeping a close eye on Belfar.

'If you all don't back off, I'm going to drop just to annoy you.' Belfar's mental bark was far worse than his bite.

'You're sounding a bit like your mate there,' Charin needled.

Belfar growled, and Wolf almost forgot how wings worked.

Varlee cackled at them both.

Clearing his throat, Wolf tried to keep his gaze from wandering to his mate but failed. 'Focus on your flying. We have a lot of ground to cover,' he snapped. They were flying Ginorti's south coast, and what had previously been a leisurely half-hour flight would now take them almost three hours at top speed.

Belfar shot him a grateful look and looped around so they were side by side. '*Anything you want to tell me?*' he sent on a narrow channel, just to Wolf.

'*As much as it makes sense, I'm regretting staying in a place where others are free to come and go as they wish.*'

'*Of course Shari is free to come as she pleases, but I told you to put the wards up!*' Even at this distance, Belfar's blush was strong enough to heat his heart.

Out of the corner of his eye, Wolf caught a flash of white on the ground, but when he looked, it was gone.

Deciding it must have been a patch of melting snow, he paid it no more attention.

Lizbeth rubbed her temples and groaned. Her headaches had been getting worse for a week now, and today she could barely stand the pain was so great.

"I'm not sure if you're aware, but I'm quite happy not seeing with traditional methods," she said into her empty house.

The light behind her eyes pulsed again.

"Yes, I'm sure," she said. "Arilla, Calem, I know you're trying to help, but you must remember I have never been able to see the way others have. This is not a boon for me. It would be a curse."

After flickering a final time, the light and the pain faded.

Slumping back on her sofa, Lizbeth sighed in relief. She had wondered if the new Realm would be as inclined to listen as Lissae had been. Thankfully, Arilla and Calem had always taken note of how others felt, rather than thinking they knew best. Lizbeth honestly didn't know how she would've coped with Innarn vision and actual vision as well. The double feedback would have been rough on her synapses.

Now the headache was a dull memory, it was time to do some baking.

The being in the white robe threw a shield over his head to prevent the Ilutri patrol above from spotting him. When they flew on, he sighed in relief and headed for the hidden place deep within Ginorti's forest.

Earth Innarnians were particular about their dead and would either bind them to trees or seal them in the ground. It was going to be hard to convince the stubborn souls to give up their resting spots and come back to the Realm of the living again.

But he was nothing if not persistent.

CHAPTER SEVENTEEN

Vebaday

Sixth day of the third week of Waeghost

ore than anything else, Cyrus wanted to kick a chair and scream into the empty lab just to hear something other than his own breathing filling the space.

Talhan was remaining stubbornly silent. While his isle had never been much for conversation, there had always been a hum in the back of his head that let him know he wasn't alone. That someone else was there to help him through. And now, with Xani and Temira gone, and Talhan quieter than the grave, his head felt empty and his heart far from full.

His gaze travelled across the mishmash of technology strewn across the workbench and fell on a box of orange crystals.

He'd do anything to have someone else back in the lab again.

Anything.

Shari looked around her room in the castle. She'd packed everything she needed for an overnight stay at her house... her uncle's house, but couldn't bring herself to commit just yet.

The whole thing felt weird—did she want to move back into her childhood room, knowing her parents weren't just down the hall anymore? Did she want to stay at the castle, where it felt like everyone was just floating through the days, purposeless?

Wisp leaned against her, and Hail nudged her jaw. She gave them both a pat. "Time to go, hey?"

Either way, she would make a concentrated effort to try.

Shifting abruptly with the two creatures to the garden of her home, she looked around. The land size was the same, but the crops were withering slightly under the dusting of snow. Shari cast a ward over them, allowing the moisture in and keeping the chill out. Almost immediately, the plants looked better.

Grinning, she went to open the door but stopped. Technically, she didn't live there anymore. She couldn't say that she was going to move back in, either. Did she really have the right to barge back in like it was still her house?

Hail chittered at her.

"You're right. I should knock," she said. Raising her hand to do just that, Shari froze when the door opened.

Belfar grinned at her. "I was tempted to let you suffer a bit longer, but I know how odd it can feel. Come on in."

Banishing the snow from her clothes, Shari stomped her feet and stepped inside.

The kitchen was empty.

The counters were bare, and anything that wasn't a photograph had been taken from the walls. Her artwork from first grade. The crooked painting of their yard that her mother had done, and the ceramic vase her father had made which had hung from a hook and been repaired more times than she could count.

Gone.

Belfar noticed her gaze sweeping the room. "Wolf's been cleaning."

Shari winced at his tone. Gentle, like he expected her to fall apart at any moment. Hail, pushing his head into her jaw, wasn't helping. Wisp was looking between Belfar and Shari as if he wasn't sure who needed comforting more.

Gritting her teeth, she smiled. "I noticed," she said brightly. "Looks good."

The worst part was that it did. The room felt bigger, brighter now the clutter was gone. It just didn't feel like home, and Shari couldn't figure out if it made coming to a decision on staying or not easier or harder.

Wolf came through the internal door, a bouquet of flowers held stem-up in one hand. "You're here," he said blankly. "I, uh, thought these would brighten the room up." He held the slightly wilted flowers out.

"The room is fine," Shari said. She didn't miss Belfar's wave of Innarn that fixed the petals. Nor did Wolf, if the colour rising on his cheeks was any indication. Hail wrapped his tail tighter around Shari's neck, and she fought not to smile in case Wolf took it the wrong way.

Wisp had no such compunction and was doing the canine equivalent of a grin. Shari did her best to ignore him.

"I didn't know what you'd prefer to eat, so I thought a bit of everything," Belfar said, sliding past her and looking at Wolf until his mate moved into the room properly.

Shari raised her brows as a feast of tiny plates appeared on the table—so many that they were almost overflowing the slab of wood. "That's quite a spread," she marvelled. She slipped the strap of her bag down her shoulder and sent it to the corner.

"Packing light?" Wolf asked.

"I don't know if I can come back," Shari admitted. "I'll try, but..." She glanced at the empty counter. "Everything is different."

General Morrow paused.

On the other side of a thicket of trees, a man in a mainlander captain's uniform was staggering from one tree to the next, looking totally lost.

Keeping an eye on the red of his jacket, the general rounded the thicket and stopped.

The man had disappeared.

Examining the ground, General Morrow could see where the boot prints had left tracks in the snow, and where they'd just vanished from.

Frowning, the general considered calling a search. After the last lot of mainlanders, he was sure Ginorti would not be happy to find a stray one wandering his land.

Particularly not in a captain's uniform.

Collis grinned as Tania flopped backwards in the garden, sending a flurry of snow into the air.

"Mum just announced it," she said. "School goes back on Adonday! As much as I didn't like *why* we were having a break, it was kind of nice." She closed her eyes and waved her arms and legs around, attempting to make an impression in snow that had already melted.

"This will be our last year of schooling," Collis soothed. "She agreed to let us both test out early."

"I can't believe you got her to agree," Tania said. Opening her eyes, she sucked in a breath.

Floating directly above her was a spectral image of a white robe.

A shield appeared between her and the what-ever-it-was, courtesy of Collis.

"What was that?" she asked softly, almost afraid the thing could hear them talk.

"Someone wants to see what you're doing. And I'm not entirely sure they're friendly," Collis said. "You need to shield, wherever you go, whatever you're doing. The shield needs to stay up."

Tania nodded. "I think that's a good idea." She looked at where the figure had just been and blinked as snow fell against the shield Collis had raised, outlining it for a moment before it slid off. "The snow is going to make it hard to remain unnoticeable, though."

Collis sighed. "We can work on that."

The outpouring of Innarn into the shield had managed to use more than she had expected. Shivering in the sudden cold, Tania sat up and wrapped her arms around herself. "Can we work on it inside?"

Nodding, Collis helped Tania to her feet. She let him lead her into the house and paused in the entryway to look over her shoulder.

She couldn't shake the feeling that she was being watched.

The heat of the spitting volcano didn't seem to bother the being in the white robe as he leaned over the magma flow. Stretching out a hand hidden in the folds of a sleeve, he plucked at the air. Plasma arched, hitting the magma, and the shimmering soul of a short, white-haired male appeared.

Slower than the others, a body formed, wrapping the soul in sinew, flesh, bone, and skin.

'Do you wish for a second chance?' the white-robed being asked.

Running his fingers through new strands of hair, Milo smiled. 'Absolutely.'

Chapter Eighteen

Zoeday

Seventh day of the third week of Waeghost

Shari shifted her weight restlessly.

It felt odd without Wisp and Hail by her side. The two sat against the wall—Wisp exuding menace and Hail scowling so hard, she struggled not to giggle at how cute he was.

Her gaze swept across to the Returned, who looked at her, totally silent as they waited for instructions.

"Remmy mentioned the other day that some of you were having trouble with controlling your Innarn, and I thought I'd show you how I keep mine under wraps," Shari said, glancing to the side as Collis and Tania entered the training grounds. "I use a mirror shield," she continued. "It basically reflects the world around me but uses a fair amount of Innarn to keep stable. Good if you're wanting to drain your Innarn at a regular pace." She chanced a grin and received more than one smile back.

"Tell me there's not a motus," Remmy groaned dramatically, throwing his head back and letting his arms flop by his sides.

"I didn't even know how to do a motus until recently," Shari admitted. "So, no, it's just pure force of will."

"Brilliant!" Remmy smiled at her. "How do we do it?" he asked.

Tilting her head, Shari focused on her mirror shield and let it spin into view around her. "It's similar to a regular shield that you'd use in battle. One that keeps all unfriendly Innarn away, but it also lets the outside world see what it expects. For me growing up, that was a Blank."

There was a rumble of surprise, and Shari remembered, too late, that the Returned hadn't been around for that part of her life. As surprise turned to anger, Shari sighed, loud enough that they all froze.

"It was the easiest way to keep everyone safe. It took a fair bit of tweaking to allow Jonathan to still know where I was without allowing everyone else to do the same." She looked out over the crowd. "With all of you wanting to keep track of each other, I'm sure the amount of Innarn expended will be so much more. Now, who wants to try first?"

Remmy stepped up. "Better be me, since I dragged you into this," he said.

"Show us your shield," Shari said.

Shaking his shoulders out, Remmy's Innarn shield sprang into being– a swirling, shifting thing that was made of more Earth than she was used to.

She prodded the shield and nodded. "Great. Now make it so we can't see it but it's still active."

Slowly, Remmy nodded his head and parts of his shield disappeared, only to flicker back to life again moments later. Sweat sheened across his forehead.

"Keep going," Shari said. "Who else wants to try?"

One by one, the Returned sorted themselves into lines, shields flaring to life and flickering as they tried to make them go invisible.

By the end of the session, more than one had managed the task, Remmy and Tania amongst them.

"Shari, this is brilliant," Tania said. "I don't feel like I'm going to burn up anymore."

"I feel settled in my own skin for the first time since we got here," Remmy admitted.

Shari beamed. She *could* help others without a blade in her hand.

Yessna smiled, making sure to keep her fangs out of sight, as one of the mainlanders succeeded in creating controlled fire. "Well done," she purred.

It had only taken one of them combusting from the inside to see that not using their new powers wasn't an option.

She was training a group in Fire Innarn on the beach of their island, closest to Rakemyst, which, through sheer size, was rapidly becoming the mainland. The irony was not lost on her.

Shading her eyes with a paw, Yessna froze. On the opposite shore, there were two figures standing in the shadows of the trees.

But she could have sworn they were the identical dark-skinned cyclops.

The ones who were both dead.

'*Nerina,*' Yessna sent.

The healer was at her side in an instant. Yessna pointed to Drah and Kerk.

They were gone.

Jonathan walked through the bookstore. There were so many memories lost in these shelves.

Zac cleared his throat. "Have you read the latest Everon Castor?" he asked.

"No, I haven't had time," Jonathan admitted.

"Maybe you'll be able to now," Zac said.

Now there aren't patrols every night. Now there isn't a new emergency cropping up every meal. Now Shari is starting to heal.

"Maybe." Jonathan grinned. "Although Castor is overrated," he teased.

Behind the desk, Eva gasped. "You take that back!" she said. "He's what keeps this shop running!"

Jonathan's grin grew. She wasn't wrong.

Before he could say anything, the bell over the door rang and Talhan's Linked entered the shop.

"Found you," Cyrus said.

Jonathan regretted his earlier thoughts—apparently, trouble was now finding them in the store again.

Cyrus crossed to Zac. "I wondered if you'd work with me in the lab again? I'm going stir crazy there by myself. Was thinking of reactivating the femto crystals—"

Three voices chorused "No!"

He nodded, his eyes troubled. "I figured there might have been some sort of latent sentience, so I'm going to melt it to slag and consign it to a pocket-Realm where nothing else exists."

"Good idea," Zac said. Jonathan grabbed his hand to help him hide the trembling. "I'd love to come back. There were a few things I was working on with Temira that I could continue."

"Sounds perfect." Cyrus grinned. His gaze dipped down to their joined hands. "Tomorrow, maybe?"

"I'll see you then." Zac smiled.

Jonathan waited until Cyrus had left the store. "Now you've saved me from the Crystal Intelligence twice."

Zac shook his head in warning. "Don't even joke about it."

Shari smiled at the others. After dinner with Wolf and Belfar, the chaos of the castle felt more like home.

Dealon had brought back a pot of something from the tavern that smelled divine, and had summoned the others, who were slowly arriving and taking their places around the table. Hail was sitting next to Shari's plate, lapping at a tiny bowl of soup. Wisp was under her chair, gnawing at something she didn't want to think too hard about.

Once the castle residents were seated, Dealon cleared his throat. "Thank you all for coming tonight," he said.

Elani threw a bread roll at him, which Talofa intercepted. "Don't aim at the chef," Talofa scolded, waving the roll at the archer.

Shari grinned.

"I know things change and we all have responsibilities we can't avoid, but I want us to try to meet up once a week for dinner," Dealon continued as if nothing had happened.

"If you're cooking, I'll be here," Raven said. "Can we invite others?"

Shari could see the endless dinners taking place in her mind's eye. The faces around the table getting older, new ones joining them, families starting, scars appearing, and slowly, the others fading until there were just a few of the original crew left. Oddly enough, the faces of the other Altoriaes were at the table as well, and Shari shook her head to dispel the image. Maybe they were there in spirit?

Rubbing the bumps off her arm, she grinned at Dealon and raised her cup. "To new traditions," she said. The others joined in, just as Mu walked through the door, carrying something bundled up in his arms.

"What have you found now?" Elani asked.

"Look at this little guy," Mu cooed.

Shari raised her head and sucked in a breath. Cradled in Mu's arms like a baby was a miniature fulni, complete with two heads.

"Wh... where did you get that from?" Shari asked, her mouth suddenly dry. Hail, sensing her distress, raised his head and growled, frost spreading under his paws at the table. Wisp appeared in front of Mu, fur standing on end as a deep rumble filled the room.

Startled, Mu juggled the fulni.

As Shari struggled not to gawp at the pair, the beast grew as she was watching, almost doubling in size.

'*Samuel?*' If her send was on the wrong side of a shriek, Shari figured he would forgive her this once.

The being in question shifted in, his scales already covering his chest and arms, a snarl on his face as he scanned the room for danger. Gaze alighting on the baby of an extinct race, he froze.

And licked his lips.

'No, *Samuel.*' Shari felt a hysterical giggle rising in her throat. '*You can't eat the last member of an extinct race. Also, why is there a fulni in the kitchen?! How did it get here?*'

'*Good question*' he sent, unable to tear his gaze away from the rapidly growing beast. "Might want to take that outside," he said to Mu.

Sneeze walked down Samuel's arm and nestled next to Hail, the two draci oblivious to anything outside of their conversation.

"But it's cold out," Mu protested, even as he had to put the fulni on the ground.

The others at the table were staring at the beast in horror as, one by one, they realised exactly what Mu was carrying.

"Soon, it won't fit through the door anymore," Samuel warned. Something in his tone seemed to get through.

"Fine," Mu sighed.

Before he could change his mind, Shari shifted them to the training ground, leaving Mu behind.

The fulni let out a mournful bellow.

Which was answered.

Eyes wide, Shari looked at Samuel.

'*So, I could eat this one,*' he mused.

'*Stop thinking with your stomach! What are we meant to do?*' Shari asked. One fulni was bad enough, but if more had survived, they would decimate everything on the Realm to sate their unstoppable hunger. They'd done it multiple times before and eaten entire Realms.

With one as new as Carilla, Shari didn't have a choice.

'Pocket-Realm.' Samuel nodded decisively. *'Safely contained and tied to this Realm rather than a single individual. Without being able to get through the gateway, it's our only chance.'*

Shari nodded and eyed the beast. Its head was now the same height as her own. Something smashed against the doors of the training ground, and she jumped.

'Better make one quick, or we're going to be in trouble,' Shari sent.

'I think that job is for you,' Samuel countered. *'Safer that way, too.'*

Glaring, Shari knew he was right. The fulni licked a stripe up her arm. Shari shook it off. *'Don't let me get eaten,'* she warned.

Shifting to the far stands, Shari closed her eyes and gathered her Innarn. She hadn't had to create a pocket-Realm from scratch since she'd been a child and was worried that she'd forgotten how. First, a doorway. Settling it into the wall of the castle seemed like the right thing to do. And she'd be able to shrink it later so the fulni wouldn't be able to get through. Something... metal, maybe.

Opening her eyes, Shari nodded, satisfied with the metal door that had an image of the fulni's face carved into the surface. Crossing to the door, she opened it to the wall of the castle.

This was where things could go wrong. She was essentially carving out a new space over the top of something that already existed. If Shari got this incorrect, the entire castle could collapse. She looked up, taking in the mishmash of elemental stories that made up the building, and gulped.

Better get it right then.

'Shari,' Samuel warned. *'They aren't going to wait much longer.'*

'Distract them,' Shari sent. Laying her hands on the cobbled stone, she felt the wall, memorising each crack and crevasse. Gathering her Innarn, she pushed. A new space appeared, large enough for a single adult fulni.

Taking in the walls, Shari shoved, and the space expanded outwards, stretching beyond what she could see. Trees sprung up, shrubs and plants, bugs and birds. A few meatier creatures appeared as well, and Shari wondered which Realm she remembered the loose-limbed, bear-like animal from. With claws as long as her forearm, she decided she didn't want to know.

What else?

Water.

Focusing, Shari created a stream, and pushed some of the land higher, making it harder for the fulni to get to everything in one vicious circuit.

'*Shari!*'

She had never heard Samuel sound so panicked before. Turning, she realised why.

A herd of fulni were heading right for her.

With her concentration broken, Shari could feel the rumble of the ground as their hooves pounded closer.

She took off running, using Innarn to help her sprint towards the middle of the new Realm, always staying just ahead of the pack. Their fetid breath hot on her back, Shari leaped over the stream and shifted back to the doors, slamming them closed behind her and shrinking them down so she would have to duck to get through.

Samuel wrapped his arms around her in a fierce hug. "When are you going to stop doing that to me?"

Too out of breath to respond, Shari hugged him back. '*Got them all?*' she asked. Wisp and Hail appeared, both leaning into her, surrounding her with a feeling of something Shari had thought she'd never have again.

Family.

'*Yes. And they almost got you,*' he growled.

Shari looked up at him. '*You would have never let that happen.*' She rested her head against his chest and felt him sigh.

'*That doesn't mean you should take needless risks,*' he said.

'Me, or the rest of the Realm? Seemed pretty needed.'

'You.'

She glanced at him blankly.

'You or the Realm? The answer is always you.'

Ducking her head again, Shari refused to let him see her cry.

The white-robed being sighed. Crystal was even less willing to release the souls it held than the Earth was. Still, if they were needed, he would make sure they came. Plasma twisted, bouncing from crystal to crystal until one sang the sweet song of release.

Pallid grey skin stretched over flesh, and the being frowned.

'I'm *whole again*,' the soul said, running a hand over her legs. She looked up at the darkness hidden within the hood. '*I can feel my legs!*' she laughed.

'*Then help to open the doorway, so others may join us.*'

Rising on trembling feet for the first time in centuries, Xani nodded. '*Of course.*'

Chapter Nineteen

Adonday
First day of the fourth week of Waeghost

Anika looked at the towering bereni trees of Ridden Hall and sighed. Until the attack by Anriluka, she'd ruled the school.

Maeve, her former best friend and all-time wanna be, shoved her shoulder as she teetered past in high heels she'd never gotten the hang of.

"Watch it, Blank," Maeve sneered.

Anika grimaced. *She'd* taught Maeve that.

Shari and Tania appeared by her side.

"Ready?" Tania said brightly.

"For another few months of torture? Sure," Anika said drily. "And didn't you test out early?" she asked Shari.

"You can leave, but you never truly escape." Shari lowered the pitch of her voice and wriggled her fingers. The giant white beast at her side huffed.

Laughing, Anika shook her head. "If I were you, I wouldn't want to come back," she admitted.

Shrugging, Shari just said, "It's one of my duties."

"Is it? If we're not on Lissae anymore?" Anika asked.

"Stop being insightful. It's weird." Shari wagged a finger at her.

Anika laughed brightly.

"Well met," Aram said, arm wrapped around Liz. "Ready for the last dash until freedom?"

"Can't wait!" Anika smiled. Out of the corner of her eye, she saw Maeve scowling at their group. If her former friend couldn't get with the times, Anika wasn't about to make her.

The headmaster walked past them, calling out greetings as she went. "Shari, excellent. Meet me in my office after parade, please. And bring Samuel with you."

Anika joined in the chorus of "Ooohh," delighting in Shari's blush.

"I'm sure it's nothing," Tania said soothingly.

Shari nodded and looked relieved.

Would she ever have that level of trust in someone?

Shari was mentally poking Samuel throughout the parade, where every student sat politely as Liza and the teaching staff told them that even though they were on a new Realm, their education was still important.

She wasn't wrong, but the teachers were going to carry that message through every lesson for the next month until even they were sick of hearing it.

At the end of the parade, Shari obediently followed Liza to the principal's office, where they met Samuel at the door. As they entered the room, their draci were quick to fly at each other, connecting in midair and perching on top of an unused chair. Shadow and Wisp curled up underneath it, black nestled against white fur.

"Make yourselves at home. I promise this will be quick," Liza said.

Glancing at Samuel, Shari shrugged. Her Innarn pulsed out, checking the room for traps before she took a seat.

'*Why did you check?*' Samuel asked.

Shari winced. Of all the beings in the Realms, Samuel was one of the ones most likely to recognise what she'd done. '*An Eni took over my last principal. You can never be too careful.*'

Samuel scoffed. '*The Eni are extinct.*'

'*So were the fulni,*' Shari countered.

He tipped his head in silent acknowledgement.

"Thank you for meeting with me. Here." Liza slid over a parchment to each of them. "Sign these, and you're free to go."

"What's this?" Shari asked, scanning the document.

"We're releasing you from your duties. The elders and the teachers got together and decided that, seeing we are not of Lissae anymore, there's no need for either of you to continue teaching if you do not wish to do so."

"And if we want to continue?" Samuel asked.

"Tutoring is a highly valued profession." Liza met his gaze easily. "I know there are a handful of students who look up to you both, and I did suggest that you held office hours for a while where they could come to you with any issues, but I was overruled."

"What if we do it informally?" Samuel pushed.

"What you do in your free time is up to you." Liza winked.

'*She's saying yes in the only way she can,*' Shari sent to him.

Samuel's frown morphed into an expression of understanding. "Ah. Of course."

"Thank you, for everything that you've taught the students," Liza said. "I know that they enjoyed your lessons."

Shari signed her name and passed the pen to Samuel. He did the same on his parchment. Together, they slid the paperwork back to Liza.

"Thank you for allowing us to teach," Shari said. "There's a few things I'd like to collect, if that's alright?"

"Of course," Liza said, and waved a hand to dismiss them.

Standing, Shari collected the two draci and led the way from the room, with Samuel, Shadow, and Wisp following close behind. Sneeze and Hail continued to chitter to each other like the rest of the Realm was an afterthought.

'*You've never left anything in the office,*' he sent.

Ignoring him, Shari walked straight past the door to their former office, heading for the tallest branches of the school.

There was, as always, no one there.

"What's this?"

"The place I'd come to be alone," Shari said. "I'm going to miss it."

Samuel leaned against the railing, looking out over the oval in the middle of the trees. "It's peaceful," he said softly.

Shari hummed in agreement. Although she'd been technically done with school for a while now, it felt odd that she wouldn't be coming back at all. After patting the trunk of the tree fondly, she slipped away, the others following in her wake.

At the entrance of the school, she stopped. Hail clambered back onto her shoulder, sending a mournful goodbye to Sneeze. Shadow licked Wisp's nose and padded to Samuel's side.

The school grounds held so many memories for her, both good and bad. And this would be the last time she left.

'*I wish you well,*' she sent to the trees.

A breeze ruffled through the leaves, and a sighing voice seemed to say, '*Farewell, Altoriae.*'

"So, what will you do with the rest of your day?" Samuel asked.

"Check on the fulni," Shari said.

"I could do that for you." He tried to play it casual, but from the eye roll he received, he'd failed.

"Check, not eat," Shari said, but there was no bite in her words.

"Are you aware how quickly they can breed?"

"I doubt they've added to the herd within a day," she said.

"No, but within a month, their numbers will have doubled," he said seriously. "I don't know how, but the population that returned were all adults."

Shari frowned. "Returned... Do you think this has something to do with Anriluka?"

Samuel shook his head. "She's gone, banished even from the Spirit Realm. Whatever is going on, it's nothing to do with her."

They walked a few steps in silence, but Samuel could almost hear Shari thinking.

"The Weavers called on the resting souls of the Spirit Realm," she said slowly. "What if they don't want to go back?"

"Do you think they have the power to summon others?" he asked.

Stopping in her tracks, Shari's gaze fixed onto twin cyclops heading straight for them. Wisp was rumbling a warning at her side. "Yes, I think they do."

"Well met," one said.

"Altoriae," the other finished.

"Wondered if you could—"

"Tell us where the others—"

"Are?" they finished together.

"You're meant to be dead," Shari said bluntly.

"Takes more than a fight—" Drah said.

"To keep us down," Kerk finished.

'*I might not be allowed to eat the fulni, but can I eat them?*' Samuel growled, sick of the twin speak already. Drah and Kerk always had annoyed him.

'No!' Shari sent. "I can move you there, if you like?" she said faintly.

"Thanks, very—"

"Appreciated."

'*Yessna, incoming. See if they're as real as they look, will you?*' Shari sent, and shifted the twin menaces away. "Well, that's not what I was expecting to do today," she said, staring at the spot where the twins had stood.

"Honestly, eating them would be no trouble at all," Samuel said. He could feel Sneeze nodding his head against his jaw.

Shari smacked him. "Go check on the fulni," she grumbled. "I'll talk to Jonathan."

Samuel gave her a mocking bow. "As you will it."

"Don't start," she warned, scowling.

He laughed as she shifted away. The moment she was gone, the smile fell from his face. How had the twins returned after they'd both fallen in battle? Sneeze rumbled, as if he was worried too.

The fulni would have to wait. He had research to do.

Yessna was in the middle of helping a group of mainlanders control their newly discovered Air Innarn, when her fur stood on end.

Looking around for the disturbance, she jolted as Drah and Kerk appeared on the other side of the clearing.

The Ferah froze, sending rapidly to the rest of the U'sala.

"Who are you?" Yessna asked loudly, trying to get the twins to focus on her as the others appeared silently in the trees surrounding the glade.

"Kerk and Drah," the twins said together.

"You're dead," Yessna said. "I saw you both fall."

The mainlanders standing between Yessna and the twins started skittering backwards, away from the confrontation they could no doubt sense brewing.

"Looks like–" Drah said.

"It didn't stick," Kerk finished.

Henot was creeping up behind them, using the long grass to his advantage. He appeared and prodded Drah's arm with his dagger.

The twin cursed and looked around, but Kibon had already shifted Henot away.

Blood dripped from the wound.

"Surely there are—" Drah said, scowling.

"Better ways to test us?" Kerk finished, ripping part of the bottom of his tunic off and using it to bind his brother's wound.

It was such a Kerk thing to do. Don't summon cloth, don't ask someone else, just use what you already have.

"It's really you," Yessna said.

Slowly, the other U'sala approached, and hugs and backslaps were given to each twin.

"If you're here, then who else is?" Wubi blurted.

Drah and Kerk shared a look.

"Well, there were some beings—" Kerk started.

"Who we might want to look out for." Drah finished.

"Training's cancelled," Yessna snapped at the mainlanders. "We need to come up with a plan."

"I came across a dead being. Two of them, actually," Shari said.

Jonathan choked on a mouthful of azehal. After he stopped coughing, he ignored Shari's smirk and said, "That's new, but not unexpected. Were they friendly?"

Shari nodded, stroking Hail's back as he curled into a ball in the palm of one hand. "The twins from the U'sala. They seemed the same as they were before, although Drah had regained his foot." Wisp leaned heavily against her, and Shari dropped her hand to give him a pat as well.

Sitting back in his seat, Jonathan hummed. "I wonder how that happened?"

"Honestly, I just shifted them straight to the U'sala. I figured they would be able to tell me if it was actually the twins or not," Shari said.

"And the verdict?"

"It's them. Drah isn't sure how his foot is still attached to his leg. Said that was how he pictured himself, and that's what the spirit pulled on when he returned." Shari stared blankly at the bookcases lining the walls. "I don't know if this is a good thing or not. What if someone like Milo, or Kodan, or the Crystal Intelligence comes back?"

As much as he didn't want to say it, Jonathan couldn't help the next words that fell out of his mouth. "What if they all do?"

The fog lying low on Rakemyst parted as the being in the white robe moved slowly through the maze of plaques, looking for a particular one.

For a moment, he stood beside one which read *SilverCloud Dawn*, but moved on. Eventually, he stopped by one reading *Meyron*.

A hand hovered over the plaque, Plasma dancing across his fingertips. Satisfaction seeped from the white-robed being.

Meyron would be the perfect soul to bring back.

CHAPTER TWENTY

Inthday

Second day of the fourth week of Waeghost

Block, duck, twist, strike. Shari moved through the training patterns with Jonathan by memory alone, letting her mind wander.

Shari hadn't realised how much she'd wanted to stop fighting until picking up her sword again. Now, she wanted nothing more than to put it down and walk away. Maybe get lost in some of Ronah's new forests. Or maybe she'd explore the other islands for a while, discover their secrets and write a book about it.

Twist, strike, stab, block, duck, twist, strike.

Nothing was there.

The flat side of a sword pressed against her throat. "Distracted?" Jonathan asked. He shielded against the icy blast Hail aimed at his head. The draci refused to stay away from Shari during training, no matter how much she'd tried to bribe him.

Wisp barked a warning at the draci, startling Jonathan. Shari used the distraction to shift before the blade could turn and pressed the knuckles of her glove against his kidneys. "Only as much as you are."

"Very glad you've sheathed your blades for the moment," Jonathan said, throwing his sword to the side.

Stepping back, Shari dropped her hands. With the Innarn flowing through the Realm at the moment, there was no way Jonathan could create anything that she wouldn't be able to counter. "I kind of thought I'd be done. Be able to walk away."

Jonathan took his time picking his sword up and sheathing it. "You still can. I'm sure we'll be able to handle it. You deserve a break, Shari."

Hail landed on her shoulder as she looked away from him, taking in the empty stands of the training ground where beings so recently watched the candidates try to outsmart each other for a chance to work alongside Jonathan, learning how to protect her. Wisp padded over to her side.

"I don't feel as if I can," she said. "These spirits—from what Yessna sent, Drah and Kerk weren't the only ones who returned. And just because we haven't seen them yet doesn't mean they aren't wandering amongst us. Who's to say Terrance or Therdon aren't waiting to strike?"

"Why don't you do a scan for them?" Jonathan asked.

Shari blinked twice. "Because that would be the smart thing to do," she said, sinking to sit on the ground. Trusting Jonathan would watch over her, she sent out her Innarn, cataloguing all the beings and creatures she came in contact with.

The expected ones were all there, along with creatures she'd only ever seen images of, and more beings who were grateful to be back. Most had unfinished business or wanted a second chance, but there were a few, like the one sneaking up behind Jonathan at the moment, who had decided murder and mayhem were the way to go.

Opening her eyes, Shari shifted silently, appearing directly behind Milo. Last time the odious Daen had died, it had been via volcano. This time,

Shari went for the quicker route and shifted his still-beating heart directly out of his body.

He stood, still suspended. As Jonathan turned in search of where she'd gone, Milo collapsed.

Jonathan looked at her as she stared down at the organ in her hands. Horrified, she dropped it, backing away from the corpse and scrubbing her hands on the rear of her pants. Hail chittered in concern in her ear. Wisp nudged the heart with his nose and stepped away, snout wrinkled.

"That's why I want to stop," she said. "Because what will I do if I don't?"

Shifting the body away, Jonathan took her in his arms and held Shari while she wept.

Wrapped in shadows, Samuel inspected Shari and Jonathan's technique during training. He was glad he'd left Sneeze with the hatchlings when he watched as the most unstealthy being in the Realms attempted to sneak up on Jonathan—saw the Guardian roll his eyes and miss when Shari shifted behind the poor attempt of an assassin.

Saw the beating heart shift into Shari's hands.

Shuddering, Samuel ducked and slipped through the door to check on the fulni. The traitor's death was too close to something he had been forced to do. While Milo deserved his demise—both versions of it—Ruker and Gazn had not warranted theirs.

Perhaps a little fulni hunting in their honour was in order?

Samuel stalked clear of the doorway. Making sure it was closed, he nodded and transformed. Great, golden wings flared out, and he took to the sky, flying through the pocket-Realm and keeping an eye out for the fulni. The herd were doing surprisingly well but had yet to multiply. There were a few females with distended bellies, which meant it was only a matter of time.

There would be no hunting today. The memory of Ruker and Gazn would just have to wait.

Something tickled in the back of his mind. If the fulni had been relegated to memory, how was the herd back here? Samuel could remember every beast he'd ever hunted, and there were a few with unique enough markings that he knew they had not died on Ronah. Or anywhere on Lissae at all.

So how were they back?

Maybe it was time for him to read that diary Asterion had found himself.

Cyrus stepped off the walkway and froze. Xani was standing outside the Techno Centre.

But it couldn't be.

Xani had never left her chair and couldn't move her legs, as far as he knew. There was also the small matter of her death to contend with.

How could she possibly be here?

Poking at a device on his arm, Talhan's Linked hissed as it took a small sample of blood.

"All clear," his B.I.R.D.s mechanical voice said.

In slow motion, the not-Xani started to turn towards him.

Panicked, Cyrus slapped a hand on his B.I.R.D.s outer shell and used Talhan's crystal to pull them both into his lab in the depths of the Techno Centre, leaving Xani on the surface outside. "Lock it down," he told the B.I.R.D.

The device hovered over to a button on the wall and *booped* into it. A klaxon sounded immediately.

With an impatient huff, Cyrus silenced the noise in his lab. Upstairs, shutters would be falling—the building going into lockdown. Scans would run over every inch of the inside, and any unauthorised beings would be instantly shifted to a holding facility upon detection.

He'd made sure that Xani was not on the list of authorised beings well before they'd left Lissae. As much as it had hurt at the time, Cyrus was glad he'd done it now.

After pulling the sample out, Cyrus ran it through the machine, tapping his arm with a finger as it whirled and hummed. A gentle chime sounded when it was done. Looking at the display on the screen, Cyrus cursed.

There were still femto crystals in his system.

After the Crystal Intelligence, he'd been tracking how long they would last in his bloodstream and he had yet to see a decrease in the numbers.

He looked at the pulsing box of crystal sitting on his workbench.

There was only one thing for it.

Using Innarn to lift the box, he compressed it as much as possible, forcing the femto crystals back into one solid mass instead of millions of tiny particles. Hesitantly, Cyrus crossed the room to the wall which held a variety of small vault doors.

"What are you doing?" a voice said.

Cyrus jumped and looked over his shoulder. Zac stood in the doorway, frowning at him.

"The building is in lockdown. I came to check you were safe," Zac said.

"Zac, I think I'm hallucinating," Cyrus said, spinning a wheel on one of the doors. "I saw Xani outside." Grunting as he pulled the door open, his Innarn guided the box of former femto crystals into the tiny space.

"The dead are coming back to life," Zac said.

"Do you remember what happened last time?" Cyrus asked. "Xani is quite possibly one of my favourite beings in all the Realms, but we can't risk the Crystal Intelligence getting her. Or me." He slammed the door shut and spun the wheel the opposite way. There was a horrid screeching, grinding noise from inside the vault, which stopped when he stepped away.

"What did you do?" Zac asked.

"Removed temptation," Cyrus said. "Without the femto crystals, the Intelligence has less of a chance of taking over. I ran the numbers, and the bigger the piece, the harder it would be to create sentience inside it."

"What about those of us who already have femto crystals in our blood?" Zac asked slowly.

Sometimes Cyrus forgot that Zac actually knew his way around the lab. "We'll just have to be extra vigilant," Cyrus said grimly.

"And what about Xani?"

Cyrus swallowed, hard. "I guess it's time to go and say hello." He crossed the room to the button which would reverse the lockdown. "I don't suppose the Altoriae could be on standby?" he asked.

Zac quirked his brows. "Already sent the message."

Nodding, Cyrus slapped the button, and the faint wail of the klaxon stopped. "To the surface?" he asked. As soon as Zac nodded, he brushed his Innarn against the crystal and pulled, setting them down on the sidewalk a safe distance away from the last spot he'd seen Xani.

She was gone.

Muran carefully walked around the oldest of the grave markers, heading towards the newest ones.

This place reminded him so keenly of Ronah's cemetery, yet it seemed a parallel place, with markers more than his years. Some were so weathered the inscribed words were lost to time. Others were of bright, shining stone, the dirt before them freshly dug. There were quite a few others, although grass seemed to be growing over the mounds at the start of the long row.

"A hundred odd dead in the last year," Muran said, voice rusty from disuse. "And how many of your souls reside in the Spirit Realm?"

He reached out a hand and brushed against a marker reading *Andrew Shansky*. "Hmm, still there then? Why don't you come back and say hello?"

The air above Andrew's marker shimmered, and slowly, the shape of a man took form. He looked around with wide eyes until his gaze fell on Muran.

"Where are we?" Andrew asked.

"Not on Lissae, yet still on Ronah," Muran said.

"How?"

"I'm not sure. I've found an empty village just inside the trees." He nodded to the tree line behind him. "You're welcome to get your bearings there."

"But–" Andrew cut himself off, looking longingly at the bridge which led to the town. "Yeah. Right. Should probably get cleaned up, at least." He raised his arm and wrinkled his nose at the torn and dirty sleeve.

"Go on then," Muran said. "There are a few others waiting."

"Others?" Andrew took one more look at the bridge before heading for the village. "Thanks," he threw over his shoulder.

Muran grinned. "Now, let's see who else is waiting."

Jonathan was walking home when someone dropped out of a tree above his head and wrapped firm thighs around his neck.

He did the only sensible thing and slammed a dagger into each of his attacker's legs. Cursing, they tightened their grip.

'Mind if I borrow a knife?' Jonathan asked Samuel, who was waiting at his door, only a few houses down. Even with his tunnelling vision, he saw Samuel's head snap up, and his apprentice was at his side in an instant, ripping the assassin away from him.

"You!" Samuel snarled.

Turning, Jonathan grabbed Samuel's hand before he could deliver the killing blow. Sneeze blew sparks on him, clearly disappointed his human had been stopped.

"Briar?" he asked.

She spat on him.

Samuel growled at her, yanking her hands more firmly behind her back. "The failed mainland assassin." Samuel's grin had a nasty edge to it. She kicked and screeched, but he didn't let go.

Waiting until she slumped in Samuel's grip, Jonathan moved cautiously closer. "We aren't on Lissae anymore," he said.

"Liar," she snarled. "We're still on Ronah."

"Yes, but after your last attempt, something happened and the islands moved away from Lissae."

Briar frantically scanned his face, then collapsed for a moment. Arching her neck, she said, "You may as well kill me then, because my whole life is on Lissae."

Claw at the ready, Samuel glanced at Jonathan for permission.

"No poison capsule this time?"

From Samuel's look of awe, Jonathan's expression was far from friendly.

"Well, guess what? I get to decide your fate. And I choose that you *live*." Abruptly, he shifted her away, into the middle of Talhan, where she stood the best chance of assimilating with the living.

"Why would you do that?" Samuel asked.

"How is death punishment when they chose it?" Jonathan said. "Besides, not everyone has to die."

He just hoped he wouldn't regret it.

CHAPTER TWENTY-ONE

Kerday

Third day of the fourth week of Waeghost

hari gratefully accepted the cup from Fenix. She took a sip and tried to ignore the way it set her throat on fire. Hail wrapped his tail around her neck, and the cold soothed her instantly. She lowered her hand to her side, and the rest of the drink disappeared down Wisp's gullet.

"You said you had news," Fenix said, taking their seat.

The box containing Milo's heart was burning a metaphorical hole in her pocket. "I... uh... Have you noticed anything... odd, since we left Lissae?" Shari asked. Why Jonathan thought she was the right person to tell Fenix what had happened, she didn't know.

"Cantash is silent, like the other islands. Many of the Daens have reported significant boosts in their Innarn abilities, and there are a number of new plants we've never seen before growing in the western fields," Fenix listed off, but looked puzzled.

"Well, the thing is—" Shari took a deep breath. "You know how the Weavers called on the spirits to help with the mainlanders?"

Cantash's Linked nodded.

"Turns out they didn't quite have the ritual down pat. The spirits stayed. And they're waking more up, all across the islands," Shari blurted. Hail nudged her ear, sending a shock of cold through one side of her head.

Fenix frowned but sipped at their drink.

"Not all the spirits are friendly," Shari continued. "One tried to hurt Jonathan yesterday. Or maybe he was going for me, I'm not sure."

Frown deepening, Fenix traced the tip of a finger around the rim of their cup. "A spirit turned being?" they asked.

Shari nodded.

"And you're telling everyone?"

Wincing at the hopeful lilt in Fenix's voice, Shari shook her head.

"Which means it's someone I dearly wanted to see..." They paused, and Shari shook her head again. "Or someone better off dead. Where is he now?"

"Dead. Again," Shari said, taking the box out of the pocket in her bag. "His remains were burned a second time, but I saved this, just in case..." *Who in their right mind would want to hold on to the heart of their tormentor?* She paused.

Fenix held their hand out.

"I don't know if you want to open the box," Shari said, her voice small. She flinched at the look Cantash's Linked gave her and handed it over. Hail chittered sympathetically. Wisp leaned against her so hard, it felt like he was trying to meld his fur with her flesh.

Slowly, Fenix lifted the lid and nodded. "This is all that's left?" they asked.

Shari's head bobbed in confirmation.

A sudden blast of heat melted the box, leaving Fenix holding the stone-black heart of their former aide. "Rather suits him, doesn't it?" Weaving a box of Air Innarn, they suspended the heart in the middle and placed it on the mantel. "This time, I think I'll keep him where I can see him."

"That sounds like a smart idea," Shari said. She hadn't known what to expect from the mild-mannered Linked, but Fenix baking and mounting the heart had not even been on her list of potential outcomes.

Collis was on his way to Tania's house when a man walking across the street caught his attention.

He was moving like he had swords strapped to each hip—arms wide away from his sides, so he didn't bump into the hilts. Every time Muran had woken up after dying, he'd walked like that, like it took him a while to get used to his body again. Collis always suspected it had something to do with being the Altoriae, but even after three hundred odd years, he'd never worked up the courage to ask.

Now, seeing the stranger across the street with Muran's walk, Muran's hair, Muran's... face.

The man was facing Collis.

And he was no stranger.

"Well met, you," Tania said, her arms wrapping around his middle.

Collis mechanically returned the hug, eyes locked on Muran's duplicate, who gave him a crooked grin. A crowd crossed between them, and when they had dispersed, Muran was gone.

Tania leaned back from him. "You look like you've seen a ghost," she said.

"I think I might have."

Anika smoothed her fingers over her top, wishing she had even a touch of Innarn to remove the micro wrinkles that had formed.

Raven wouldn't care, she knew that. But still. He was coming to help her move the last of the memories from her parents' house, and no doubt she'd sport more wrinkles before they were done. That didn't mean she couldn't look nice when he arrived.

A knock boomed through the house, and Anika frowned. Quickly, she crossed to the door and flung it open. "Someone's eager," she said, and stopped.

Standing on the doorstep was not Raven, as she'd expected, but her father.

Her very dead father.

Shrieking, Anika slammed the door closed and leaned against it, twisting her wrist so the waiting blade fell neatly into her hand. Her heart was pounding so hard against her ribs, she mistook it for the banging on the door.

Gripping her crystal pendant in her free hand, Anika whispered, "Help. Please help," and hoped that Raven would get the message.

The air compressed in front of her, and Raven appeared, bow at the ready. "Who do I need to kill?" he asked.

"My father?" she said.

He lowered the bow. "Isn't he already residing with the spirits?"

The banging on the door started up again, shaking her body with the force of it. "Not anymore."

"Altoriae, we have a problem," Raven said aloud.

It took Anika a moment to realise he was sending but speaking for her benefit.

Shari appeared next to Raven, the rest of the guild popping into being around them.

"What's wrong?"

"Anika's dead father is knocking on the door." Raven gestured with his bow.

"Well, let him in then." Shari grinned.

"Are you mad?" Anika hissed. "He's meant to be dead!"

"There was a failsafe built in to help populate new Realms," Shari said. "It allows spirits to return, if they want."

Elani, somehow balancing on the railing, tilted her head. "All spirits?"

"Only those who want to come back, I think," Shari said.

"You aren't particularly convincing," Anika said.

"Move, and we'll ask. If he tries to attack, well—" Raven gestured to the army around him.

Thinning her lips, Anika nodded and stepped quickly out of the way.

The door burst open. "Anika!"

Anika found herself impressed. Rany Thorne had an arsenal of weapons pointed at him and barely flinched as he frantically searched the faces before him. His gaze caught hers and he rushed forwards, arms outstretched.

Only to stop when the tip of an arrow notched under his chin.

"What, exactly, are your plans with Anika?" Raven asked, muscles taut as he kept the arrow ready to fire. It might not do much damage at such close range, but it'd still hurt.

"I think I should be asking you that," Rany snapped. "Last time I saw my daughter, we were on a battlefield. I just want to make sure she's alright."

"The daughter you kicked out of your home?" Shari asked.

Anika shivered. The Altoriae should not be able to speak so quietly and exude so much menace at the same time. Maybe she'd been getting lessons from Samuel?

"My brother forced me to. Said it would be for the best. I've since set him straight about that."

Shari's glance flicked to Anika, before returning to Rany. "And will your brother be joining us?"

"Not a chance," Rany said. "The Thornes are strong. We made sure he wasn't welcome in the Spirit Realm, and he left before we were woken."

"Who woke you?" Shari asked.

"Muran Curtis."

Anika's jaw dropped at the same time Shari's weapon dipped. "The sixth Altoriae?" she asked.

"I was shocked too," Rany admitted.

Glancing over at Shari again, Anika shook her head. The Altoriae had already shifted away, no doubt going on the hunt for her predecessor.

"Welcome home," Anika said weakly as Rany finally crossed the room and wrapped her in a hug.

Shari shifted out before she could think. She'd never had a connection to Muran, and had thought, when she was younger, that it was her fault. After talking to a few of the Returned, and pouring over the *Handbook*, she'd figured it was because the souls of the others were in the Spirit Realm, ready to guide her, but Muran's had been trapped in the pocket-Realm with the Returned.

Shari paused. By that logic, it was possible that the souls of the other Altoriaes were now walking around on the island somewhere. Shari didn't get too much of a chance to think that through, as Brinley's send screamed through her shields.

'Help! Vannali is under attack!'

Shifting to the second cry for aide that night, Shari doubted there was ever a chance she'd get to give up fighting.

CHAPTER TWENTY-TWO

Narday

Fourth day of the fourth week of Waeghost

Sitting in the tavern, Shari swirled her drink around, looking into the depths of her glass as if it contained a mystical secret.

Vannali had not, in fact, been under attack last night. Brinley had been spooked by some menacing shadows on her walk home. Shari couldn't really blame Vannali's Linked. With all the dead beings popping up, things were a bit tense at the moment.

Tonight was meant to be the second meeting of The Lonely Orphan Society. But there were very few who had shown up. Anika had breezed in an hour ago, started the meeting, then told the others her parents had returned. She'd been teary-eyed but had said that it felt wrong to run a society when she didn't meet the requirements.

Shari had a strong feeling that she was going to be in a club for one again.

Wisp leaned against her side, looking at her like he was sick of her dramatics. Hail chittered at her, and she sighed. Raising a hand, she patted the draci as the door to the tavern hesitantly opened, and a mousy-haired man entered, looking around.

Joana, who'd been clearing a table, looked up to welcome the newcomer and promptly dropped all the dishes she was holding.

Flicking her Innarn out, Shari caught them before they could shatter and sent them back to the kitchen, cleaned and ready to use again.

"Toby?" Joana whispered.

"Mum," the man said, rushing to her.

Tania had told Shari what happened on the beach, how Chamele's experiments had killed Tobias.

It looked like Joana's son had returned for a second time.

Shari just hoped that everyone was as friendly as he was.

The sedolic pack lifted their noses as one, their pincers clacking with glee.

They were all aware of what a new Realm meant.

Fresh meat.

Shari caught sight of movement outside of the tavern. Peering through the window, she spotted a pack of green, scaly dog-like animals with two large pincers each on their chest. They were moving in a huge group through the main street.

Beings were starting to take notice, by the sound of the screams.

Groaning, she downed the rest of her drink and stood, placing Hail on the table. "Wait here," she said. The draci looked at her with big eyes. "I'll not see you die tonight," she said. Wisp put a gentle paw on Hail's tail when the draci tried to dart forward. "Watch him for me," she ordered Wisp. The Shadow Bringer nodded.

Walking into the street and leaning against the door as she warded it shut, she sent, '*Guild, to me. Weapons ready please. We have a sedolic infestation to deal with.*'

Jonathan appeared on her right. "I was wondering if they would reappear."

Innarn lashing out, Samuel snarled. "I loathe these creatures."

"Well, go for it then," Shari said.

Samuel looked over the top of Shari's head, searching for Jonathan's permission.

"The sooner I don't have to look at another sedolic, the better," Jonathan said.

That was all Samuel needed.

He handed Sneeze to Shari, and in three long steps he was clear enough of the awning to change form. When he roared, Shari covered her ears.

The sedolics had no such option and merely trembled in fright.

'*Might want to move the squishy ones you want to keep,*' Samuel suggested, as three more Q'Aralide, in varying sizes, appeared in the sky behind him.

Shari shifted everyone back into the tavern. Hail immediately flew to her shoulder and started scolding her until he spotted Sneeze.

"Looks like we get to watch instead of being on the menu tonight," Shari quipped, and wished she hadn't when Jetonyx grabbed a sedolic by the middle with a claw and ripped the pincers straight off the screaming creature.

"Yay us," Elani said, deadpan.

Looking at Jonathan, Shari threw up a shield to prevent the noises of the dying animals reaching their ears. She'd had enough of that sound for several lifetimes.

Joana and Toby were moving amongst the crowd, sharing jokes and cheering with the other Returned every time one of the creatures met their grizzly end. Remmy, cheering with the others, caught Shari's gaze.

Slowly, he made his way to her. "We're so used to being their snack. It's good to see them feeding someone else for a change," Remmy said, nudging Shari when she winced as the hatchlings used one as a tug toy.

Shari took a moment to think about what it must have been like. Waking up to be chewed on by these basalt lovers, only to have to do it all over again the next time they died. "I imagine it'd be quite vindicating, in a way."

Remmy, looking out the window, hissed suddenly. "Daivi."

"Where?" Shari asked.

He pointed, and Shari shifted the dead Returned woman into their midst.

"Daivi?" Remmy asked. His question quieted the guild, who turned to look at the newcomer.

A guy with swirls of ink decorating the side of his face pushed his way to the front of the crowd.

"Kieran," Daivi said, tears in her eyes.

"Daivi," Kieran said, and wrapped his arms around her like he'd never let go.

Shari blamed the tears in her eyes on Tormorylth getting a scratch from a swiftly decimated sedolic, rather than the Returned gathering around their fallen member for a reunion none of them expected would happen.

Luttrell stepped through the split in the Realms and stretched, his bone armour clanking with the movement. He looked over at a few of his top troops who had elected to take the journey with him.

The massive Chirea glanced around the gloom, unable to make much out, but he could smell Innarn in the air and someone was roasting meat nearby.

"It's good to be back," he said, the skull over his head shadowing his grin. He turned to his warriors. "Shall we go introduce ourselves?"

Yessna was tending the fire when a sound she hoped to never hear again reached her ears.

The clanking of bone.

Growling low in her throat, the Ferah sent a swift message to the others, raising the wards to keep the mainlanders safe.

She had some vermin to deal with.

The others shifted in, one by one, using the shadows to their advantage.

'*What do we have?*' Kibon asked.

'*Chirea,*' Yessna sent back.

Wubi swore. He must have been hanging around the mainlanders, as he had a few new words in his arsenal.

'*The Chirea killed Varox,*' Nerina sent. '*Time to make them regret that decision all over again.*'

How had she forgotten Varox's death at the hands of these insect feeders?

Nerina swung her sword menacingly. Yessna felt like groaning. Nothing good ever came of allowing their healer to go into battle, but with the killers of her mate in clear sight, there was little chance in stopping her.

The twins grinned at each other grimly. '*Into the fray,*' they sent and stepped backwards, blending into the shadows.

The clanking of bone armour stopped, and the biggest Chirea looked around at their little group. He easily outnumbered them, three to one.

"Looks like we'll be eating well tonight," he boomed.

And copped a fireball to the chest.

Yessna whirled around, ready to face the threat at their backs, only to see Therion, trembling hand still glowing.

The mainlander was scowling at Luttrell. "You'll have to go through us to get to them."

Luttrell twisted his broadsword to point the tip forward. "Oh, we can do that, snack," he snarled.

Henot's frantic send of '*Since when do the Chirea eat their victims?!*' was almost lost amidst the pounding feet and clanking bone.

'*It doesn't matter. Not like they're going to get the chance,*' Kibon sent, even as he skewered one of the stampeding bone warriors right through the eye.

'*Clear!*' Felton warned, and a red line fell across Yessna's vision, sending her and Wubi scrambling backwards. The Chirea, thinking they were retreating, came closer. Felton, grinning like a loon, set off a series of Innarn bombs, blowing bits of bone and guts all over the field.

Wubi picked a chunk out of his beard. '*Every time,*' he grumbled, lip curling with disgust. Raising his arm, he swung his spiked chain, and let it loose. It tangled through the legs of three Chirea and bringing back far more shin bones than he was ready for.

'*Not fresh,*' Yessna noted. '*I don't think they've killed since they've come back.*'

'*Good,*' Nerina. '*They'll go back to the grave hungry.*'

'*They don't actually eat the flesh of their victims,*' Felton sent.

'*Except they did under Luttrell's rule,*' Kibon countered.

In all the time they'd been fighting together, Yessna didn't think she'd ever seen so much hatred from Nerina. The healer screamed, slicing her way towards the one who towered over the others.

It was happening in slow motion.

Nerina's expression was contorted into one of loathing, her focus on the big tu'zar in front of her, totally oblivious to the Chirea coming at her from the side.

Therion wasn't though. A fireball smashed into the smaller Chirea, sending the excess skull on his head flying just as he swung his sword.

Ducking his blow, Nerina jammed her sword straight up, giving Luttrell's bowels a new exit point.

The other Chirea let loose the most soul-breaking sound Yessna had ever heard as their leader dropped like the sack of dung he was. As one, they raised their weapons, skulls tipped back to look at the night sky.

Nerina sliced clean through the spine of the Chirea who had attempted to sneak up on her, separating neck from spine with surgical precision.

As the head bounced to the ground inside the helmet, the fight began in earnest once more.

Chapter Twenty-Three

Rasshday

Fifth day of the fourth week of Waeghost

Samuel peered at the hatchlings and frowned. "Behave," he warned.

'*You can trust us.*' Jetonyx looked at him solemnly.

Scowling, Samuel closed the door behind him and set off, Sneeze on his shoulder and Shadow by his side. He didn't have a particular path in mind, but Cylanthar was nudging at the inside of his skull. Who was he to ignore a deity?

Letting his mind wander, Samuel strode through the streets of Ronah, wondering how in all the Realms he'd been lucky enough to end up exactly where Oalark wanted him, but without having to worry about her suffocating presence wrecking everything he'd worked for.

He jerked to a stop, Cylanthar's bells chiming lightly in his head. Samuel looked around and found himself utterly unsurprised to be standing outside Lizbeth's house.

His first friend. The one who had seen him for who he was and knew he could be better.

The front door opened, and Lizbeth stepped out. "Samuel! Perfect timing. I just pulled a batch of cookies out of the oven."

Shadow trotted towards Lizbeth and leaned his head against her legs, looking at her with big eyes until she bent to pat his head.

"You don't have to feed me, you know," he said gruffly. "I enjoy your company without food."

Colour dusted her cheeks red. "I enjoy your company too, but the need to bake is ingrained in me, I'm afraid. You'll just have to put up with the cookies as well."

Samuel laughed. "Just so long as you know our friendship isn't conditional on baked goods."

Sneeze blew sparks in solidarity.

Lizbeth gave him the smile that made his heart melt. "I never thought it was."

Bruised and bleeding, the U'sala slumped to the ground.

'*Reckon we're going soft,*' Kerk sent.

'*Have to be,*' Drah added.

Yessna tried to muster up the energy to growl, and merely waved a dismissive paw in their direction.

"Did we win?" Therion asked, his speech slightly slurred.

'*What happened to him?*' Yessna sent.

'*Took a blow to the head not long after Luttrell dropped. Concussion, bruising, and a few stitches. Head wounds bleed like a—*' Nerina broke off, and looked up, raising a sword in one hand as mainlanders started pouring into their clearing.

"Why are there misshapen skeletons on the ground?" Ishta asked, standing at the head of the pack, a sword held in one hand.

'*Chirea...*' Yessna started to send and sighed. "The Chirea," she rasped. "Nasty tu'zars who eat your flesh and wear your bones as armour.

Sometimes before you're even properly dead." As soon as the words left her mouth, she winced and avoided looking at Nerina. While they were pretty sure that hadn't happened to Varox, it must still play in the healer's nightmares on occasion.

"Why weren't we informed? We're soldiers—we could have helped." Ishta looked furious.

Therion staggered to his feet, his skin taking on a concerning green tinge. "Ishta, you didn't want to help against these. There's no—" He burped wetly. "No training coulda prepared us for that." He waved a hand to encompass the massacre of bodies and turned to throw up in the bushes.

Wrinkling her nose, Yessna pulled her tail out of the way and cast a discreet bubble of air around her head so she wouldn't have to smell the sick, lest she join him too.

Tania smiled at Oakley, who was ever so carefully gathering moss.

"Well met, fellow Linked," she said brightly.

Oakley looked up and sighed. "Well met," he said.

"What's wrong?" she asked.

Ginorti's Linked sighed again. "It felt like I just got him back, and now he's gone again."

It took Tania a moment to figure out what Oakley meant. "Ginorti?"

Nodding, Oakley placed his gathered moss on a nearby log. It was covered in precisely positioned items. A blue mushroom cap, the emerald moss, spiral-shaped leaves, tiny iridescent yellow cones, and more items Tania couldn't identify.

"And you are...?"

"Trying to do anything I can to wake him up," Oakley said. "Maybe if I find the right thing, he'll be alright."

Tania dropped to her knees beside him and laid her hand on his arm. "They're tired. All the islands. And I know it's weird not having them natter at us all the time, but I can still feel Ronah. I have to trust that she'll wake up when she's ready. I'm sure Ginorti will too."

Oakley nodded slowly. "I hope so," he said.

"You're still going to go and find more things, aren't you?" she asked.

"Yeah," Oakley admitted.

"Well, let me help you carry them then."

Ginorti's Linked attempted a smile. "Thanks," he said, getting to his feet.

Tania smiled brightly until he turned away.

Wringing her hands, she could only hope that she was right.

Cyrus swore.

Xani was outside the Techno Centre again, and this time he couldn't avoid her.

"Well met," he said, mustering up a smile.

'Well met, Cyrus. Have you seen Temira?'

He flinched. It had been bad enough when Xani died the first time. Cyrus didn't know if he had it in him to help the second technomancer through the death of the first. 'She... she didn't make it to the new Realm.'

Xani's eyes went cold. 'Tell me what happened.'

'Temira struggled after... Her healing degenerated. I must have seen her dead dozens of times.' Cyrus paused. There was nothing quite like watching your mentor testing a prototype, being thrown across the room and waking to stuff her intestines back inside her skin. 'She was lost without you,' he admitted. 'I think she gave up.'

'I returned,' Xani sent. 'She could too.'

'Possibly. I haven't seen her yet,' Cyrus said.

Tilting her head, Xani looked right through him.

Cyrus had forgotten the feeling of Xani peering through his soul.

'You don't think she will.'

'No,' he said, blinking against the gathering tears. 'I *don't*.'

Xani sighed. '*I wanted to be able to finally beat her in a foot race,*' she sent.

Laughing, Cyrus shook his head. '*Maybe in the next life?*'

All traces of humour left Xani's face. '*The Crystal Intelligence?*'

'*Dead. You took it out.*'

Xani smiled. '*That is something that can stay deceased.*' She looked over Cyrus's shoulder. '*Looks like not everything got that message.*'

Oily black uniformed soldiers were marching towards them.

'*Uh, Shari...*'

Shari shifted with Jonathan to the square in front of the Techno Centre and groaned.

The square was full of soldiers.

"What if we just try to be nice?" Shari muttered out the side of her mouth.

She was glad Hail and Wisp had been sleeping when she'd left. The last thing she wanted was for her creatures to get hurt.

Samuel, wearing his Q'Aralide form, dropped heavily into the square behind them, batting away projectiles like they were gnats. The three hatchlings were circling above them, their shadows causing the soldiers to shiver in fear.

"Or we could do it the hard way," she said.

Captain Rappen stepped forward, his uniform looking worse for wear. "Give up, aberrations," he snarled. The leaves in his hair and mud on his clothes made it look like he'd traversed the length and breadth of the islands, just to try and intimidate them.

Kemanyr dropped from the sky and ripped his head from his shoulders, her wings straining to get her airborne again.

Shari's mouth fell open. She snapped it closed straight away as the youngest hatchling spat the head out, muttering about the vile taste. It bounced a few times, until the captain's sightless eyes looked up at her as his body collapsed across the square.

'*Kemanyr, that's nasty. You don't know where that's been,*' Sanithane sent.

If it were up to Shari, she'd probably say a few extra things, but she didn't.

Soldiers were screaming or retching at the sight.

Sanithane roared, and the square fell silent.

'*Fight, and die again,*' Kemanyr broadcasted, her youthful voice making the soldiers look around. '*I've seen your end. It's worse this time.*'

The mainlanders were muttering amongst themselves.

'*Are you fighting because you believe that those different from you do not deserve to live? Or because some fool in a red jacket told you to?*'

All three hatchlings were circling lower now, their shadows causing more than one person to grip their weapon tighter.

'*Live and be free in a Realm where peace will find you. Or fight and die today. The choice is yours.*'

'*I didn't know Kemanyr was so eloquent,*' Shari sent on a tight band to Sanithane.

'*Neither did I.*'

'*Don't be rude,*' the hatchling sent. '*Shift those out who lower their weapons please. Then cover your eyes.*'

Shari glanced at Jonathan but did as Kemanyr asked. In the end, there were only a handful of soldiers who remained, gripping their weapons like they were a lifeline.

'*Eyes,*' Kemanyr sent.

Obediently, Shari closed her eyes. A wave of Innarn like nothing she'd felt before swept over her.

'*Safe now,*' Kemanyr sent.

When Shari looked, the little hatchling was sitting next to a puddle of blood where the captain's body had fallen, calmly cleaning her claws.

Deciding discretion was the better part of valour, she didn't ask what had happened to the remaining soldiers, or the captain's body.

Instead, she was just grateful that it was one less fight she had to have.

CHAPTER TWENTY-FOUR

Shari should have kept her thoughts to herself.

Whatever it was that had sparked the new mainlanders to attack Talhan had spread across the islands.

'*Shari!*' Tania was sending frantically.

'*Altoriae!*' Oakley sent, followed quickly by Zana, Fenix, Domic, and Brinley.

'*Shift them all to Ronah now,*' Shari ordered, picturing the swathe of empty land between the main street and the castle.

"I hope you're ready for this," she muttered to Jonathan and sent to Sanithane at the same time.

They arrived in chaos: screaming, flashes of Innarn, and more tentacles than Shari ever wanted to see again.

"I forgot about the U'tan," she said. '*Any chance they can be reasoned with?*' she sent to Samuel.

Bitter laughter filled her head. '*Snack time!*' he sent to the hatchlings, the thought echoing back to Shari.

"Well, that's one way to kill them in an enclosed space," she muttered, watching as Tormorylth slurped one up by a waving tentacle.

She looked around the battlefield roiling with bodies. It wasn't just beings she had fought, but ones that were older than her time as well. The clothing some of the Lissaens were wearing was reminiscent of things you'd see in the history books.

"Once more into the fray," Shari said, wading in, sword flashing as she attempted to protect herself rather than aiming to kill.

One particularly insistent being, a dark-haired male, gave her a cocky grin and plastered his back against hers.

He felt so familiar, and Shari was sure she'd seen him before, on another battlefield... "Muran," she whispered.

Sanithane remained above them, sending plumes of Innarn into the masses, which were more designed to detain than to kill.

Shari had never been prouder of him.

More and more fighters Shari had never met—but felt like she'd known her whole life—crowded around, until there were twelve of them in a circle.

The bodies before her parted as if they didn't have a choice, and a woman with pointed ears strode directly towards Shari, the tip of her weapon aimed for Shari's heart.

Raising her sword, Shari stood her ground. The woman was taller than Shari had expected, and she had to tilt her sword higher to rest in the hollow of the spirit's throat.

The ground rumbled in warning underneath their feet.

They both froze.

Off to the side, barely more than an arm's length away, a low wooden wall appeared, rising as the stunned fighters watched.

Around them, a house was growing.

"You want them to live here, amongst us?" Shari said, incredulous.

There was a pleased purr from underneath her feet.

"Is that why the islands are so much bigger now?" she asked.

"I think so," Muran rasped from beside her. "Not all of us came back, you know? We were given the choice."

"Then why are you fighting us?" she asked.

"We were not the ones to throw the first blow. One of yours did," the woman in front of her said. She moved in a blur of speed too fast for Shari to follow, and between one heartbeat and the next, the tip of a blade was at her throat.

'Who are you?' Shari asked, but she felt like she already knew the answer. The blade pressed closer in clear warning as Shari raised her glove. She slowly lowered her hand again and waited, barely daring to breathe, for the answer to her question.

Abruptly, the blade disappeared, but the danger the woman emanated didn't lessen in the slightest. "Kay'imi."

From Shari's other side, a woman said, "Petuar." *The second Altoriae.*

"Askanar."

"Feyka."

"Lerah."

"Tanika."

"Shael."

"Crista."

"Jali."

"Abby."

"Fiona."

Shari turned, showing her back to the most dangerous being on the Realms, and looked at the other Altoriaes who had fought with her one by one.

"Why are you here?" she asked, her voice thick through the lump in her throat.

"To help make this new Realm safe for all," Kay'imi said, stepping up behind her.

The fine hairs on her neck rose, and Shari could feel the heat of the first Altoriae against her shoulders. "You all chose this?"

Tanika laughed. "Just like you, we spent most of our lives fighting. It'd be nice to figure out what others do."

Stepping outside the growing dwelling, Shari decided to take a leaf from Grace's book and used the air currents to rise above the battlefield. *'Stop!'*

Her broadcast was loud enough that more than one being smacked themselves with the hilt of a weapon as they tried to cover their ears.

Lissaens lowered their weapons immediately. The spirits refused, until Kay'imi appeared by her side, scowling at them. They scowled back but put their weapons down.

Is she where Grace gets the bad temper from? Shari thought wildly.

Expectant faces were peering up at them, and it took her a moment to remember what she was trying to say. *'There appears to have been a miscommunication somewhere,'* Shari sent. *'Our new Realm wishes for peace. For the fighting to stop.'* Something warm rubbed against her arm, and Shari knew her mother was near, agreeing with her words. *'In honour of my parents' sacrifice, I ask you to lay down your weapons and greet your new neighbours.'*

The beings on the battlefield looked doubtful, but Shari still had more Innarn than she knew what to do with. She gathered the weapons and shifted them into her pocket-Realm and out of reach.

Collis looked at who he had been battling a moment before and did a double take.

"Indijo?" Collis asked.

"Collis?"

The two were laughing and clapping each other on the back, rapidly sending stories of their time apart.

Slowly, others were extending hands and greetings. A few beings tried to go for stealthy attacks but were swiftly stopped, usually by someone on their side.

Kay'imi lowered herself to the ground, and Shari followed suit.

'I hope this was what you meant,' she sent to her parents. There was a pleased rumble underneath her, and Shari sighed.

She'd settle for a rumble if she couldn't get a hug.

Looking around the past Altoriaes, Shari forced a grin. "Welcome to our new Realm."

All across the former battlefield, Jonathan watched in awe as connections were being made.

An Ilutri took to the sky, winging towards Rakemyst, but he froze when a female cried out, "Meyron?"

Landing again, he rushed into the arms of the woman who must have been his mate, holding her close.

Elani and Amara, returned from the dead, were wrapped tightly around each other, heads bent close together as the pair reconnected. Eva, her blue hair a beacon, hastened to join the pair.

The Linked were holding court, ushering beings to different areas and allowing the newly growing houses to continue unimpeded.

A white-robed figure from across the field caught Jonathan's gaze, and he shifted next to them.

"Was this all you?" Jonathan asked.

A hand appeared and pushed the hood back, revealing long silver hair and pointed ears.

"Kodan?" Jonathan gasped. Of all the beings he expected to have stepped through the veil, the former U'sala who'd caused them so much grief was not one of them.

"All I ever wanted was a place for beings to belong," Kodan said. The light plasma Innarnian had smoke rolling gently from his exposed skin. "I've done that now." He looked around and smiled. "I did aspire to be your apprentice, you know," he said to Jonathan. "Being able to help just one Realm? Sounded ideal." Blisters appeared on his face—the Realm was clearly too dark for him to survive. "Looks like I've done that now," he said.

Before Jonathan could stop him, Kodan threw off his robe and burst into flames.

Zac stared at the pile of ash next to Jonathan. "That was dramatic."

Jonathan didn't know what to say. Of all the beings in the Realms, he would not have suspected Kodan of being able to organise a mass uprising turned migration.

The clean-up took less time than Jonathan had thought it would. At the end of the day, dozens of new houses had appeared, in different styles than he was used to, although the new residents appeared to be happy.

The Risen were finally dispersing to places across the islands to stay, although many were promising to keep in touch with others, despite the language barriers and different time periods they appeared to be from.

Just as Jonathan was thinking about heading home to write everything down in the book, a hoard of Altoriaes descended upon him.

Shari gave him a grin that spoke volumes about how tired she was.

"Guardian Buan, meet the former Altoriaes," Shari said, waving over the dozen beings before him.

He bowed at the waist. "Well met, Altoriaes." Mentally, he was doing calculations on how to split his time between them all, who would want to fight, how they would train, the best way to—

The one who could only be Kay'imi stepped forward, glaring at Shari. "That is the last time we are to be addressed as such. We are simply part of the Risen. None of us wish to continue the fight that cost us our lives."

"Speak for yourself," Tanika said. "I died of natural causes, thank you very much."

Shael snorted. "Natural, maybe, but not old age."

"Least I didn't trip over my laces and stab myself with my own–" Tanika retorted, breaking off at Kay'imi's glare to clear her throat.

'*This is what it's like in my head*,' Shari sent, raising a single brow for the first time.

It was Jonathan's turn to clear his throat, lest he laugh.

"If you would prefer not to hold your old titles, then so be it," Jonathan said, and caught Shari's gaze. "You've all done so much for Lissae. If any here deserve a fresh start, it's you."

Tears welled in Shari's eyes, and Jonathan knew he'd have the fight of a lifetime convincing the elders, but he'd do it. For her.

CHAPTER TWENTY-FIVE

After the battle, the former Altoriaes followed Shari back to the castle, and they crowded into the one room they had all used as a bedroom during their tenure.

Hail was glaring at Shari from his nest on the dresser. Swiftly, she scooped him up and dropped a kiss on his head in an attempt to placate him. Grumbling, Hail made sure to put holes in her arm as he travelled to her shoulder. Wisp bit onto the hem of her shirt and refused to let go, displeasure at being left out of the battle clear in every strand of fur.

Shari winced but bore their ire well.

When she turned back to face the others, they were all staring at the singular bed.

"Well, this could get awkward," Fiona said with a laugh.

A flurry of sending started up, but before the others could get too invested, Shari knocked on the dresser to get their attention.

She grinned. "I'm going to sleep somewhere else and let you lot fight over who gets to stay. Remember, this is your second chance, so no maiming or murder." Before anyone could stop her, she and Wisp slipped through the hidden door into Samuel's house and sealed it shut so they couldn't follow.

Back against the door, Shari slid down and rested her head on her knees. For most of her life, she'd felt so alone, and now there were a dozen others like her, all camping out in her bedroom, and she'd run away.

Some Altoriae she was.

Wisp licked at one side of her face, while Hail stroked the other side with gentle paws.

"Shari?" Samuel said. She felt him take a seat next to her. "Are you alright?"

"Yeah," she said, leaning against him. "Can I crash here tonight?"

"Of course," he said. "Take the bed." Gently, he helped her to her feet and led her to the huge bed in the middle of the room.

She flopped down gracelessly and groaned, too tired to even open her eyes. Hail squeaked, but the noise of the angry draci faded. Shari figured that he'd remembered this was Sneeze's house too.

Samuel used Innarn to remove her boots and her weapons.

The bed dipped, and a furry weight settled over her legs.

Cocooning herself in a blanket that smelled like him, she slurred, "G'night, Samuel," and was out like a light.

Vebaday
Sixth day of the fourth week of Waeghost

Waking slowly had always been a luxury, and today, Shari found it no different.

Except the blanket didn't smell right, and the bed was harder than she remembered.

Shari felt around, stretching her arms as wide as she could, and still wasn't able to find the edge of the mattress. Reluctantly opening her eyes, it took her a moment to place the stone ceiling above her head.

She was at Samuel's.

In his bed.

Scrambling upright, Shari untangled herself from the blanket in record speed and poked her head out the door to a blinding mountain of golden scales.

'*Don't wake them.*' Sanithane's send rumbled from the bottom of the pile. '*They're full of U'tan and probably won't move for days.*'

'*How are you going to get out then?*' Shari asked, prodding the biggest body with her toe.

Sanithane opened an eye and glared at her. '*I have my ways,*' he said. He may have been aiming for mysterious, but it was slightly hard to pull off when he had a pair of draci sleeping above his middle eye.

Wisp huffed at him from Shari's side.

'*I'm going to check on the Altoriaes and make sure they didn't stab each other over a bed,*' Shari sent.

He opened another eye. '*Now that I'd like to see,*' he sent.

'*Go see,*' Tormorylth sent. '*Sleeping now.*'

Shari covered her mouth to muffle her laughter and tiptoed back to the door that led to her room. Her old room? Well, one way to find out.

Samuel appeared by her side, a draci on each shoulder and Shadow by his side. Twisting the handle, Shari opened the door and stepped through.

The former Altoriaes had vacated the room, leaving only Kay'imi sleeping in the bed. Shari turned to shrug at Samuel, only to find him standing stock still, a blade at his throat.

"Grow a scale, and I'll still pierce your hide," Kay'imi snarled.

Shari shoved Samuel backwards and took his place before the blade. "Don't even try it," Shari growled. "Don't pretend like you weren't watching everything I was doing. Like you don't know exactly who Samuel is."

Kay'imi slowly lowered her blade. "You still defend him?"

"I always will," Shari snapped.

The first Altoriae grinned at her, blade disappearing into the folds of her skirt. "I'm glad. I'll gather the others, shall I? Meet us in the small dining room." She vanished before Shari could say anything else.

"I am glad I was too young to face her on the battlefield," Samuel said. "She's scarier than you."

"I'm not scary," Shari said.

Samuel grinned. "Not compared to her, you aren't."

Grumbling, Shari led the way before slouching in her seat while Hail nibbled at her hair and Wisp tried to cheer her up by chasing Shadow's tail.

The former Altoriaes entered as a group, Jonathan trailing in behind them.

Looking at the crowd around the circular table, Shari grinned.

The oldest living Q'Aralide, last elder of his kind, the final Guardian, and thirteen of the beings he swore to protect all in one room.

Shari rose to close the doors, but more beings filtered in.

"Eminlith!" Kay'imi said, delight colouring the word, rising to give the woman a warrior's greeting.

Petuar's head snapped up when one of the new men coughed. "Thuk!" She grinned.

'*What's going on?*' Samuel sent.

Shari beamed and blinked away tears. The other Altoriaes were not shy about sharing their emotions. '*These are their Guardians.*'

Qar sat next to Askanar, and Ullmar next to Feyla, the four exchanging stories. Estebar and Lerah curled up in the same seat, leaving Shari to wonder if Guardian and Altoriae were all they meant to each other.

Liadain clapped Muran on the back, tears streaming down her face. Ailan introduced Tanika to Clara, who had an arm wrapped around Shael's waist. Crista and Neev looked like they would never be parted again, and

Jali and Aisling were just as bad. Tabatha was fussing over Abby, and Resa was laughing at something Fiona said.

Jonathan came over and took the seat on her right. "Too much?" he murmured.

"Yes and no," Shari said. "It's good to see them happy. There are just a lot of bodies in the room."

Kay'imi noticed. "Sit down, you lot. We'll have plenty of time to catch up later."

Guardians and Altoriaes sat, side by side, the table expanding to fit them all. Food and drink appeared before them, and Shari sent a quiet word of thanks to Dealon. Wisp settled between her and Jonathan, while Shadow took his spot beside her and Samuel.

"Now, Shari. Where should we start?" Kay'imi asked.

"Am I correct in assuming that none of us want to uphold the mantle of Altoriae anymore?" There was a chorus of nods. "Then I suggest the first five of you should change your names."

Voices overlapped each other, asking why.

"You are the stuff of legend. The beings every school-aged child is taught about. If you—" she pointed to Kay'imi "—were to go out there and introduce yourself, best case, you'd be mobbed by well-wishers. Worst case, you'd have beings wanting your personal attention to get rid of the menacing spider under their eaves."

Kay'imi smirked, tipping her head at the reference to an entry in the *Handbook*. "Call me Kay then," she said.

"What about the rest of us?" Muran asked.

"With all of the Returned, you couldn't get away with a name change," Jonathan said. "And for the others, there was a fashion, for a time, to name your child after the Altoriae. There were more girls named Shael in 3850 than any other name."

"If someone asks, just say, *Oh no, not that one*," Shari suggested. Hail chirruped in agreement.

Shael laughed.

"And the Guardians?" Liadain asked.

"Disappointingly, not as well known," Shari said.

"You do see the flaw in your renaming plan, don't you?" Liadain continued. "There are many from your history. We were with them in the Spirit Realm. They will know who we are."

"Huh. Hadn't thought of that," Shari muttered.

"Perhaps a name change will convince them that we don't want to live the same life we did before?" Lerah said.

"We can but try," Petuar stated.

"How many of you would prefer to reside in the castle?" Jonathan asked.

Every single hand went up, except for Shari's, Samuel's, and Jonathan's.

"Brilliant. It's yours." Shari grinned.

"Traditionally the Altoriae..." Eminlith broke off.

"I'm not the Altoriae anymore," Shari said.

Samuel snapped upright in his seat. "Cylanthar," he swore.

Faintly, Shari could hear bells. "Sorry?" she asked.

"Nothing," he muttered, slouching again. A corner of his lips quirked up, and Shari shook her head at his dramatics.

"Feel free to reshape the castle. Although some of my guild are still here, so please take them into account when you're doing so," Shari said.

"Where will you go?" Kay asked.

"Home," she said.

She just had to figure out where that was.

Tania made the trek through the new houses with Collis by her side, making sure she stopped and greeted everyone as they went, taking a mental note of anything they needed, and matching them up with others who may be able to help.

She paused as a weathered man walked towards them, his gaze scanning those around as if he was looking for someone.

"Yirrisaunder?" she called out, not knowing why that name, out of all the ones she knew, had fallen out of her mouth.

His head snapped around, frantic gaze passing straight over her.

"I think I know where your family is," she said. "I can take you to them, if you like?"

He nodded, crossing to them quickly.

Tania shifted them all to the refugee village, right outside Yirri's house.

Alistair looked up from where he'd been chopping wood. "Here to relieve me?" he asked.

"Here to bring someone home," Tania said, waving at Yirrisaunder.

The door creaked open, and Yirri, still gripping her shawl, stepped out and stopped when she spotted them. "Yirrisaunder?" she whispered.

After teetering down the stairs, she ran her hands over her son's face, tears flowing over her cheeks. "It is you," she said. Yirri tapped him on the nose and grabbed him by the ear. Dragging him with her, Yirri stormed towards the house.

Tania couldn't tell if she was yelling at her son or calling her grandkids to come and see their father again.

She giggled and looked at Alistair. "I didn't know you were still helping Yirri out."

"I didn't know I was allowed to stop," Alistair said. He glanced over his shoulder. "She's terrifying."

"But in a good way," Tania said.

Alistair wiped the sweat off his brow.

"Thank you for helping her," she blurted.

"Are you kidding? Why wouldn't I? As scary as she is, Yirri makes the best pastries in all of Ronah." Alistair winked.

"And you won't get any unless I have more firewood!" Yirri called from the doorway.

"Yes, Yirri!" Alistair said. Rolling his eyes, he got back to work.

Yirri waved at Tania and stomped back inside.

"Another family reunited," Collis said.

"Are you thinking about Muran again?" Tania asked as they walked away.

"I didn't know he'd even made it to Ronah. I don't understand how he's with the Risen, and why he hasn't come to see us," Collis said.

"I'm sure there's a reason," Tania said.

"It might have something to do with you being so difficult to track down," a voice behind them said.

Collis whirled, Innarn gathering against his skin like a storm.

"Impressive," the dark-haired man said, cocky grin in place. "But you'll have to do better than that."

Tania blinked, and they were in the training ground. She looked around and spotted a grizzled woman leaning against the stands. The woman tipped her head at Tania and turned her gaze back to the two men circling each other.

"Seriously?" Tania muttered, and sank into a seat carved from Plasma, propping her head up to watch the two fools fighting.

"You must be Ronah's new Linked," the woman said. She was maintaining her distance, but Tania still had the impression she was close enough to do some damage if she wanted to.

Giving a non-committal hum, she looked between the two strangers and grinned. "If that's Muran, then you must be Liadain."

"How do you figure that?" she asked.

Sword and staff were clashing, giving off great sparks and melting the snow around them.

"You watch your Altoriae the way Jonathan watches Shari."

Liadain gave Tania a piercing look. "I like you," she said, and turned back to take in the two men.

Muran was broader than Collis, but the teen was taller and was using his longer limbs to his advantage. He also seemed to have a better grasp on his Innarn.

"It's almost not fair," Liadain said.

"What isn't?" Tania felt her Innarn rising and used it to create an untraceable ward around the combatants. She had a feeling the former Guardian was about to step in.

"Collis has turned into a good fighter, but he can't be allowed to win."

Tania had been right.

Liadain's Innarn lashed at the ward before bouncing back and knocking her out.

"Don't mess with my soul-match," Tania said mildly, and turned her attention back to the fight.

By the time the former Guardian woke up, Muran was standing over her, sporting a nasty-looking gash along his arm.

"You missed half the fun," he said, helping Liadain to her feet and holding still while she healed him.

"The new Linked is protective," Liadain said.

Tania gave her a deceptively mild smile. "Aren't we all?" she asked.

Collis wrapped a sweaty arm around her and dropped a kiss on the top of her head.

Looking at him, Tania forgot the rest of the Realm for a moment and just basked in his presence, until the smell hit her. "Go wash up. You two need to sit and actually talk. Preferably with the others."

"Wise too," Liadain said. "You might have knocked me out, but I still like you."

Tania grinned.

Shari was walking through the castle when she bumped into Skye.

"Well met! How are you going?" Shari asked, steadying Hail on her shoulder.

Skye looked at Wisp before she gave her a strained smile. "Good thanks. Things are..." Her bottom lip trembled. "Good," she finished lamely.

"Struggling?" Shari asked.

"How can I miss such a murderous roommate?" Skye wailed. "I don't even know what happened to her!"

"She's still on Lissae," Shari said.

"You're sure?" Skye asked.

"I am." She ignored Wisp's huff at the lie. If it helped Skye, that's all that mattered. And there was a slight grain of truth to it. Where else could her cousin have gone?

Skye nodded. "Thank you." She adjusted the strap on her arm.

Shari looked at the heavy bag. "Going somewhere?"

"Ginna from *The Shifting Island Sentinel* has offered me an apprenticeship. I'm moving to Talhan to make the commute easier."

"Hey, congratulations! Ginna is awesome," Shari said.

"I'm going to quote you on that," Skye warned.

Laughing, Shari said, "Feel free. And thank you, for everything you've done to help us all."

Skye hefted the bag again. "I'm going to head off before I start bawling. I bid thee well, Shari."

"I bid thee well, Skye." What quirk of fate had pulled them together for the brief period of time? Without Skye, she never would have met Grace. Grace would have remained chained to Chamele and forced to do who knows what sorts of atrocities.

Shaking her head, Shari continued on her way. What else did the fates have in store for her?

Jonathan sat in an armchair off to the side, trying not to smile as Muran took centre stage. Shari and Samuel were close by, waiting to hear the older Altoriae's tale. The Returned had crowded into the room, sitting on all manner of items and staring at Muran like they'd never expected to see him again.

Muran conjured a stool next to his seat, and the Returned whooped.

Remmy came forward, and with an ostentatious wave of his arm, a small table appeared. "Any particular design?" Remmy asked Muran.

He laughed. "When have you ever asked me that?"

"It's more permanent now," Remmy said.

"A door, then. So I'll always have a way back."

Jonathan felt more than heard Shari's indrawn breath.

"Alright, when was the last time we were together?" Muran spoke over the top of the noise Remmy was making. "Anriluka's downfall. The fulni took me out—"

There were a few protests, and Jonathan noted how Samuel was careful to look just as shocked as the others in the crowd. Muran didn't glance their way at all.

Jonathan wanted to roll his eyes but refrained.

"Oh, I was a tad distracted, being back home." Muran flashed a disarming smile, and everyone calmed down. "Next thing I knew, I was in the Spirit Realm. It wasn't like our nightmare." He grinned at the others. "Time would go as slow or as fast as you wanted. We could look over and check you were all going alright. I tried to search for others that we knew, back then, but could never really find them." He paused and checked on Remmy's progress.

"Daivi popped in, and we searched for a bit more, but no luck. Then there was a call, stronger than I'd felt before. A few left, and I thought that would be the end of it." He sighed. "You don't need to sleep, or eat, or do anything in the Spirit Realm. But you do kind of... lose awareness?" He glanced at Daivi, who nodded.

"When I was awake next, a being in a white robe pulled me back into the land of the living and asked for my help to split the doorway between the two Realms. There was something in me that said it needed to be done, so I did it. And here we are." He shot them all another smile.

"Is it true you brought the other Altoriaes back with you?" Kieran yelled out.

"I could never find them," Muran said.

Liadain, off to the side, rolled her eyes but otherwise remained stoic.

"How did you come across Liadain then?" Remmy asked, swiping at something on Muran's arm.

Muran laughed. "She came across me."

"He couldn't find his way out of a wet paper bag," Liadain scoffed.

The Returned were quick to jump to his defence—their stories of all the times Muran had saved them when they were lost overlapping each other.

Jonathan grinned. It looked like Muran was going to ensure the other Altoriaes had their chance at anonymity if they still wanted it.

Shari looked at Wolf and Belfar from across her childhood table, incredulous. "You're going back to Rakemyst?" she confirmed.

"Yes." Wolf winced. "I'm sorry. We tried, really. The house is just not built for an Ilutri. My wings keep getting tangled."

She had to bite the inside of her cheek to keep from laughing at the disgruntled expression Wolf wore. "I understand," she said, making no mention of the fact that her father had managed for years without a hassle. With Wolf looking as grumpy as he did, she doubted he would appreciate the slight on his flying abilities. She chanced a glance at Belfar, who clearly was thinking the same thing as she was. And the other Ilutri hadn't mentioned any issues either. Shari coughed to hide the laugh she could no longer contain. "I'm glad you're telling me, really. We've had an influx of new beings at the castle. Moving back here is no hassle for me."

Wisp barked in agreement.

"Thank you for understanding, Shari," Belfar said.

"I hope Rakemyst is more comfortable for you," she said.

Wolf nodded. "It can't be any—" He broke off and scowled at his mate.

Belfar was far better at looking innocent than Wolf was at playing dumb. "What your uncle *meant* to say was that we thank you for allowing us to stay."

"What he said," Wolf growled, bending down to rub his shin.

"When are you moving?" she asked.

"We already have," Belfar said, wincing slightly. "The house is all yours again. We just wanted the chance to say goodbye."

Shari stood from the table, the other two following suit. "Thank you," Shari said. She wasn't big on hugging, but she held her arms out just to see her uncle squirm.

Belfar laughed and shoved Wolf out of the way. "You only ever need to send, and we'll be there before you can blink," he said, giving her a quick squeeze.

Wolf gave her an awkward bow and shifted out, but not before Shari glimpsed the tears that threatened to fall.

"Aww, he's going to miss me," she said.

"We both will," Belfar said, nudging her.

"I'll miss you both too," Shari said. "Now shoo! I have some redecorating to do!"

Laughing, Belfar slipped out the back door, leaving Shari to look around the kitchen.

Wisp raised his head to glance at the door, then blinked at her sleepily.

Wolf and Belfar had already stripped the clutter away, probably in an attempt to free up some space for Wolf's wings. How he'd struggled to move in the space when his mate was the one with the prosthetic was beyond her.

Perched on the windowsill to soak up the last rays of sun, Hail lifted his head and chittered at her.

"You're right. It's time I made this feel like my home, and not like a shrine to my parents. The only real question is, where should we start?" Shari asked, rolling her sleeves up.

Chapter Twenty-Six

Zoeday

Seventh day of the fourth week of Waeghost

It was far too early in the morning, but Shari found herself stamping her feet and rubbing her hands together as she stood to one side of the training grounds, listening to the clanging of swords. The cold nose Hail was pressing against her neck was not helping, but the heat emanating from Wisp's glowing chest was keeping her legs warm at least.

The other Altoriaes had joined her, curious to see Anika's group as they trained without Innarn.

"They're quite good," Askanar said, coming to stand next to her.

"Anika has improved a lot," Shari said. "I love the daggers she's rigged up. You should see them right about... now."

Hail *meeped* and hid in her hair. Wisp lifted his head as if he was planning on critiquing Anika's technique.

Sure enough, Anika was twisting her wrists, the daggers dropping into her hands as she blocked a blow from one of the satyrs.

"I don't think she wants to fight any more than we do," Askanar said.

Shari looked at the other girl with a critical eye. "You're probably right, but Anika needs to know she can protect herself in a world where others have innate weapons she can't access."

"True," Askanar said. "Speaking of things we can't access—I was hoping you would be willing to show us the new entrance to Merthin." She gestured to Qar, who looked less than excited.

"Of course, Askanar," Shari said.

Askanar grinned. "Call me Ana. It's time for me to go home."

Qar rolled his eyes. "Yay," he said, deadpanned. "More water."

Shari covered her mouth so she wouldn't giggle.

Asterion had stopped to look at the new blooms in the town square when he felt a tugging on the leg of his pants.

"Ter! Dad is home!" Eric said, letting go of the fistful of material.

"Excellent. I'm sure you missed him." Asterion glanced around to see Louise and Andrew walking towards him, arms wrapped around each other's waists.

"Well met, Asterion," they said together.

"Well met. It's good to see you back," Asterion said.

The family wandered on, and Asterion smiled. It really was a relief to find families reconnecting. There hadn't been an attempt to place all the Risen with their kin yet, and many were still finding their own feet. To be alive again after so long... Asterion looked around the square and beamed.

He had an inkling of what that was like.

Shari nodded in encouragement as Askanar, now Ana, made her way to the glow worm cave, Qar trailing reluctantly behind.

Domic appeared the moment they vanished, Caeli at his side. "It's polite to let me know when you bring strangers to my isle," Domic said.

"Ana isn't a stranger. She's one of the Risen, from a long time ago," Shari said, fighting to keep the smile on her face friendly. Wisp held no such compunction and growled at the pair. Shari put a soothing hand between his ears.

Hail nodded his head frantically, his horns bumping into Shari's cheek.

Caeli gave her an unimpressed look. "That's not all she is."

Shari didn't waver. "You're right. It's hard to sum up one life in a single sentence."

The former candidate nodded slowly. "We've had a few Risen join us. I'm sure she'll fit in just fine. I'm assuming she'd prefer her former... status to be ignored?"

"Ana just wants to live a peaceful life." As much as Shari wanted to confirm what Caeli already knew, Ana's safety was more important than the curiosity of the Linked's soul-match.

Caeli nodded, and smiled. Ana's secret would be safe with her.

Shari grinned, keeping her tone light. "How is Akoren going? Is he taking all this growth in stride?"

"He has yet to let me know," Domic said. Caeli rubbed his arm gently, letting the Linked lean on her.

"Tania is saying much the same about Ronah. There's a book that says the islands will come good again," Shari said, trying to reassure them.

Hail curled his tail tighter around her neck.

She just didn't want to say that, in the diary Asterion had shown her, the islands had woken a final time to say goodbye.

Edward wrapped an arm around Harmony's waist and nuzzled his cold nose into her neck.

"I almost thought you'd get rid of them," Harmony said, her fingers buried in the soil of the carrot patch.

Edward laughed wetly. "Turns out I actually like carrot stew," he said.

Harmony turned in his arms. "Lucky I came back then," she said, her eyes glistening suspiciously.

"I will be forever grateful that you did," Edward said.

"Well," Harmony sniffed, "you were barely looking after yourself. I couldn't very well leave you alone." She leaned against him, her gentle tone at odds with the harsh words.

Edward held her tighter. Whatever the future held, he would be able to face it with a smile now Harmony was by his side again.

"We have a problem," Eva said in greeting.

"What would that be?" Jonathan may not have been able to spend as much time at the store as he wanted, but he'd learnt to appreciate Eva's no-frills approach. Samuel followed him, and Jonathan didn't need to look to know his apprentice had raised a brow.

"There are only two copies of Everon Castor's latest books left and no way to get any more."

Behind him, Samuel started coughing. It sounded like he was attempting not to laugh. By the sound of it, Sneeze was berating him.

Jonathan shot him a glare. "I'm sure we can figure something out."

"Not for Castor's fans. They'll be storming the store before you know it," Eva said.

"Cross-reference who has been buying copies of the last ones and see how many have missed out. We may just have to give one to the Quiver and Quill and refer people there," Jonathan said.

Eva nodded. "That'll keep me busy for at least another day," she said.

"What do you mean?" Jonathan asked. He ignored Samuel as the other man moved around the store, plucking books off the shelves and putting them back again.

"Now the Realm-saving is done, surely you'll want to take the store over again," Eva said, grabbing a cloth to wipe the already clean bench.

Jonathan shook his head. "The Realm might be saved, but there's always work to do. Like helping people get settled and figuring out what needs to change so we can all live and work together. I'm going to need you to look after the store for years yet."

Eva's shoulders dropped, and she sighed. Despite her relief, she went straight back to business. "Where are you going to get all the new books from, now we can't reach Lissae?" she asked.

Jonathan froze. "I hadn't actually thought of that."

Eva laughed. "Maybe instead of running a bookstore, you should write the stories to fill it."

"It would take far more than one author to keep all the readers on Ronah happy," he laughed, but tucked the thought away. Maybe, one day, he'd write the story of Lissae's last Altoriae.

Samuel, hands shoved into his pockets, said, "I'd give it a go. Fixing up the... book reminded me I have a taste for crafting stories. Now it feels like my fingertips will bleed ink if I don't write. Besides—" He crossed to the Everon Castor display and picked up a book, Sneeze protesting at the movement. "I have to give my readership something to look forward to."

Jonathan looked at him, aghast.

Eva's jaw dropped. "*You're* Everon Castor?" she shrieked.

Putting the book down, Samuel winked and strode out of the door chuckling.

"At least we can get more copies of his books easy enough," Eva said smugly. "And think of the export possibilities! We'll be the only store in all the Realms to stock Everon Castor's latest works!"

Jonathan groaned. The last thing Samuel needed was something else to be smug about.

Shari was about to shift home when she had a strong feeling that she needed to check on Yessna.

"One more stop," Shari said, patting Hail with one hand and Wisp with the other..

Hail chittered at her sleepily. Wisp sighed but got to his paws.

After giving the peaceful waterfall a last glance, Shari shifted to the not-so-little island where the U'sala and the mainlanders were.

The remains of the Chirea littered the ground.

'*Yessna, what happened?*' Shari sent, eyeing the mess and throwing a shield around her draci.

'*You don't want to know.*' The Ferah sounded tired, but at least she was still alive.

'*Oh, I kinda do,*' Shari sent, flicking an image of where she was for good measure.

Yessna shifted in next to her. "Gozochas. I was hoping to have this cleaned up before you found out."

"You fought the Chirea?" Shari asked.

"And won. Nerina took out Luttrell. Again." Yessna looked quite proud.

"Do you need a hand with..." Shari waved an arm to indicate the area.

"No, the mainlanders are quite keen on practicing their–"

A fireball slammed into a pile of bones nearby. Shari raised a shield quicker than she could blink.

"Sorry!" someone called.

"Aim *away* from other beings!" Yessna snarled.

"Sorry!" they yelled again.

"What is going on?" Shari asked.

Hail sneezed, and tiny snowflakes flew from his snout. Wisp lapped the flakes out of the air as they fell.

"The mainlanders, some of them have Innarn now," Yessna said.

Shari took a breath. "That would have been nice to know," she said mildly. How were they going to test beings now Lissae wasn't around to do it? They would need a whole new method of matching teachers with students...

"You are plotting," Yessna said.

"Thinking about what to do. So much is going to change now we're not on Lissae anymore," Shari said.

"I think that's the first time I've heard you admit it without crying."

Shari winced. "Not here for the mind healing right now, thank you."

"I can still be proud of your progress as your friend," Yessna shot back.

"We're friends?" Shari asked, pleased.

"Don't look so smug," Yessna grumbled, but gave her a grin.

Shari laughed and shifted away before the Ferah could change her mind.

CHAPTER TWENTY-SEVEN

Adonday
First day of the first week of Bloomcrest

Asterion looked outside at the piles of slush and shuddered. Today he'd stay in and organise the office, maybe get started on the list of Risen and see if they could match them with their descendants—if that's what they wanted to do. He might need to make a form up to see...

Thinking about what sort of questions they would need to ask, Asterion took a seat at his desk and shifted uncomfortably. Something was digging into his leg.

The diary. He took it out of his pocket and placed in on the corner of the desk so he wouldn't forget it later. Occasionally, the Guardian wanted to check something in it, and it was helpful to carry the diary with him.

One of the Risen, who reminded him strongly of a statue in Ronah's museum, gave him a smile and wandered into the Guardian's office, closing the door behind her.

Asterion grinned to himself. Slowly, the beings here were getting used to him. It was nice not to have everyone avoiding his presence.

Settling down with parchment and quill, Asterion got to work on the questions for the Risen, blocking out everything else around him.

Until a delicate hand reached across and picked up the diary.

"Can I help you?" Asterion asked.

It was the Risen who had been in with the Guardian.

"You found my grandmother's journal. I'd recognise her writing anywhere. Where did you find this?" she asked.

"On Rataeo. She was one of the first settlers there."

The female sat down heavily, a seat rushing from the floor to wrap around her and still her fall.

"Who are you?" Asterion asked.

"Kay," she said, her eyes on the book as she opened it, ever so carefully, to the first page. As she ran a finger over the smudged writing, Asterion watched in astonishment as it cleared up, a beautifully inscribed name appearing. "I was named after her," she said. "Thank you for keeping her words alive. Do you mind if I make a copy?"

"Of course not, but you must keep the original," Asterion said.

"It's not for me," Kay said. "She always had a way of ensuring the right being found her words at the right time." A wave of her hand, and a duplicate appeared, looking just as old and worn as the original. "She went missing before I was born, but her old journals survived. I spent hours as a child reading through them. It will be nice to see where she ended up."

"Not everything in there is for the faint of heart," Asterion warned.

Kay grinned. "There's a reason I was named after her," she said, and passed the original back to him.

"My thanks," Asterion said, opening the book to the first page as Kay silently slipped away.

Diary of Kay'imi.

His head snapped up, but she was already gone.

Someone was incessantly saying her name. '*Tania?*'

"Huh?" Sitting up in bed, Tania rubbed the sleep out of her eyes.

'*You're awake!*'

"I am now," she mumbled, looking around for whoever was talking.

'*I'm underneath you, silly.*'

Half asleep, Tania flopped sideways and lifted the edge of her quilt to peer under her bed.

Ronah laughed at her.

Tania sat up, all traces of tiredness gone. "Ronah?" she whispered.

'*At least you didn't ask if I have teeth this time,*' the island laughed.

"Ronah!" Tania cried. The hum in the back of her mind had returned. '*I missed you,*' she said.

'*I was right here,*' Ronah soothed.

The door to her room creaked open, and Alistair tiptoed in. "Another nightmare?" he asked.

"Ronah's back," Tania said hoarsely.

Alistair gave her a confused look.

Tania tapped the side of her head. "I can hear her again."

"That's good?" Alistair looked as if he wasn't sure what he was meant to say.

"That's perfect," Tania said. Flopping back in her bed, she let her mind wander and could feel the other Shifting Islands drifting away. They were all still growing, ever so slowly, their borders changing as they moved through the sea. Ronah extended down farther too, almost as if the island was growing roots.

'*I missed you,*' Tania sent again. '*I know you needed to rest, but I was so worried.*'

'*You don't need to worry. I'll always be here,*' Ronah sent.

Tania smiled and eased back into sleep, knowing that when she woke, Ronah would be right there waiting for her.

Shari smiled as Hail nudged her chin. The little draci had been feeling extra cold, so Shari had donned a scarf and let him curl up in the folds. Wisp, with his inbuilt heating system, was having no such trouble. Shari wondered how long it would be before the draci realised and curled up inside the glowing cavity of the Shadow Bringer's chest.

The streets of Ronah were bustling more than she'd ever seen them. Residents she had spent her life around mingled with the Returned and the Risen as easily as if they were all old friends.

They were all instinctively giving Shari the space she needed, nodding polite greetings but not saying anything to her as she moved through the town, feeling a bit like the spirits must have before they regained their bodies.

Slowly, Shari made her way to the doorway in the empty field. The stubborn thing remained shut when she tugged on it.

"We're settled; we're good now. Found all the right beings," she said to the wood. "Surely you could open, just a bit?"

It didn't budge.

"Fine," she said, a flash of inspiration coming to her.

She would try the doors at the museum instead.

Making sure Hail was still cosy, Shari took a breath and shifted.

The big white building on the hill seemed farther away than usual, but Shari was happy for the short trek. She didn't really know why she was determined to test the doors, other than the chance at some sort of peace. She was sure Yessna would say it was something else entirely, but Shari wasn't about to bring this up with the Ferah.

At least, not yet.

Entering the museum was like coming home. The glass cases were full of old friends who made her grin. Letting her eyes trail over the objects, Shari made her way to the double doors, a small smile on her face as Wisp's claws clicked on the tiled floor.

The wall where they use to sit was blank.

Crossing the room as quietly as possible, Shari then lifted her hand and touched the wall, as if it would somehow call the doors into being.

Nothing happened.

Her head fell forward, hitting the wood softly.

"I kind of thought that would work," she said, her words sounding hollow as they echoed through the room.

Hail lapped at her chin.

"What am I meant to do, if I don't fight anymore?" she asked the draci, turning and slowly sliding down until she was on the ground, letting her legs splay out in front of her. "Do I just give up? Work at the tavern? Retreat into the woods?"

Wisp sat between her legs, head level with hers, staring at her. Looking away, the dust motes visible in the beams of light coming from the high windows caught her attention.

Hail chittered at her, aggressively headbutting her chin.

She laughed sadly and scooped him up. After raising her knees, she sat Hail on them and looked him in the eye. "I'm lost. My history is full of war and violence, and without that, I don't know who I am."

Wisp licked the side of her face.

'*You Shari,*' Hail sent. '*You more than your past.*'

"Maybe if I had looked after it more–" Shari broke off. "Maybe I *can* look after it more. There's been no one to look after the museum since Anna was killed by Anriluka."

And the new doorway was close enough that she could make gardens surrounding the museum so she could keep an eye on it.

"Thanks, Hail," Shari said, kissing the draci on the tip of his nose and watching him go cross-eyed. He sneezed at her, sparks flying from his snout.

"Hey, you're looking better."

'*You happy again,*' he sent, fluttering back to her shoulder.

"Yeah, Hail, I am."

Shari kissed Wisp on his snout too before getting to her feet. She grinned. Time to take a tour and figure out what she needed to do to get the museum back up to scratch.

Collis gulped. He had to time this just right.

Hidden in the shadows, he looked across the road at Remmy, who was nonchalantly leaning against a pillar and paging through a book. The effect was ruined by the Returned glancing up at every noise.

Finally, Remmy nodded, and Collis counted to fifty in his head, giving Tania enough time to turn around before he broke cover and shifted to the front door of her house, right as it was pulled open.

Her eldest brother stared at him with wide eyes.

"Well met," Collis said, throat suddenly dry. "I know it's almost time for you all to leave, but I must speak with you."

Caleb narrowed his eyes. "If you've hurt my sister..." he said threateningly.

"Far from it," Collis said. He felt a ping from Remmy, letting him know that the other man had left his post and was following Tania, making sure she got to school safely. "Please?"

"What's the hold up? Oh, Collis," Jordan said, "we were just about to leave."

"He wants to talk with us," Caleb said, not taking his gaze off Collis.

"Come in, then. We'll have to be quick," Jordan said.

Collis gave a grim smile and wiped his sweaty palms on the back of his pants, carefully stepping past Caleb. Tania's parents and siblings were gathered in the lounge room.

"How can we help?" Liza said.

"Do you understand what a soul-match is?" Collis asked. He shoved his shaking hands into his pockets then pulled them out again, worried it would come across as rude.

"Yes," Liza said. "My parents were soul-matched. You and Tania are too, aren't you?"

Collis nodded. "She is already my whole Realm. I wanted to ask if I may make her my family?"

Tania's youngest sister squealed, even as her brothers gaped and scowled at him.

"Say yes, say yes!" Jessica chanted, tugging on her father's arm.

Liza, tears in her eyes, reached out and grabbed his hands. "Tania means the Realms to us, and I know she means even more to you. How could we say no?"

Jessica shrieked and jumped on him, hugging him tight. "That means you're part of our family too!" She beamed at him.

Collis smiled back, and looked around the room at Tania's brothers, who were grinning at him.

It had been a very long time since he'd had a family.

"I'd ask soon, if I were you," Christopher, Tania's middle brother, said. "Jess can't keep a secret to save herself."

"Can to!" she said, letting go of Collis to shove Christopher's arm.

What had he gotten himself in for?

CHAPTER TWENTY-EIGHT

Inthday

Second day of the first week of Bloomcrest

The three hatchlings stood in their squishy forms, toes burning in the early morning frost as they looked out at the rutenberry saplings.

Jetonyx grinned. As fun as it had been to help protect Carilla, it would be nice to not have to fight again. The U'tans had upset his stomach, and he'd spent a miserable day regretting ever laying eyes on a tentacle.

But this... This was better than anything. Their seedlings had grown, and in the first rays of morning sun, tiny bundles of green fruit could be seen hanging lower than the leaves.

Tormorylth licked her lips.

'No, Tormo,' Jetonyx sent. '*We need to wait until they're ripe.*'

She sagged. '*I know. How long does it take?*'

'*We should ask Sweet Treats,*' Kemanyr sent, grinning at them.

'*Kem,*' Jetonyx groaned.

'*Jet,*' she moaned back at him, poking out her tongue.

Mock growling, he held up his fingers in a mimicry of claws and chased her around the field, careful that neither of them knocked into the fragile plants.

Puffing, Jetonyx pulled to a stop next to Tormorylth, who looked guilty and faintly sick.

'*The green ones do not taste as good,*' she sent.

Jetonyx rolled his eyes. '*Of course they don't,*' he sent. '*They aren't ready yet. Go back inside and change. You'll feel better.*'

His nest mates disappeared, and Jetonyx stopped to take in the beauty of the moment. The sun colouring the clouds pink and orange, sparkling frost making everything look like tiny touches of Innarn were alighting on it, and the plants that held their future in fruit that was yet to come.

It finally felt like he could breathe.

Shari swung into Jonathan's office in the back room of the store, feeling lighter than she had in years. "Guess what," she said.

Samuel glanced up and frowned. "We're going to need far more information if you wish us to guess something."

"Figure of speech, Samuel," Jonathan said idly, scrawling something across a piece of parchment.

Wisp trotted over to the Guardian's side and rested his head in Jonathan's lap.

From Samuel's shoulder, Sneeze blew a flurry of embers her way.

Shari laughed. "I figured it out!"

Joining in her excitement, Hail chittered and flared his wings.

"Again, more information is required." Samuel smirked slightly, and Shari whacked his shoulder.

"Quit playing," she groused. "I figured out what I'm going to do now."

"And what would that be?" Samuel drawled. "We have the Guardian turned Realm leader, the Apprentice turned sell-out author slash rutenberry farmer slash elder, and the Altoriae turned..."

"Curator," Shari said, flopping into her armchair.

Hail gave a little *oof* that made Shari coo at him in apology.

"Curator?" Jonathan looked up. "Perfect," he said, giving her a grin, and he scratched Wisp under his chin.

"Protector of the Realm still." Samuel nodded.

"Hardly," Shari scoffed.

"Without our history, who exactly are we?" Samuel asked.

Sneeze, properly awake now, realised that Hail had joined them. The two draci flew to each other and started chittering and cleaning, nestling together on a haphazard stack of books.

The noise from the draci woke Shadow, who slunk out from under Samuel's chair and caught sight of Wisp. The two canines curled together in between their humans.

"I can't think of anyone better to look after our history," Jonathan said.

Shari sank back and smiled. She finally felt like she had found her right place in the Realms. That it didn't involve wielding a weapon made it all the sweeter.

Lizbeth smiled as the hatchlings went bounding by, scales nowhere in sight.

It was slightly disappointing that they were more welcome in their 'squishy forms,' but the islands just weren't built to have the three of them wandering the streets side-by-side, even after the unexpected expansion.

Samuel scowled as he strode after them, and Lizbeth could feel his aura pulsing in agitation. Sneeze was the only calm spot around him.

"Something wrong?" she called from her seat outside the tavern.

He turned, a snarl ready, before he recognised her and came to slouch into the chair opposite. "The hatchlings will be the death of me," he declared.

If Samuel had been anyone else, Lizbeth would have made a quip about children following in their parents' footsteps, but she didn't think he would appreciate the sentiment.

Before she could come up with the right words to say, Samuel was growling, a rumble that seemed to fill the air around them. *'Your toothpick is heading this way.'*

"My...?" Lizbeth frowned and let her Innarn flow out, trying to sense who he was looking at.

Her niece, the one who worked in the Techno Centre on Talhan, was approaching. She stopped at the table, the sound of her gloves sliding against each other indicating her upset. "Well met," Mara said softly.

Lizbeth was impressed by how easily she was ignoring the growling Q'Aralide. "Well met," she said cautiously. The last time they had spoken, they had not parted on good terms.

"I, ah, came to apologise," she said. "In the battle against the Crystal Intelligence, I crossed into the Spirit Realm. You were my favourite relative, and I kept an eye on you." She tucked a strand of loose hair behind her ear but kept her eyes downcast. "I almost rejoiced when Innarn started to fade. I wanted to reach out and say I *told you* so, but it hurt to watch the confidence I loved so much be shattered."

Lizbeth gripped her cup, her throat too tight to speak.

"When we had the chance to return, I came back. To you. I needed to apologise. You don't have to say anything," she hurried to add. "I just needed you to know."

"Thank you," Lizbeth rasped.

Her niece gave an aborted bow. "I bid thee well," she said, and scurried away.

Samuel let her sit in silence, and when Lizbeth reached out her hand, he was right there to take it.

Tania was practically jumping out of her seat. Alistair might not have understood what she meant when she said Ronah was back, but the other Linked would. They were meeting in one of the rooms in Rakemyst's tower, and Tania could barely sit still.

"Something to share?" Zana asked, handing her a plate of fruit.

"Ronah's back," Tania blurted.

All the other Linked froze. Only their heads moved as they turned to look at her.

"She's back?" Fenix asked.

Tania nodded frantically. "Have your islands spoken to you?" she asked. *Surely she wasn't the only one.*

One by one, the others shook their heads.

"Try," she begged.

Zana sat down on the floor right where she had been standing and closed her eyes. Tania felt her trembling send, and an answering rumble from Rakemyst. The eldest Linked's eyes flew open. "Rakemyst is back."

Cyrus leaned against a pillar, taking a hunk of crystal out of his pocket and rolling it in his hand. "Talhan," he beamed.

Fenix and Oakley looked at each other and sighed. They had both been through so much since their islands had joined—poisoning, kidnapping, torture, betrayal. Tania wasn't sure if they'd be game enough to reach out to their islands again, lest their hearts be broken once more.

Beaming, Fenix nodded their head. "Cantash is back."

"Ginorti too, the tired old thing," Oakley laughed in relief.

Everyone turned to look at Domic, who shrugged. "Well, Akoren is like the tides. He'll speak to me when he's ready."

"Or you could reach out," Tania suggested. *Please reach out.*

Heaving a sigh, Domic slumped in his seat, arms crossed. For a long minute, nothing happened.

Maybe I was wrong. She chewed on her lip, wishing desperately to take back her words. She was so lost in her thoughts, she almost missed what Domic said.

"He's here."

Beaming, she turned to Brinley.

Vannali's Linked looked around the room with tears in her eyes. "She's not."

The room fell silent as the Weaver left in a cloud of white robes.

Chapter Twenty-Nine

Kerday

Third day of the first week of Bloomcrest

Anika smiled at Raven. "That is the most perfect idea!" she said, doing her best not to jump up and down.

"I'm glad you like it," he grinned bashfully. "You'll be able to reconnect with your parents by moving back in but use your house to make and sell your creations. And you've got a fallback if something goes wrong."

The words were said lightly, but Anika could hear the dark undertone. "I don't think I have much to worry about going wrong when you're around," she said.

Raven pulled her in for a hug, the quiver of arrows clinking as he kissed her on the cheek. "I'll be here for as long as you want me to be." He smiled.

"I'll always want you here," Anika said. "But right now, you want to go hunting, and I'm very curious as to what you can find that will dye this purple." She shook out the bolt of cream-coloured cloth.

"I'll see what I can find," Raven said, giving her another kiss and whistling as he walked out the door.

Anika stared after him, a sappy smile on her face—until there was a knock on the door.

"Come in. It's open," she called.

Silver hair and pointed ears flowed into the room, and Anika's eyes widened.

"Well met, Anika," Ginna said.

"Wh... well met." Anika hoped her voice wasn't trembling too much.

"I was wondering if you'd have time for an interview today?"

"I, uh... Sure!" Anika dropped the cloth like it burned and led the way to the seating area. "Excuse the boxes," she said. "I'm rearranging things at the moment."

"Oh, you should see my place!" Ginna laughed. "It's a total mess," she leaned in closer, "and my desk is even worse."

Anika laughed and glanced at her sewing desk, the side littered with bits and pieces of unfinished products.

"So," Ginna said, "how does it feel to be the foremost fashion designer on Carilla?"

Brinley lifted her robes free from the morning dew. Every day, she started with a walk, and, until the event of the new Realm, she had endured Vannali's incessant chattering in her head.

And now? How she missed it.

'*Why would you miss it when I'm right here?*'

Brinley stumbled, tripping on a rock sticking out of the path that she'd been successfully dodging for years.

In her head, Vannali laughed at her.

'*Rude*,' Brinley thought.

'*You're the one with only two legs*,' Vannali chuckled.

'*And you laugh, yet you have none,*' Brinkley finished the thought. '*You're back?*' Brinley asked.

'*Of course. I'll always be here when you need me.*'

Sniffing, Brinley raised the hood of her robe so no one would see her tears. '*I've needed you for weeks since crossover.*'

Vannali tutted. '*Sometimes, we need to heal before we can help others.*'

'*I've missed you.*' Brinley sank to the ground, burying her fingers in the mossy banks of the path.

'*I've missed you too,*' Vannali sent.

'*Linked,*' Brinley announced, '*Vannali is back!*'

Cheers, joy, and happiness flowed through their messages. Laying flat along the path, Brinley found she couldn't stop grinning.

Tania curled up next to Collis on the couch in her lounge room. "Vannali is talking again," she said, unable to stop herself from smiling.

"That is excellent news," he said, stroking her arm. "I think the islands like to keep their Linked ready for anything."

Tania sucked in a breath and held it in her cheeks for a moment, before puffing it out. "I don't think there was much that could prepare us for a whole new Realm."

"What about a whole new family?" he asked. A ring was held in the fingertips of his other hand. "Not now, but when you're ready."

"Are you asking if I'll make a family with you?"

"I'm asking if we can make one together," Collis said.

"Yes!" Tania shrieked, twisting around to hug him.

Her family spilled into the room, laughing and shouting.

Tania had never felt more loved than right at that moment.

Cyrus looked across at Xani and laughed.

The Technomancer of Lissae had a butterfly perched on the end of her nose, the bright orange wings standing out against her grey skin. Xani was going cross-eyed, trying to see the creature.

She lifted her hand.

'*Don't touch it—the wings are fragile,*' Cyrus warned.

She froze, hand raised, as she looked at him for guidance.

'*Just wait,*' he sent.

Slowly, the butterfly moved its wings.

'*It tickles,*' Xani marvelled.

Cyrus grinned. He couldn't imagine what it was like to be able to feel again after spending centuries paralysed.

'*I could feel my face.*' Xani looked away from the butterfly to roll her eyes at him. '*I have just never had a butterfly land on me before.*'

'*You are far too perceptive.*' He mock-scowled at her.

She sighed as the butterfly flew away. '*I'm glad I'm back, you know.*'

'*Me too.*' Cyrus beamed at her.

The guild had gathered around the castle dining room for their last dinner together, although they didn't know it yet.

Shari looked at each face, meeting each person's gaze, before she couldn't help herself any longer. "I don't think I want to fight any more."

"But you're the Altoriae," Talofa blurted.

"And the Altoriae protects Lissae." Shari glanced out the window. "We're not of Lissae anymore."

"What will you do?" Dealon asked.

Hail and Wisp pressed against her, lending Shari the courage to answer. "General Morrow vowed to take over when I needed to rest, and I think that's what needs to happen now."

"What will we do?" Talofa asked, her voice small as she wrapped all four arms around herself.

"Well, the guild doesn't have to abandon," Shari said with a wry smile. "Carilla still needs protecting. You should probably choose a different name, though."

"Don't think we didn't notice that neat little sidestep," Elani said, picking under her nails with the tip of a knife. If it weren't for the white-knuckled grip, Shari would have assumed the archer to be uninterested in the conversation.

She sighed. "I was planning on looking after the museum. It's been a while since there was a curator, and while I may be done fighting, that doesn't mean I want to lose our history, where we're from."

"That sounds perfect for you," Mu said. "We'll be able to collect things for you to look after."

"Not living things," Shari said, alarmed.

The group laughed, even as Mu flushed. "That was *one* time!"

"That was a baby fulni!" Elani said drily.

They laughed again, and Shari settled back in her seat, glad that her former guild had taken the news so well.

EPILOGUE

Carilla

Adonday

First day of the first week of Withergreen

2 N.R.C. (New Realm Created)

Shari shook the blanket out and laid it in front of the doorway in the empty field, using her Innarn to levitate the basket of goodies Dealon had given her that morning. Wisp put a paw on one corner of the blanket, and Hail helpfully flew to the opposite corner and sat down neatly, tucking his tail around his claws.

Just over a year had passed since the creation of Carilla, and she was celebrating what would have been her parents' anniversary.

Jonathan and Samuel came through the opening in the hedge, both carrying baskets of their own. Shadow was trailing after them, looking at Samuel like he'd hung the moon.

"I managed to spare some rutenberries for you," Samuel said, swinging the smaller basket down on another corner. Sneeze poked his head out, lips stained blue. "I can't promise they all made it here though," Samuel scowled.

The draci rolled his eyes and leaped from the basket to join Hail.

Jonathan laughed. "I'm afraid my offering isn't nearly as fresh," he said, pulling a bottle of quass juice from his basket. "In honour of your parents," he said, placing it in the middle of the blanket.

"Thank you. I'm glad you both managed to come," Shari said, settling down and taking out all sorts of treats.

Samuel grinned at her. "The hatchlings send their apologies. Harvest has just started, although I'm sure we're only going to get about a third of the crop. Personally, I wouldn't miss our family picnic for all the Realms."

Shari smiled and once he was seated, leaned into his side. "I'm so glad I can call you both family," she said, giving Jonathan a fond look. "And speaking of family–" Shari gave her former Guardian a mischievous grin and knocked on the door.

As it swung open, Samuel and Jonathan's jaws drop. After putting her hand through the door without looking, the being in the grey cloak slapped it heartly.

"Told you," she said.

'*I thought Jonathan would at least be able to keep his composure,*' Mitch grumbled. Underneath the hood, she knew he was grinning.

"How?" Jonathan asked.

'*Special permission, and more paperwork than you ever want to think about,*' Mitch sent.

Shari prepared a plate and passed it through to him.

'*The door only opens to this room.*' Mitch indicated the plain grey room around him. It was in a darker part of the portal than Shari was used to, but it made sense. '*I'm the only one who can open the door, and the only one able to leave this room. You do not want to know the amount of Innarn buzzing around to make this possible.*'

"Any idea of when we'll be able to..." Jonathan gestured at the portal.

Mitch lowered the hood and raised his brows. '*Do you really want to?*'

Jonathan shook his head. "No, but others may wish to know."

'*Try to tell them, and the words will slip away like water through a sieve. It's part of the Innarn.*' Mitch took a bite and moaned. '*You have no idea how bad the food is here. Compliments to the chef.*'

"Dealon is amazing," Shari agreed, taking a bite. "I know you can't tell us much, but... is Grace alright?" she asked.

'*It took a while, but she is. Going from strength to strength and keeping beings on their toes.*'

"Why would anyone do that?" Samuel asked, feigning ignorance. He'd become a lot better at understanding idioms.

"It's Grace," Shari said. "We can only be glad she's not stabbing people."

Mitch laughed. '*I never said that.*'

They talked and laughed, catching up on things big and small until Mitch looked over his shoulder, as if he could hear something they couldn't. Nodding, he placed his plate just outside the door. '*Jonathan and Samuel got their surprise today. Now it's time for yours, Shari. But it means I'll have to go.*'

"But—" she protested.

'*Trust me, you don't want to miss this. Besides, I'll see you again next year. I bid thee all well.*' He closed the door before they could respond.

"What was so important that he needed to go?" Shari huffed.

'*Well met, Shari.*'

She knew those voices. She hadn't heard them in over a year.

Shari reached for the ground, burying her hand in the grass until she could feel the earth beneath. '*Well met, Mum, Dad. I've missed you.*'

'*We'll always be here, watching over you. We love you, Shari.*'

Laughing, Shari fell backwards, letting the grass cushion her fall. '*I love you too.*'

Hours later, when the picnic had been packed up, and Samuel and Jonathan had gone home, Shari wandered through the halls of her museum, Hail wrapped around her neck and Wisp by her side. Of all the things she'd expected to happen today, talking to her parents hadn't even been on the list, but she was glad it had.

Her feet trod a familiar path, and she found herself back in the room where the doors to Lissae had once stood.

Sometimes, all it took to change a life was a trip to the museum and a charging minotaur.

GLOSSARY

A

Aberration – A slur used by mainlanders to refer to Innarnians.

Adonday – First day of the week on the Realm of Lissae. The other days are **Inthday, Kerday, Narday, Rasshday, Vebaday,** and **Zoeday.**

Akoren – One of the sentient Shifting Islands on Lissae. Originally home to Lissae's deities, she is inhabited by the **Wisara** and refugees from the mainland who required a place to stay after the civil war.

Altoriae – Protector of the Realm of Lissae. Traditionally a female role, although there has been one male Altoriae. Previous Altoriaes have included Kay'imi, Muran Curtis, Jali Thorne, and Fiona MacAde. Forces of nature cannot kill her. They must swear to uphold the seven duties of the Altoriae.

Altum – The home Realm of the Q'Aralide. Now destroyed.

Apprentice, The Guardian's – The Guardian's Apprentice is to take over the role of Guardian once the current holder of the title falls in battle or dies of old age.

Azehal – A drink favoured by the Guardian. A rutenberry-flavoured stimulant drink, typically served hot with sweetener and milk.

B

Beads – A form of currency on Lissae created out of **ziom**. The technical name is **ziom beads**.

Bereni trees – Trees that are grown to be used as buildings. The size and design of the tree can be controlled by an Innarnian or by one of the sentient islands.

B.I.R.D. – Stands for "Bio Instructor for Relative Distance." Designed by Xani of Talhan to ensure beings would stop bumping into things if they were absorbed in their crystal slab. The B.I.R.D. device acts as both a guide and a guard.

Blank – A person who can't use Innarn.

Bloomcrest – The third month of Winter. Preceded by **Waeghost** and followed by **Withergreen**.

Blyknot – A curse used by Samuel. See **Curses**.

Books 'n' More – A store on Ronah that the Guardian runs when he's not saving the Realm of Lissae.

Buta sprouts – A small, round root vegetable that tastes like ten-day-old socks.

C

Cantash – One of the sentient Shifting Islands on Lissae. He is home to the Daens.

Carilla – new Grey Realm.

Castle, Ronah's – The centre point of Ronah and the traditional home of the Altoriae, the Guardian, and their respective families.

Cedore – A curse used by Samuel. See **Curses**.

Crystals – Hold energy which is turned into electricity. Often installed in clusters to gain more power and last longer. Different coloured Crystals do different things. White Crystals are used for communication. Black Crystals gather power and Orange Crystals connect currents to create fences. Crystal necklaces are given to young children and Blanks for them to manipulate the Crystals.

Curses – Several curses are common on Lissae, including: Adeon's fire; By the Life of Lissae; Ke'ra's Flash; Zoemer's Rocks; Rasshnae's Floods; Vebnah's Breath; Na'reh's Ghosts. Other curses from the Realms include: ketarr; dathae; tu'zar; tongue of a Ne'fora; whale's ass; basalt-chewing hemmit-loving buzzard; cestoray; slime vattar; hanotqe; slime-filled cedore; feseor; gozochas; thrice-damned; fizzpot; trusnuck, blyknot.

Cylanthar's bells – The ringing of Cylanthar's Bells happens when events which have the potential to change her disciples' lives occur. See **Cylanthar**.

D

Daborang – A spiced tea of Yessna's making.

Deities – Lissae has six deities who are said to have lived on Akoren: Adeon, Ke'ra, Na'reh, Rasshnae, Vebnah, and Zoemer.

Ducibus' Hall – The place between Realms, guarded by the **Ducibus**. Also referred to as the **portal.**

E

Elders – Those who have, through age and experience, managed to survive the Realms long enough to guide their people. They also act as advisors to the mayor.

Elements – Lissae has seven main elements that Innarnians can manipulate: earth, air, fire, water, plasma, spirit, and technology.

F

Ferah – Humanoid beings with cat-like features, including fur, tail, whiskers, and claws.

Firepeak – The second month of Summer. Preceded by **Swellsun** and followed by **Suncrest.**

G

Ginorti – One of the sentient Shifting Islands on Lissae. He is home to the Satyrs.

Gozochas – A curse used by Yessna. See **Curses.**

Guardian – The rank for the person who is in charge of training and caring for the Altoriae, and for Lissae. In cases of emergency, the mayor and elders defer to the Guardian.

H

Hazelcrown – The second month of Autumn. Preceded by **Sunfall** and followed by **Stormwake.**

Healers – Similar to Earth's doctors, they heal patients who are sick or injured, usually using Innarn, although they also use the old methods.

Healers Centre – Also called the **Hospital**. A place on Ronah or Rakemyst to go when sick or injured.

I

I bid thee well – A traditional phrase when two or more people part ways.

Innarn – Predominately elemental magic which is present in all Realms to varying strengths. Innarn is split into three main groups: Dark, Grey, and Light. Each variant of Innarn has its own specialties. See **Elements** for more information. There are also other disciplines of Innarn, including Animal, Crystal, Mental, Realm, and Time.

Innarnian – (said Inn-*ar*-ni-an) A person who can use Innarn.

Inthday – Second day of the week on the Realm of Lissae. The other days are **Adonday**, **Kerday**, **Narday**, **Rasshday**, **Vebaday**, and **Zoeday.**

Ioyitmar – Light desert Realm. Some refugees found their way to Lissae after civil unrest.

J

Jinkor – A fixed island on Lissae.

K

Kerday – Third day of the week on the Realm of Lissae. The other days are **Adonday**, **Inthday**, **Narday**, **Rasshday**, **Vebaday**, and **Zoeday**.

L

Linked – A soul joined with that of one of Lissae's Shifting Islands. As the Shifting Islands are sentient, it was decided long ago that they should link with a being on their island to ensure that they remain in touch with the current needs of their population, and not remove themselves from the trials and tribulations of everyday beings.

Lissae – A Grey, sentient Realm who is defended by the Altoriae. Comprising six continents, seven sentient Shifting Islands, and multiple fixed islands, she is home to ten races. She is said to be a Mother Realm. There are two moons in her orbit.

Lissaen – A person who lives on Lissae.

Littlesun – The second month of Spring. Preceded by **Withergreen** and followed by **Raincrest.**

Lonely Orphan Society, The – Created by **Anika Thorne**, the short lived group comprises of beings who have lost their parents. Few members remain. Also referred to as **LOS**.

LOS – See **Lonely Orphan Society, The**.

M

Mainlanders – A name for those residing on the mainlands or fixed islands of Lissae.

Merthin – Akoren's underwater city. Home to the **Wisara**.

Months – Lissae has three months for each of the four seasons. Summer has **Swellsun**, **Firepeak**, and **Suncrest**. Autumn has **Sunfall**, **Hazelcrown**, and **Stormwake**. Winter has **Nightcrest**, **Waeghost**, and **Bloomcrest**. Spring has **Withergreen**, **Littlesun**, and **Raincrest**.

Mother Realm – The only Realm capable of giving birth to new Realms. Highly guarded and sought after.

Motus – The movement used to create Innarn. One must have thought, intent, and movement correct for the Innarn to work. Motus can be an individual construct, or a widely recognised form. Forms of motus used: Air; Sleep; Wind Blast; Wall of Stone.

N

Narday – Fourth day of the week on the Realm of Lissae. The other days are **Adonday**, **Inthday**, **Kerday**, **Rasshday**, **Vebaday**, and **Zoeday**.

Nightcrest – The first month of winter. Preceded by **Stormwake** and followed by **Waeghost**.

P

Patrol – Any Innarnian resident over fifteen is required to help the Guardian and the Altoriae patrol the Realms to watch for any possible threats.

Pocket-Realm – A small Realm that is attached to a larger one.

Portal – The place between Realms, guarded by the **Ducibus**. Also referred to as the **Ducibus' Hall**.

Q

Quass juice – a sweet bubbly orange drink, served cold.

Quiver and Quill Tavern – The tavern previously run by the Altoriae's parents on Ronah. Currently run by **Joana**.

R

Raincrest – The third month of Spring. Preceded by **Littlesun** and followed by **Swellsun**.

Rakemyst – One of the sentient Shifting Islands on Lissae. He is home to the Ilutri.

Rasshday – Fifth day of the week on the Realm of Lissae. The other days are **Adonday**, **Inthday**, **Kerday**, **Narday**, **Vebaday**, and **Zoeday**.

Rataeo – A virtually uninhabited Dark ice Realm with a time speed double Lissae's. It is home to the **U'tan**. Most of the animals are relatively harmless, except for the **metsari**.

Realms – Planets which inhabit various parts of the multiverse on three main levels: Dark, Grey, and Light. There can be many sub-levels and a mix of Dark and Grey, or Grey and Light within the same level. Dark Realms are places with little to no natural sunlight. Most lights in these Realms are made by Innarn. Grey Realms are places with a similar amount of light to Lissae and Earth's equator. Light Realms are places where there is an abundance of natural light.

Returned – The name given to those from Ronah who survived being eaten by Anriluka.

Ridden Hall – The school on Ronah.

Risen – The name given to those who formerly resided in Lissae's **Spirit Realm**, and are now residents of Carilla.

Ronah – One of the sentient Shifting Islands on Lissae. She is home to a variety of races and the traditional home of the Altoriae. Traditionally, Ronah selects a being to be her spokesperson. Ronah is one of the six gateways to the Realms.

Rutenberry – The frosted, dark-purple skin of the rutenberry hides the chocolate-like fruit inside. It can be eaten raw, although the skin can be bitter. Skinned, mashed, and cooked, it can be added into cakes, biscuits, and other sweets, including drinks.

S

Send/Sent – The word used for telepathic communication.

Sentient – Able to perceive or feel things, capable of thought and communication.

Sentinel, The Shifting Island – The major source of news for the Shifting Islands of Lissae. Available on your crystal slab with the low-cost subscription of 3 ziom beads a day!

Shifting – The Innarn art of mental teleportation from one space to another.

Shifting Islands – The name of the group of islands that travel around Lissae's seas, seemingly on a whim. They are sentient beings who care for the residents who make them their home. See: **Akoren**, **Cantash**, **Ginorti**, **Rakemyst**, **Ronah**, **Talhan**, and **Vannali**.

Spirit Realm – A pocket-Realm belonging to Lissae, where spirits go once their flesh fades.

Stormwake – The third month of Autumn. Preceded by **Hazelcrown** and followed by **Nightcrest.**

Suncrest – The third month of Summer. Preceded by **Firepeak** and followed by **Sunfall.**

Sunfall – The first month of Autumn. Preceded by **Suncrest** and followed by **Hazelcrown.**

Swellsun – The first month of Summer. Preceded by **Raincrest** and followed by **Firepeak.**

T

Talhan – One of the sentient Shifting Islands on Lissae, and the only one to start with an all-human population. He now accepts immigrants from all races on Lissae.

Techno Centre – Located on Talhan, it is the hub for all of Lissae's crystal and technological advances. The building also holds the Healing Centre, and the labs of the technomancer and Talhan's Linked.

Technomancer – The head of the Techno Centre has been given the nickname of technomancer due to the number of times her advances have brought the seemingly deceased back to life.

Tuklopia – a Grey Realm where the current Guardian was ambushed in an attack that many thought took his sight.

U

Ulnan – Temira's home Realm. It was destroyed, and all that remains is a burned door in the Ducibus' Hall.

Ulnanian – A race from Ulnan. The only known surviving member is Temira.

V

Vannali – One of the sentient Shifting Islands on Lissae. She is home to the Weavers.

Vebaday – Sixth day of the week on the Realm of Lissae. The other days are **Adonday**, **Inthday**, **Kerday**, **Narday**, **Rasshday**, and **Zoeday**.

W

Waeghost – The second month of Winter. Preceded by **Nightcrest** and followed by **Bloomcrest**.

Wards – Innarn shields designed to protect specific areas.

Well met – A traditional greeting throughout the Realms.

Withergreen – The first month of Spring. Preceded by **Bloomcrest** and followed by **Littlesun**.

X

Xin – A pale mauve drink of swirling silver liquid favoured by the Weavers. The heated drink gives off steam and is an excellent way to warm up on a cold night.

Xteria – An island turned continent in the Realm of **Rataeo**.

Z

Ze/Zir/Zim – A gender-neutral pronoun.

Ziom – The hardest metal in the Realms, found on Lissae. Used for the creation of housing frames, precious jewellery, and weapons.

Ziom beads – A form of currency on Lissae. Also referred to as **Beads**.

Zoeday – Seventh day of the week on the Realm of Lissae. The other days are **Adonday**, **Inthday**, **Kerday**, **Narday**, **Rasshday**, and **Vebaday**.

BEINGS AND CREATURES

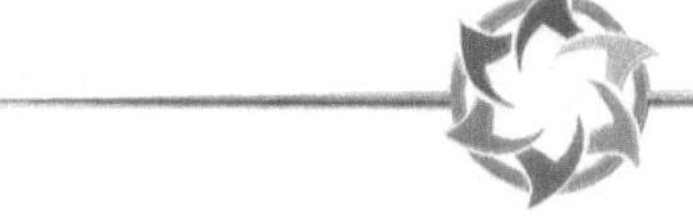

A

Abby Thorne – The eleventh Altoriae. She lived until she was 91 years old when she died from an attack. One of the Risen.

Ailan – Guardian of the seventh Altoriae. One of the Risen.

Aisling – Guardian of the tenth Altoriae. One of the Risen.

Akoren – One of the sentient Shifting Islands on Lissae. Originally home to Lissae's deities, she is inhabited by the **Wisara**, and refugees from the mainland who required a place to stay after the civil war.

Alistair Hollingsworth – of Ronah. Youngest son of Liza, stepson of Jordan. Brother of Caleb, Christopher, Tania, and Jessica Hollingsworth. Former candidate for the Guardian's Apprentice.

Amara – currently of Ronah. Formerly of Cantash. Former candidate for the Guardian's Apprentice. Member of the Altoriae's Guild. One of the Risen.

Ana – See **Askanar**.

Andrew Shansky – of Ronah. Father of Eric Shansky, husband of Louise Shansky. One of the Risen.

Anika Thorne – of Ronah. Student at Ridden Hall. Blank. Stylist to the thirteenth Altoriae. *Wields a mean stiletto. She's quite impressive, actually.*

How does she continue to annoy me, even after she's gone?

Anriluka – An U'tan from Rataeo who is older than Lissae's calendar. She almost devoured Ronah's entire population before Muran Curtis' Guardian banished her back to her home Realm. Anriluka was finally defeated by Shari Dawn, the thirteenth Altoriae, in the spring of 4059.

Aram Thorne – of Ronah. Student at Ridden Hall. Classmate of the 13th Altoriae. Currently dating **Liz Ribeck**.

Arilla Dawn – of Ronah. Mother of Shari Dawn, wife of Calem Dawn. Owner of the Quiver and Quill Tavern. *Very sorry about the arrow.*

I was aiming for your daughter.

Ashlen – One of the Returned, and a member of the Altoriae's Guild

Askanar – The third Altoriae. She lived until she was 51 years old when she died in an attack. One of the Risen. Now known as **Ana**.

Asterion – formerly of Atlantis. A former professor who donated his mind to become myth embodied. Currently residing on Ronah. *Clumsy does not become you, but apparently results in the birth of a new Realm.*

B

Belfar – of Rakemyst. Mate of Wolf Dawn. Second in command of Elder SilverCloud's guards.

Brayden – of the Wisara. A spokesperson.

Briar – of the Mainland. Tries to assassinate the Guardian. *Failed. Twice in a row. What are they teaching assassins these days?*

Brinley – of Vannali. Vannali's Linked.

C

Caeli – of Akoren. Former candidate for the Guardian. Soul-matched to **Domic Iabor.**

Caleb Hollingsworth – of Ronah. Eldest son of Jordan, stepson of Liza. Brother to Jessica, Christopher, Alistair, and Tania.

Calem Dawn – of Ronah. Father of Shari Dawn, husband of Arilla Dawn, son of SilverCloud, and brother of Wolf Dawn. Owner of the Quiver and Quill Tavern. *He sacrificed everything to keep Shari safe. I can respect that.*

Cantash – One of the sentient Shifting Islands on Lissae. He is home to the Daens.

Captain Rappen – of Jinkor. Formerly under Elder Chamele's command. One of the Risen.

Chamele – of Jinkor. Elder. *Good things come to those who wait... like the death of this pathetic being.*

Charin – of Rakemyst. One of the patrol members in Wolf's group. Spouse of Varlee.

Chirea – A race of warriors who use the bones of their fallen enemies to make their armour, weapons, and other items. The Chirea show status and power through the amount of bone armour they have collected. They use golden arrows soaked in a special mixture created by the Q'Aralide to steal Innarn. They are also known for poisons and soaking their weapons in potions that make healing by Innarn impossible.

Christopher Hollingsworth – of Ronah. Middle son of Liza and Jordan Hollingsworth, sibling of Caleb, Alistair, Tania, and Jessica Hollingsworth.

Clara – Guardian of the eighth Altoriae. One of the Risen.

Collis Iuvo – of Ronah. Unofficial leader of the Returned. Sworn guardian and soul-match of Ronah's Linked. Member of the Altoriae's Guild.

Crista Davis – The ninth Altoriae. She lived until she was 32 years old when she died via an attack. One of the Risen.

Should say – of trouble and mayhem.

Crystal Intelligence – of Lissae and Atlantis. *Never trust a talking crystal. And for the love of the Nine Hells, never take a machine from Atlantis!*

Her bells are both a blessing and a curse.

Cylanthar – The Q'Aralide deity of destiny. She makes her presence known by the ringing of bells when events which have the potential to change her disciples' lives occur.

Cyrus Petram – of Talhan. Talhan's Linked.

D

Daen – A short, fierce, and loyal race with amazing control over the Fire Element.

Daivi – of Ronah. One of the Returned, and one of the Risen.

Can make even vegetables taste delicious.

Dealon – of Ronah. Formerly of the Wisara. Former candidate for the Guardian's Apprentice. New member of the Altoriae's Guild.

Domic Iabor – of Akoren. Akoren's Linked. Soul-matched to **Caeli**.

Draci – Tiny dragon-like creatures that grow no bigger than a human's palm. The draci are native to Cantash, and those who have not found a being to bond with live in the gardens.

Drah – of Ronah. Formerly of the U'sala. Twin brother to Kerk.

Regained missing foot. And a second chance at life.

Ducibus – The Ducibus guard the gateways between the Realms. No one really knows what they look like, as they all wear dark cloaks. There is a theory that they come from different Realms and comprise many races. They ensure the safe travel between Realms and that those who aren't meant to get through, don't.

E

Edward Thorne – of Ronah. Husband of Harmony. Elder of Ronah. Grandfather of Anika Thorne.

Elani – of Ronah. Formerly of Ginorti. Member of the Altoriae's Guild.

Elizabeth (Liz) Ribeck – of Ronah. Student at Ridden Hall. Named after her aunt Lizbeth. Classmate of the 13th Altoriae. Currently dating **Aram Thorne**. See **Liz Ribeck**.

Eminlith – Second Guardian of the first Altoriae. One of the Risen.

Eobustus – Native to Cantash, the coal-black equines with manes of fire are a physical representation of energy and heat transference. They use heat from their surroundings to gather energy, then convert that energy into other things—movement, Innarn-boosting, running without rest. They are the fastest creature in all the Realms—provided they've had a good feed of magma or the sun is at full strength.

Eric Shansky – of Ronah. Son of Louise and Andrew Shansky.

Esse – Tania's escape-artist chicken. *Snack with blue feathers*

Estebar – Guardian of the fifth Altoriae. One of the Risen.

Eva – of Talhan. Orphaned. Now works at Books 'n' More.

Everon Castor – Author of the bestseller *From Ember to Flame*.
Good to know I can do something other than hurt beings.

F

Felton – of Ronah. Formerly of the U'sala. Explosives expert.

Fenix – of Cantash. Cantash's Linked.

Ferah – Humanoid beings with cat-like features, including fur, tail, whiskers, and claws.

Feyla – The fourth Altoriae. She lived until she was 153 years old. One of the Risen.

Fiona MacAde – The twelfth Altoriae. She lived until she was 24 years old when she died from an attack. One of the Risen.

Frointh – Forgotten Lissaen deity of Crystal. His statue can be found in Ronah's museum.

Fulni – An animal similar to Earth's buffalo but carnivorous and with two heads. The last fulni herd went extinct over two hundred years ago. Their tails are attached to a major artery, and if the tail is removed, they will bleed out in seven seconds.

G

General Morrow – of Ginorti. Head of the Satyrs army. Father of Liza Morrow. Grandfather of Tania Hollingsworth.

Ginna – of Lissae. Reporter for *The Shifting Island Sentinel.*

Ginorti – One of the sentient Shifting Islands on Lissae. He is home to the Satyrs.

Grace – of Jinkor. Former slave of Chamele. The Altoriae's cousin. Formerly known as Lissa. *Left behind on Lissae.*

H

Hail – One of Cantash's draci. *Has claimed Shari as his human.*

Halfair – of Ronah. One of the Returned.

Hantra – Earth spirits summoned by the Wisara. Unable to be controlled or stopped by the Shifting Islands as they were given bodies made of the earth. They are slow-moving and persistent, and their only goal is to do what the summoner has told them to. The only way to kill a Hantra is to remove both arms before decapitating it. Raising the Hantra is taboo on any of the Shifting Islands.

Henot – of Ronah. Formerly of the U'sala. Gnome.

I

Ifera – Formerly of Ioyitmar, now of Carilla. Granddaughter of Whitmore.

Ilutri – Winged humanoids from Lissae. They are usually found on Rakemyst and are high-level Innarnians. They include some of the finest archers on the Realm.

Indijo – of Ronah. Collis's childhood best friend.

Ishta – of Jinkor. Part of the mainlanders' troops. New Innarnian.

J

Jali Thorne – The tenth Altoriae. She lived until she was 19 years old when an accident caused her death. One of the Risen.

Jessica Hollingsworth – of Ronah. Youngest daughter of Liza and Jordan Hollingsworth, sibling of Caleb, Christopher, Alistair, and Tania Hollingsworth.

Jetonyx – of Ronah. Golden Q'Aralide. *turned Ritenberry farmer.*

Joana – of Ronah. One of the Returned. Mother of Tobias. Currently running the **Quiver and Quill Tavern.**

Jonathan Buan – of Ronah. Guardian to the thirteenth Altoriae. Owner of Books 'n' More. *Who knew it would take a new Realm to loosen the Guardian up?*

Jordan Hollingsworth – of Ronah. Husband of Liza Hollingsworth. Father of Caleb, Christopher, Alistair, Tania, and Jessica. Deputy Headmaster of Ridden Hall.

K

Kay'imi – The first Altoriae. She lived until she was 1217 years old when a lone Ahana archer killed her. One of the Risen. Now known as Kay.

Kemanyr – Youngest Q'Aralide. *Golden, loves rütenberries and embarrassing her elders. Me. She loves embarrassing me.*

Kerk – of Ronah. Formerly of the U'sala. Twin brother to Drah. ~~Deceased~~ *Returned to the living.*

Kibon – of Ronah. Formerly of the U'sala. Long-range weapons expert.

Kieran – of Ronah. One of the Returned. Has a swirl of ink on the side of his face.

Kodan – Formerly of the U'sala. One of the Risen. *Has somehow managed to redeem himself. Colour me shocked.*

L

Laura – of Ronah. A student from Ridden Hall with exceptionally Dark Innarn for one born on Lissae. *Under my protection. Don't even think about hurting her.*

Lerah – The fifth Altoriae. She lived until she was 334 years old when she died due to an attack. One of the Risen.

Liadain – Guardian of sixth Altoriae. One of the Risen.

Lissa – Sarina's daughter. Cousin to the Altoriae. Now known as **Grace**.

Liz Ribeck – of Ronah. Student at Ridden Hall. Named after her aunt Lizbeth. Classmate of the 13th Altoriae. Currently dating **Aram Thorne**. See **Elizabeth (Liz) Ribeck**.

Liza Hollingsworth – of Ronah. Daughter of General Morrow. Wife of Jordan, mother of Caleb, Christopher, Alistair, Tania, and Jessica. Headmaster of Ridden Hall.

Lizbeth Ribeck – of Ronah. *The hatchlings called her sweet treats, and she heard. Never have I been more mortified.*

Louise Shansky – of Ronah. Mother of Eric, wife of Andrew Shansky.

Luttrell – of the Chirea. Former leader. Defeated by *first* Amara of Lissae, *then by Norina of the Usala. Take that, you big bone head. Maybe if you respected females a bit more, they'd stop killing you. Oh, wait...*

M

Maeve Riley – of Ronah. Student at Ridden Hall. Gossip queen.

Mara Ribeck – of Talhan. Formerly of Ronah. Healer of optics. Augmented sight. Niece of Lizbeth Ribeck. Chose her career to help her favourite aunt.

Meyron – of Rakemyst. Felled in the initial attack by the Chirea. Used to have a golden feather. One of the Risen.

Milo – of Cantash. *Deceased. Twice.*

Mitchel – of the Ducibus. Formerly of Ronah. Sentinel of Carilla's gateway.

Mu – of Ronah. Formerly of Nindonia. Member of the Altoriae's Guild.

Muran Curtis – The sixth Altoriae. He lived until he was 45 years old and was eaten by Anriluka. One of the Returned, and the Risen.

This man will just not stay dead

N

Neev – Guardian of the ninth Altoriae. One of the Risen.

Nerina – of Ronah. Formerly of the U'sala. Healer.

O

Oakley – of Ginorti. Ginorti's Linked.

Oalark – ~~Queen of the Q'Aralide.~~ *May she turn in her grave, knowing I am in charge of the future of the Q'Aralide race.*

P

Pala – Leader of the Ducibus and sentinel of Lissae's gateway.

Palon – Native to Lissae, the palon is a small, six-legged creature descended from wolves. They have soft fur and long tongues, with a preferred diet of insects.

Petuar – The second Altoriae. She lived until she was 1005 years old when an accident caused her death. One of the Risen.

Pustish – of Vannali. Creatures of myths, the pustish are tiny bats who are said to guard Spirit Innarn from misuse.

Q

Q'Aralide (said Que-*ral*-die) – A vicious Dark race who wield Spirit, Earth, Plasma, and Air Innarn. Approximately thirty feet tall, their social status depends more on their colour and abilities than anything else. Apart from their Innarn, their breath is something to watch out for, as it can strip the flesh and the life from someone in just one exhalation.

Qar – Guardian of the third Altoriae. One of the Risen.

R

Rakemyst – One of the sentient Shifting Islands on Lissae. He is home to the Ilutri.

Rany Thorne – of Ronah. Father of Anika Throne. *And a perfect example of how not to treat your hatchlings.*

Raven – of Ronah. Formerly of Freeson. Former candidate for the Guardian's Apprentice. New member of the Altoriae's Guild. Excellent tracker.

Remmy – of Ronah. One of the Returned.

Resa Sunab – Guardian of the twelfth Altoriae. One of the Risen.

Ronah – One of the sentient Shifting Islands on Lissae. She is home to a variety of races and the traditional home of the Altoriae. Ronah's current Linked is Tania Hollingsworth. *Is it odd to admit I missed the crying? I do hope the hunk of dirt has fully recovered*

S

Samuel Caragnton – currently of Ronah. Formerly of Altum. Golden Priest of the Q'Aralide. The Lissaen Guardian's Apprentice. Also called **Sanithane** when in Q'Aralide form.

Sanithane – See **Samuel Caragnton.** *I will rewrite the future of the Q'Aralide.*

Satyrs – A humanoid race from Lissae with legs and tail similar to a horse. They are usually found on Ginorti. They include some of the finest crack troops on the Realm.

Sedolic – Green, scaly, dog-like animals with two large pincers at their front. They are a favoured food of the U'tan.

Shadow – of Ronah. The only creature to be one of the Returned. *My pardon*

Shadow Bringer – Sent to watch over others, sometimes to protect, often to kill. *In another life, I used them frequently—to the detriment of my prey*

Shael Robertson – The eight Altoriae. She lived until she was 73 years old when an accident caused her death. One of the Risen.

Shari Dawn – of Ronah. ~~The thirteenth Altoriae of Lissae and creator of the Altoriae's Guild.~~ *Free to make her own choices, at last.*

SilverCloud, Elder – of Rakemyst. Father of Calem and Wolf Dawn. Grandfather to the thirteenth Altoriae. Head Elder of Rakemyst.

Skye – Former aide to Elder Suni. Former carer of **Grace**.

Sneeze – ~~A creature of immature draci.~~ *A menace to all. My draci.*

T

Tabatha – Guardian of the eleventh Altoriae. One of the Risen.

Talhan – One of the sentient Shifting Islands on Lissae, and the only one to start with an all-human population. He now accepts immigrants from all races on Lissae.

Talofa – of Ronah. Formerly of Sulanta. Member of the Altoriae's Guild.

Tania Hollingsworth – of Ronah. Ronah's Linked. Daughter of Liza, stepdaughter of Jordan. Sister to Caleb, Christopher, Alistair, and Jessica. Soul-matched to Collis Iuvo.

Tanika Riley – The seventh Altoriae. She lived until she was 46 years old. The only Altoriae to die via natural causes. One of the Risen.

Temira – of Talhan. Formerly of **Ulnan.** Also called the technomancer, Temira is Head Healer and head of the Techno Centre.

May Cylanthar guide your soul.

Terrance Thorne – of Ronah. Anika Thorne's uncle. Deceased.

Do I regret what I did? Not even a bit.

Therdon – of Rakemyst. Former candidate for the Guardian's Apprentice. Killed by the thirteenth Altoriae for tampering with the minds of others.

Ugh. This one. Stay dead already!

Therion – of Jinkor. Part of the mainlanders' troops.

Thuk – Guardian of the second Altoriae. One of the Risen.

Tobias – of Ronah. One of the Returned. Joana's son. Also known as Toby. Deceased due to experimentation by Chamele. One of the Risen.

Tormorylth – of ~~Atrium~~ *Ronah.* Q'Aralide. *Before I know it, she will be taller than me!*

Tuscaro – A small grey bird with a white beak, native to Vannali. This bird is said to only sing in true love's presence.

U

U'sala – A group of beings from all over the Realms who have banded together to protect the Realms from creatures who wish to change them for their own benefit. Currently a small sub-set, led by Yessna, reside on Ronah.

U'tan – A race of extraordinarily powerful strategists who reside on Rataeo.

Ullmar – Guardian of the fourth Altoriae. One of the Risen.

Ulnanian – A race from Ulnan. The only known surviving member is Temira.

V

Vallan – A creature bred for its hide and meat. Vallan flesh is particularly delicious roasted.

Vannali – One of the sentient Shifting Islands on Lissae. She is home to the Weavers.

Varlee – of Rakemyst. Third in command of Elder SilverCloud's guards. One of the patrol members in Wolf's group. Spouse of Charin.

Varox – Fallen member of the U'sala.

W

Whitmore – Formerly of Ioyitmar, now of Carilla. An elder, and a Water Innarnian.

Wisara – Primarily ocean-dwelling beings whose bodies–although humanoid–look like the tangled roots of lotus flowers. Wisara tell the Tales of Lore. They travel the oceans and live in **Merthin**.

Wisp – A **Shadow Bringer**, sent by **Mitchel** of the Ducibus to watch over **Shari Dawn**.

Wolf Dawn – of Rakemyst. Mate of Belfar. Brother of Calem Dawn, and uncle to the thirteenth Altoriae. Commander of SilverCloud's guards. Previously known as LoneWolf Dawn.

Wubi – of Ronah. Formerly of the U'sala. Wielder of the spiked chain.

X

Xani – of Talhan. Also called the technomancer, Xani was Head Healer and head of the Techno Centre. ~~Deceased.~~ *One of the Risen.*

Y

Yessna – of Ronah. Former commander of the U'sala.

Yirri – Refugee now living on Ronah. Mother of Yirrisaunder.

Yirrisaunder – Refugee living on Ronah. Son of Yirri. One of the Risen.

Z

Zac Husdon – of Talhan. Formerly of Ronah. Techno apprentice.
If anyone can put up with Jonathan, it's Zac.

Zana – of Rakemyst. Rakemyst's Linked. Eldest of the Linked, and an accomplished diplomat.

Map of Vannali

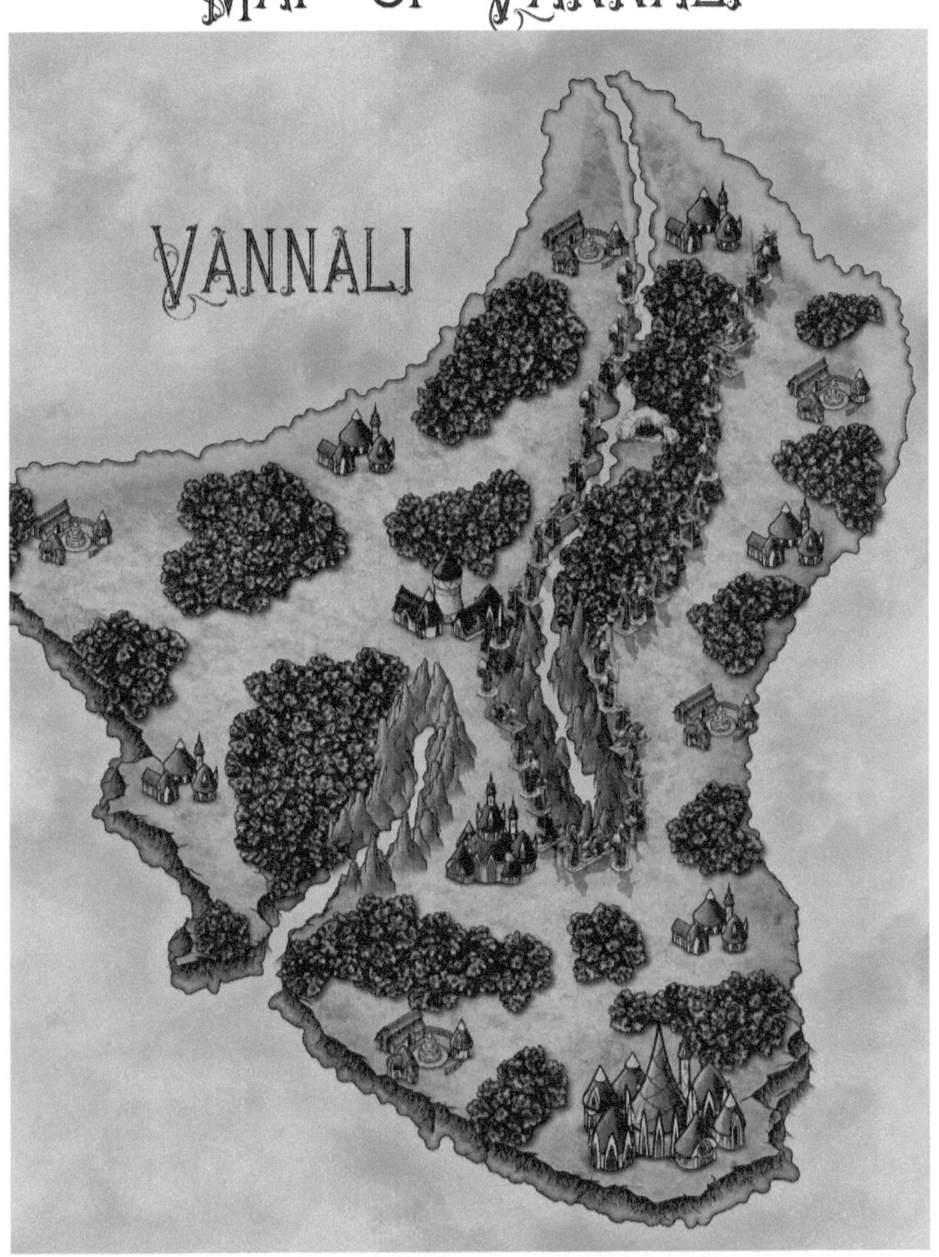

Sulanta
Opestila
LISSAE
Deep Sea
Vendalbara
Tevon
Rohinda
Yaston
Vutana
Kenorvia
Jinkor
Neloni
Muhara

LISSAE

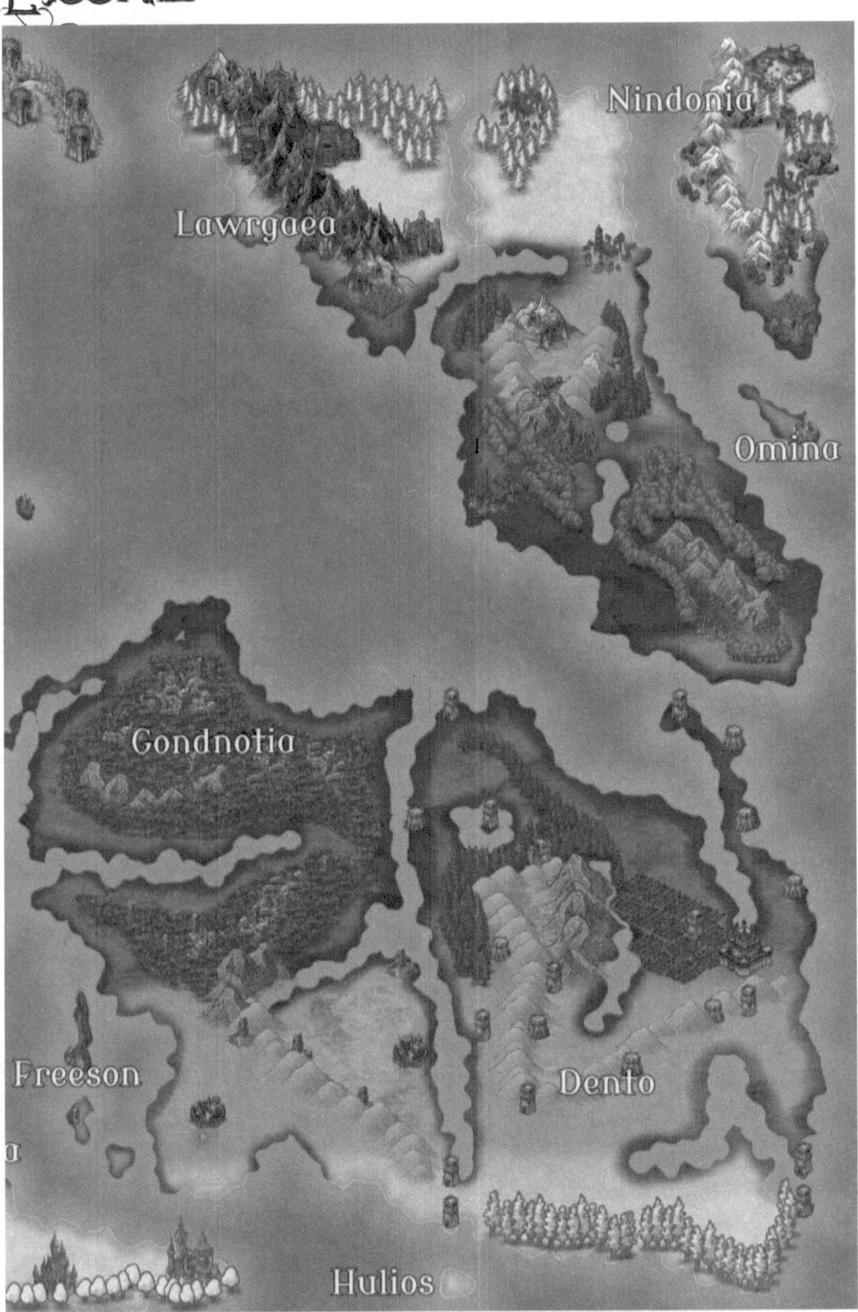

ENJOY THIS BOOK?

You can make a big difference.

Reviews are the most powerful tools in my arsenal when it comes to getting attention for my books. They help me gain visibility, and they can bring the Realm of Lissae to other readers who may appreciate the journey.

If you have enjoyed this book, I would be incredibly grateful if you could spend just a few minutes leaving a review (it can be as short as you like) at your favourite bookstore, or on the Goodreads page. You can jump right to the page by clicking below.

Find it in your preferred bookstore - books2read.com/vannali

Goodreads - goodreads.com/book/show/214136674-vannali

Thank you very much.

ACKNOWLEDGEMENTS

Can you believe it? The story is done. I have never cried so much when writing a story.

This book would not have become what it is without you. Yes, you. Whenever I thought about stopping (although, how could I with that ending in Akoren?!), I would remember that there were people waiting to read the next part of the story. You are absolutely the reason this book exists, and I can't thank you enough for coming along for the ride.

Yes, I still have amazing people who kept me motivated, caffeinated, and going even when I wanted to stop. To my family and friends, who put up with my manic schedule, random mutterings, late dinners, messy house, and the occasional bout of running away so I could write something down, you all rock! You really are the glue that held my sanity together.

To my amazing team of beta readers, I love how, when I put out the call with the insane schedule I had planned for the rest of the series, you all rallied behind me. Jodie, Ruth, Kathy—you all are indispensable to Lissae. Sending you a Wisp of your own!

Anna from CREATING ink, I can't thank you enough for putting up with my random *I broke it, now I fixed it, here's the new file* emails. You make the editing process such a pleasure, and I love working with you. As always, mistakes in the final version are my own fault and not an indicator of your work.

I can't thank Vanesa enough for the stunning covers she continues to create. Lissae wouldn't look the same without her.

Special thanks to Alex for naming Hail. Your enthusiasm is contagious—never stop being you. Thanks also to Cyrus, Michelle, and Lisa for some of the new character names. That list from so long ago has kept me going when I have no idea what to name the new character who just jumped, fully formed, onto the page.

Jodie—you organised things so I wouldn't have to, and you kept me on track with your comments and SupaNova salads.

Laura, I love that we can get together and laugh and cry at the same time. We are superwomen, booktok girlies, and wonderfully imperfect people cosplaying as functional adults. We got this.

Danielle, your encouragement has shaped the worlds both in the book and the one outside it. I'm so very honoured to be your friend.

Corin and Ren, I do hope I didn't scar you too much (more)! Love you to the moons and back.

Danny, thank you for picking up the slack, the cups of tea, the dinner, and keeping things going when you saw how my days were mapped out. I hope you're enjoying the books as much as I had fun writing them.

To the amazing team at Sunshine Coast Libraries who always seem so excited to hear about what I've been up to in the writing world—endless gratitude for all your encouragement, particularly Karen, Codie, and Nat for listening to me yammer on during lunchtime and putting up with me randomly shouting words or groaning when I remember I haven't done the thing. (Turns out I did do the thing—I just forgot about it). You've been with me the whole time this book was in process and have been so gracious about it. And Karen, from day one, you were my biggest cheerleader at SCL—thank you isn't enough. Your encouragement really means the Realms.

I cannot forget you, the reader! Thank you again for exploring the Realms within these pages. There are still a few short stories to come, and an awesome surprise to finish the series off.

Until next time, happy reading and I bid thee well.

ABOUT THE AUTHOR

R. Lennard is the Australian author of the young adult fantasy series *Lissae*. She is an avid fantasy and sci-fi reader, and in her spare time, she works as a librarian. She enjoys learning about ancient civilisations, cosplaying, and drinking endless cups of tea.

Residing on the beautiful Sunshine Coast in Queensland, Australia, Rebecca enjoys the natural beauty of both the beach and the bush. She lives with her family and is ruled over by her cat.

Rebecca is known as 'the Tetris Queen' and is usually the one to pack the fridge after a big grocery shop, or the car when going away.

To find out more about Rebecca, head to rlennard.com

After More to Read?

The *Eni Inside* is a short story prelude to the Lissae series included in the 3rd Australian Pen anthology, *The Evil Inside Us*.

The headmaster of Ridden Hall, Lawrence Anderson, went out on patrol, but never returned. Instead, a being bent on taking over Lissae came back in his place.

Full of stories about dark secrets, you'll want to join the masses and buy your copy of *The Evil Inside Us* now!

Available at: lissae.com/short-stories

What would you do when you had nothing to lose?

Orphaned, Jonathan Buan travels halfway around the Realm to defend his father's honour.

He finds more than he expected—more pain, more death, and more people to call his own.

Can he save them all, or will he become a demon's snack?

Find out what Jonathan was like before he became the Guardian.

Buy *Guardian* to bend the elements to your will today!

Available at: lissae.com/short-stories

**When a sentient Realm asks you to be her protector,
how can you say no?**

Shari Dawn appears to be just another teen, until a band of wandering Wisara visit her home–Ronah–a sentient, Shifting Island of Lissae.

Now her secret identity has been uncovered, Shari must learn how to control her powers, preparing to be tested in a prophecy passed down from the ancients, which will determine her role in the future of the Realm.

But sinister forces infect the dreams of Ronah's people. With a team she didn't want by her side, Shari must decide who lives and who dies.

The fate of the Realm is in her hands...

Buy *Ronah* and step into Lissae today!
Available at: lissae.com/ronah

How do you live after being eaten by a monster?

After he died, Collis found himself in a nightmarish Realm full of creatures who wanted to eat him. Waking up after the fiftieth time he'd died wasn't any easier than the first.

Stuck in a pocket Realm, Collis and the residents from Ronah must defend themselves against the deadliest creatures from across the Realms. But survival comes at a cost.

And if they die? They reform. Over and over. Just how are they going to escape?

Find out in *Returned*.

Available at: lissae.com/short-stories

A misplaced arrow could cause a war...

Wracked with guilt, Shari must face the joining of two Shifting Islands with her sword at the ready.

But as the search for the Guardian's next apprentice is still underway, fear strikes her heart. Not all the candidates are who they claim to be. And a fearsome new foe is out for revenge.

Can Shari lower her defences enough to let someone else in? Or will the decision cost her more than she's willing to give?

Buy *Rakemyst* and fly into Lissae today!

Available at: lissae.com/rakemyst

His choice could change the very fabric of the Realms...

The most feared being to walk the Dark Realms was once a mere hatchling. Scrawny, weak, and half-mortal, Sanithane strives to gain enough power to ensure his tormentors never bother him again.

But when his queen sets an impossible task, Sanithane has to choose—his kin, or his life?

Find out the story behind the Golden Priest in *Shadows*.

Available at: lissae.com/short-stories

Something is watching them from the shadows...

After a devastating betrayal, Shari longs for life to return to the way things were.

But she has little time to dwell on normality. A disturbing new foe rises, and former enemies become allies in the fight to save Lissae.

Juggling school by day and patrolling by night, it will only take one slip up to bring everything crashing down. Shari must battle her way to the heart of her problems... or die trying.

Buy *Talhan* and discover the heart of Lissae today!

Available at: lissae.com/talhan

There's something hiding in the Dark.

It's seeking Shari relentlessly and it's got only one thing planned for the Altoriae…

When a spy impersonates Shari, Samuel is summoned home to chair the Dark Conclave. It's the most dangerous meeting in all the Realms; a place where blinking out of turn will lead to being eviscerated, and Shari, it's number one enemy, accompanies Samuel under the guise of protecting him.

While Shari is away, the mainlanders have declared war, and Jonathan alone must confront them. With trouble brewing on both sides of the gateway, how will Shari overcome the Darkest of Realms and keep Lissae intact at the same time?

Buy *Cantash* and fan the flames of Lissae today!

Available at: lissae.com/cantash

The clouds hang thick as the Light Realms start their attack...

Scooped up from the portal, Shari must survive the Lightest of Realms. Can she find her way back to Lissae, before her Innarn is forcibly removed?

Having survived the Dark Conclave, Samuel returns to Lissae–alone. The Altoriae who went missing from his side holds the key to bringing back his race, but he's forbidden from searching for her.

Jonathan is struggling to keep the peace between those on the Shifting Islands and on the mainland.

Now his apprentice is back, they must decide–do they search for Shari, or prepare for war?

Buy *Ginorti* and discover the trees of Lissae today!

Available at: lissae.com/ginorti

There's something in the silence.

As Shari struggles to come to grips with who she is after her time away, Akoren and the Wisara draw closer, and Innarn is disappearing from Lissae.

Can Shari, Jonathan, and Samuel figure out what's going on, or will the ancient stories about the silence be the end of them all?

Don't miss out on the thrilling continuation of the Lissae series, where the thing hiding in the silence threatens to consume everything in its path.

Buy *Akoren* and discover the silence of Lissae today!

Available at: lissae.com/akoren

READING ORDER

Guardian*

Ronah

Returned*

Rakemyst

Shadows*

Talhan

Guild*

Cantash

Sanctum*

Ginorti

Tempest*

Akoren

Weaver*

Vannali

Grace*

Lissae Chronicles*

The Altoriae's Handbook

*Part of the Lissae Chronicles

Keep up to date with the Lissae series and receive exclusive extras by signing up for the newsletter at:

lissae.com/welcome